實用商業美語

——實況模擬

Vol. II. —應用篇—

杉田敏 著　　張錦源 校譯

三民書局 印行

國家圖書館出版品預行編目資料

實用商業美語II──實況模擬／杉田
敏著，張錦源校譯.－－初版.－－臺北
市：三民，民86
　　面；　　公分
ISBN 957-14-2576-1（平裝）

1.英國語言－讀本

805.18　　　　　　　　　　　　86003019

國際網路位址　http://www.sanmin.com.tw

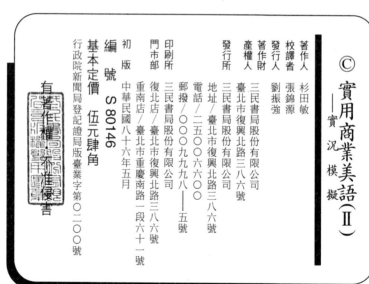

© 實用商業美語（II）
──實況模擬

著作人　杉田敏
校譯者　張錦源
發行人　劉振強
著作財　三民書局股份有限公司
產權人　臺北市復興北路三八六號
發行所　三民書局股份有限公司
　　　　地址／臺北市復興北路三八六號
　　　　電話／二五○○六六○○
　　　　郵撥／○○○九九九八－五號
印刷所　三民書局股份有限公司
門市部　復北店／臺北市復興北路三八六號
　　　　重南店／臺北市重慶南路一段六十一號
初　版　中華民國八十六年五月
編　號　S 80146
基本定價　伍元肆角
行政院新聞局登記證局版臺業字第○二○○號

有著作權　不准侵害

ISBN 957-14-2576-1（第二冊：平裝）

序

　　從日系國際食品公司跳槽到 ABC 食品公司的主角澤崎昭一，如願以償地到了紐約的總公司上班。然而，一開始的交通事故以及紐約的毒品和犯罪問題，都給他帶來了一些壓力。不過，他仍以其與生俱來的挑戰精神克服了這一切。

　　突然間，ABC 食品公司被 A.C. 勞雷菸草公司購併了，還被迫要與附屬於該公司的尼爾森食品食料公司合併。合併後新公司的總裁是亞力士‧迪馬哥。外界的評論說他是「能幹但冷酷無情」。而他的企業哲學則是「不賺錢就走路」。

　　儘管外界對他是這樣的評價，但澤崎竟意外地對他有好感，因為他認為「此人絕對可以重整 ABC 食品公司」。此外，澤崎也覺得，若要學習「競爭」與「利潤」並重的美式經營，這是個絕無僅有的良機。

　　公司合併後，澤崎不僅未被列入裁員名單中，而且還與布雷‧溫謝爾同被調派至新公司位於芝加哥的總部。但在飛往芝加哥的途中，澤崎依然覺得忐忑不安。

　　「這是個競爭激烈的新公司，我有辦法與那些美國同事共事嗎？」

　　「對於這些急劇的變化，我有足夠的應變能力嗎？」

　　「企業的存在是以『物慾』為其目的嗎？」

　　不過，這些問題在本書的末了都已不再是主角澤崎的煩惱了。

　　此外，本書也提及了「自尊心」和「遠見」，這是特別針對人心的內在問題所作的探討。盼望諸君能透過故事情節，知道澤崎為何擔憂，並與澤崎一同思索。

杉田　敏

本書的使用方法

　　要想用英語跟老外「暢所欲言」並不容易。即使你買了幾本會話書籍，且一字不漏地背誦下來，但你接下來卻會面臨到無法「照本宣科」的問題，因你無法掌握實際談話內容。在本書中，會有各種狀況的模擬，告訴你要如何在不同的情境中與人展開對話。本書更以商場上的實際對話為例，引導讀者去思索學習會話之道。

預習

　　先仔細閱讀「課文內容」，並將概要記住。若要使用另售的錄音帶，則一開始盡量不要看課本，試著專注地用耳朵聽。Sentences 是故事中所使用句子的採樣，這也是大腦的暖身操。

課文・翻譯

　　試著於閱讀完「狀況」之後，在心中描摹該場景。若是配合錄音帶使用，則先不要看劇情內容，嘗試用耳朵聽。如果覺得會話速度太快而無法理解，千萬不要立刻放棄，可以多聽幾次。

字彙

　　基本上，只要有初步的字彙能力，便足以應付大部分的商務英語會話了。但若自己需要遊走多國，則應該要背誦基本商務用語的廣義解釋及其正確發音。在 Vocabulary Building 中則藉由例句來學習活用法。並請讀者參考本書末了的單字表。

習題

　　在不改變例句結構的原則下，代入 a)、b) 詞組，練習另造新句。

簡短對話

與內文的說法和談話進行方向不同的對話。

總結

會話應盡量具有實用性，且能反映國際商業環境。所以每一課在總結的地方都會有異國文化的應對之道、社會語言學知識、以及各種重要的商業情報。

CONTENTS

PROFILE

～故事中出現的主要人物～

● **Shoichi Sawasaki** / 澤崎昭一(37歲)

本系列的主角,他在轉至 ABC 食品公司一年後,就被調派到紐約總公司。他仍以其天生的積極與幽默,來適應新的企業環境。

● **Eric Turner** / 艾瑞克‧透納(45歲)

公司的行銷副總,昭一的直屬上司。他是哈佛大學的 MBA,一個講求實際且充滿活力的企業家。

● **Roz Weathers** / 羅絲‧威德斯(32歲)

昭一在紐約總公司的行政助理,是位能幹的女性。

● **Hank Owens** / 漢克‧歐文斯(38歲)

昭一在紐約總公司的同事。

● **Bradley Winchell** / 布雷得利‧溫謝爾(37歲)

昭一在紐約總公司的同事。

● **Maria Cortez** / 瑪莉亞‧古岱茲(28歲)

有波多黎各血統的美籍女性。專門負責拉丁裔的市場行銷。

● **Ray Weston** / 雷‧威斯敦(54歲)

ABC 食品公司的 CEO(總裁)。他以不矯揉做作的溫和性情,和重視團隊精神的經營方式,博得了公司裡眾多員工的尊敬。

● **Alex DeMarco** / 亞力士‧迪馬哥(43歲)

他是合併後新公司「尼爾森 ABC 食品公司」的總裁。外界對他的評價是「冷酷無情」。他是位天才型的經營者。

Welcome Wagon in New York

（歡迎莅臨紐約）

◆ Lesson 18 的內容 ◆

　　澤崎在上司茱莉‧亨利的安排下，調任紐約總公司。雖然他以前也到過此地出差，但這次的情形與上次迥然不同。澤崎在抵達紐約甘迺迪機場時，行李居然不知去向。這樣一個新生活的開場，頗令澤崎有前途多舛之感。

Oh, they'll find it.
I'm Roz Weathers,
your
administrative
assistant.

Welcome Wagon in New York (1) (歡迎蒞臨紐約)

●預習 — *Sentences*

- Welcome to the Big Apple.
- They're only half true.
- Here's your ID badge.
- My friends call me Shoichi.
- How've you been?

●*Vignette*

[*Reception area at ABC Foods' New York headquarters*]

Weathers: Good morning, Mr. Sawasaki, and welcome to the Big Apple.

Sawasaki: Hello, thank you.

Weathers: How was your trip?

Sawasaki: Fine, except for my lost luggage at JFK.

Weathers: Oh, they'll find it. I'm Roz Weathers, your administrative assistant.

Sawasaki: Oh, yes. I've heard many things about you.

Weathers: They're only half true. [*Laughs*] Here's your ID badge. But you'll have to drop by Security for a picture sometime today— on the first floor. They'll issue your elevator security card too.

Sawasaki: Thanks, Ms. Weathers.

Weathers: Please call me Roz.

Sawasaki: Sure, Roz. My friends call me Shoichi. Last time I was here, I was told that without an elevator card I couldn't get any higher in this building than this second floor reception area.

Weathers: Yep. Security is especially particular about who gets off on the R&D and executive floors. Shall I take you to your new office on 28?

Sawasaki: I'll follow your lead.

Weathers: Let's go then. By the way, the executive offices are on the 31st and 32nd floors and the . . .

Winchell: Hi, Roz. How've you been? Oh, hello there. I'm Bradley Winchell.

*   *   *

[ABC 食品公司，紐約總公司的接待處]

威德斯： 早安，澤崎先生。歡迎來到紐約。

澤崎： 妳好。謝謝妳。

威德斯： 一路行來如何？

澤崎： 很好，只除了我在甘迺迪國際機場把行李搞丟了。

威德斯： 哦，他們會找回來的。我是羅絲‧威德斯，你的行政助理。

澤崎： 哦，是了，我聽過很多關於妳的傳聞。

威德斯： 那些話只有一半是真的。[笑] 這是你的身分識別章。但你今天還是得找個時間順道到警衛處去照張相 —— 在一樓那裡。他們也會發給你出入電梯的安全卡。

澤崎： 謝謝，威德斯女士。

威德斯： 請叫我羅絲好了。

澤崎： 當然，羅絲。我的朋友都叫我昭一。我上一次在這裡的時候，有人告訴我，在這棟大樓如果沒有電梯卡的話，頂多只能在二樓的接待處晃一晃，再要高一點的地方就去不了了。

威德斯： 是啊。而且安全警衛會特別留意那些上到研發部和主管辦公室樓層的人。要我帶你到你在二十八樓的新辦公室嗎？

澤崎： 妳帶路吧！

威德斯： 那我們走！順便一提，主管辦公室在三十一和三十二樓，而…

溫謝爾： 嗨，羅絲。妳好嗎？哦！你好。我是布雷得利‧溫謝爾。

＊　　＊　　＊

Lesson 18 Welcome Wagon in New York (1)

Words and Phrases

reception area	接待處；櫃臺	yep	〔俗〕是的
headquarters	總公司	be particular about	對…特別謹慎
Big Apple	紐約市的別稱	R&D (research and development)	
lost luggage	遺失的行李		研究開發
JFK (John F. Kennedy)	甘迺迪國際機場	follow someone's lead	跟從某人的引導
administrative assistant	行政助理	by the way	順帶一提
drop by	順道拜訪 (停留)	hello there	嗨，你好
Security	警衛處		

Vocabulary Building

- **except for**　　除了…以外
  Your proposals are excellent, except for the budget section.
  (你的提案好極了，就只預算部分不怎麼高明。)

- **I've heard many things about you.**　　我聽過很多關於你的傳聞。
  cf. I've heard many people speak highly of you.
  (我聽過很多人說你很好。)

- **half true**　　一半是真的
  cf. I've heard a lot of half-truths and innuendoes, but is there any evidence that Rob has stolen money from the company?
  (我聽到了不少似真又假、別有所指的話語，只是，到底有沒有甚麼證據可以證明羅伯真偷了公司的錢？)

- **Call me [Roz].**　　〔口語〕叫我…；以…稱呼我。
  cf. My first name is Rosalyn, but everybody calls me Roz.
  (我的名字是羅莎琳，不過大家都叫我羅絲。)

▶ *Exercises*

請勿改變例句的句型, 用a)、
b)詞組代換下列例句。

(解答見 261 頁)

1. Fine, except for my lost luggage at JFK.

   a) if it weren't
   b) not bad

2. I've heard many things about you.

   a) learned
   b) rumors

3. Shall I take you to your new office?

   a) install the phone in
   b) the conference room

◆◆◆◆◆◆◆◆◆◆◆◆◆◆ 簡短對話 ◆◆◆◆◆◆◆◆◆◆◆◆◆◆◆

Sawasaki: We spent a good half hour at the baggage carousel waiting before the first bag finally appeared.

Weathers: Yes, often you have to wait a pretty long time, but then they start coming fast and furious.

Sawasaki: That's just the way it was yesterday at JFK. But when all the other passengers from my flight were reunited with their luggage, and I found myself standing there all alone.

Weathers: I hope you didn't have to wait too long to file your claim at the lost luggage counter.

Sawasaki: Well . . . there were only about 50 people ahead of me in line, a lot of whom didn't seem to speak much English.

---

baggage carousel (在機場中)來回運轉以供旅客提取行李的輸送帶　　**fast and furious** 又快又急　　**JFK** (=John F. Kennedy International Airport) 甘迺迪國際機場　　**be reunited with** 與⋯再度會合　　**file one's claim** 提出申訴　　**lost luggage counter** 行李掛失處

Lesson 18

Welcome Wagon in New York (2) （歡迎蒞臨紐約）

●預習 — *Sentences*

· We must go for a run sometime.
· Here's your room with a view.
· Aren't those the World Trade Center buildings?
· The system is compatible with Tokyo.
· You'll find the manual in the top drawer.

●*Vignette*

Winchell: We must go for a run sometime. Enjoyed meeting you, Su-chi Sa-wa-ki, right?

Sawasaki: Close. It's Sho-i-chi Sa-wa-sa-ki.

Winchell: Of course, Sa-wa-sa-ki.

Sawasaki: Good. Japanese names can be hard to say.

Winchell: I'll practice. Sayonara.

Weathers: Now here's your room with a view.

Sawasaki: Excellent.

Weathers: This used to be the South African business development manager's office. ABC Foods' divestiture last spring changed his address.

Sawasaki: Aren't those the World Trade Center buildings that I see over there in the distance?

Weathers: Yes.

Sawasaki: This desk looks like an airplane cockpit. I use a computer, but I'm not sure . . .

Weathers: This workstation is modular so you can rearrange it as needed. There's a color monitor, a 40-megabyte hard drive, and it has an integrated phone modem for on-line data and E-mail services. The system is compatible with Tokyo, and you'll find the manual in the top drawer.

溫謝爾：　我們一定得找個時候一起出去吃個飯。很高興見到你，Su-chi Sa-wa-ki，對嗎？

澤崎：　很接近。是 Sho-i-chi Sa-wa-sa-ki。

溫謝爾：　當然，Sa-wa-sa-ki。

澤崎：　很好。日本名字會不太好念。

溫謝爾：　我會練習的。莎喲哪啦。

威德斯：　這就是你的辦公室，還可以眺望遠處。

澤崎：　棒極了。

威德斯：　這裡以前是南非事業開發部經理的辦公室。去年春天 ABC 食品公司讓售了這個事業部，所以他也跟著搬家了。

澤崎：　我看到那邊遠遠兒的有些建築物，是世貿中心大樓嗎？

威德斯：　是啊。

澤崎：　這個桌子看來像是飛機的駕駛艙。我雖也使用電腦，但我不確定…

威德斯：　這個工作站是組合式的，所以你可以依你的需要重新組裝。有彩色螢幕，一部 40 mega 的硬碟，還有整合式的電話數據機，可以取得上線的資料並提供電子郵件的服務。這系統與東京是相容的，你在最上層的抽屜可以找到使用手冊。

Lesson 18　Welcome Wagon in New York (2)

Words and Phrases

go for a run　　一起出去吃個飯
Enjoyed meeting you.　　很高興見
　到你。
practice v.　　練習
airplane cockpit　　飛機的駕駛艙
modular [ˈmɑdʒʊlə]　　組合式的

integrated　　綜合的; 統合的
phone modem　　電話數據機
on-line　　線上的; 網路上的
E-mail (electronic mail)　電子郵件
compatible [kəmˈpætəbl] with　　與
　…是相容的

Vocabulary Building

- **Close.**　　很接近。
It was a close call.
(真是千鈞一髮。)

- **Excellent.**　棒極了。
cf. Beautiful.
(帥呆了。)

- **divestiture** [dəˈvɛstətʃə]　　(控股公司)放棄或出讓某一子公司
cf. The company has already divested itself of all its interest in Latin America.
(那公司已經出讓了它在拉丁美洲的一切權益。)

- **in the distance**　　在遠處
cf. Ever since Joyce was named a board member, her former colleagues have kept their distance.
(自從喬依絲被任命為委員之後, 她以前的同事就開始跟她疏遠了。)

16

▶ Exercises

請勿改變例句的句型, 用a)、b)詞組代換下列例句。

(解答見261頁)

1. Japanese names can be hard to say.

   a) difficult to pronounce
   b) Oriental

2. Aren't those the World Trade Center buildings that I see over there in the distance?

   a) Catskill Mountains
   b) mist

3. This desk looks like an airplane cockpit.

   a) resembles
   b) is built

◆◆◆◆◆◆◆◆◆◆◆◆◆◆ 簡短對話 ◆◆◆◆◆◆◆◆◆◆◆◆◆◆◆

Sawasaki: You seem to be a lot more advanced in OA here in New York than we are in Tokyo.
Weathers: Advanced in a way?
Sawasaki: I said in "OA."
Weathers: "OA"?
Sawasaki: It's short for office automation—all this high-tech gadgetry and the systems that make it work. Don't you say "OA" in English?
Weathers: Maybe some people do, but it's a new one to me.

---

short for …的縮寫   **high-tech** 高科技的   **gadgetry** 小巧的機械裝置

Lesson 18

Welcome Wagon in New York (3)（歡迎蒞臨紐約）

●預習 — *Sentences*

- I'll book a table for you at Tavern on the Green.
- I suppose that's all right.
- Take a taxi from your hotel at a quarter to 7.
- You're looking very well.
- My wife says I'm getting too well-rounded.

●*Vignette*

Sawasaki: Speakerphone and automatic memory dialer.

Weathers: Oh, I almost forgot. Here's a message from Eric Turner, your new boss. He wanted to take you out for lunch today, but he's still tied up in a meeting with the Department of Commerce in Washington. He'll take the shuttle back this afternoon. Eric wanted to know if you had any dinner plans.

Sawasaki: No, no plans.

Weathers: All right. I'll book a table for you at Tavern on the Green in Central Park— 7 o'clock. OK?

Sawasaki: Central Park? I suppose that's all right.

Weathers: Don't worry. Take a taxi from your hotel at a quarter to 7.

Owens: Hello, Shoichi. Welcome to New York.

Sawasaki: Hank Owens! Hi. It's good to be here.

Owens: You're looking very well.

Sawasaki: My wife says I'm getting too well-rounded.

Owens: Not at all. Is Etsuko here with you?

Sawasaki: No, she'll be moving with the children during their school break.

Owens: After the culture shock wears off, I think they'll enjoy the States.

澤崎的上司艾瑞克・透納人還在華盛頓出席商務部的會議，但他卻給澤崎留了話，說是想和他吃晚飯，地點是中央公園的某知名餐廳。而澤崎也碰到了舊識漢克・歐文斯。

澤崎： 免執聽筒裝置和自動記憶撥號。

威德斯： 哦，我差點忘了。艾瑞克・透納，你的新上司，留話給你說他今天想帶你出去吃午餐，可是他現在仍在華盛頓，跟商務部的會議還沒開完。他今天下午會搭定期往返的班機回來。艾瑞克想要知道你晚餐有沒有甚麼別的計畫。

澤崎： 沒有。沒有甚麼計畫。

威德斯： 好。那我會替你們在中央公園的「果嶺酒店」訂位 ── 七點。可以嗎？

澤崎： 中央公園？我想應該可以吧。

威德斯： 別擔心。六點四十五分的時候從你下榻的飯店搭計程車過去就行了。

歐文斯： 哈囉，昭一。歡迎來到紐約。

澤崎： 漢克・歐文斯！嗨！來到這裡真好。

歐文斯： 你看起來氣色很好。

澤崎： 我太太說我變得太胖，圓滾滾的。

歐文斯： 哪兒有！悅子有跟你一起來嗎？

澤崎： 沒有，她會在孩子學校休假的時候和他們一起搬來。

歐文斯： 在文化衝擊慢慢消失後，我想他們會喜歡上美國的。

Lesson 18　Welcome Wagon in New York (3)

Words and Phrases

speakerphone　　免執聽筒裝置

automatic memory dialer　　自動記
　憶撥號

be tied up　　(因會議)分不開身

Department of Commerce
　商務部

shuttle　　定期往返的巴士(或飛機)

book a table　　(在餐廳)預先訂位

I suppose that's all right.　　我想應
　該沒問題。

well-rounded　　(身材)豐滿的

school break　　學校假期〈指較短的
　休假〉

Vocabulary Building

● **I almost forgot.**　我差點忘了。
cf. Before I forget, next Monday you'll need to come in an hour earlier since we have a meeting.
(趁我還沒忘記，下星期一我們有個會議，你需要提早一個小時到。)

● **boss** *n.* 上司; 老闆　*v.* 支配
cf. Mitch tends to boss his coworkers around too much.
(米奇常常會過度支使自己的同事。)

● **take someone out**　帶某人出去(吃飯等)
I'd like to take you out to dinner sometime next week to celebrate your tenth anniversary with the company.
(下禮拜我想找時間帶你出去吃晚餐，慶祝你進入公司十週年。)

● **wear off**　慢慢消失
Take this medicine right away, and the pain will wear off.
(馬上把這藥吃下去，痛苦就會慢慢解除。)

(解答見 261頁)

▶ **Exercises**   請勿改變例句的句型, 用a)、
b)詞組代換下列例句。

1. He wanted to take you out for lunch today.

   a) have lunch with you
   b) was hoping

2. I'll book a table for you at Tavern on the Green.

   a) reserve
   b) the two of you

3. She'll be moving with the children during their school break.

   a) coming over
   b) kids

◆◆◆◆◆◆◆◆◆◆◆◆◆ 簡短對話 ◆◆◆◆◆◆◆◆◆◆◆◆◆◆

Weathers: We don't keep much on paper these days. Almost everything is computerized for readout on the screen. If you have time today, I'll show you where particular topics are stored and how to retrieve them.

Sawasaki: That would be a big help. I notice that reference books and files are kept on shelves behind everybody's desk. Any particular reason for that?

Weathers: They don't want any of them in their line of vision. They distract their attention.

Sawasaki: I see.

Weathers: It's the same reason we keep pens, staplers and tape dispensers in a single drawer. They can also disturb your line of sight. And make more clutter.

---

readout (從記憶裝置中)讀出資料   **on the screen** 在螢幕上   **store** *v.* 儲存(資料、檔案)   **retrieve** 叫出(檔案、資料)   **reference book** 參考資料   **line of vision** 視界   **distract** 分散(注意)   **stapler** 訂書機   **tape dispenser** 膠帶臺   **clutter** 散亂; 雜亂

Lesson 18

Welcome Wagon in New York (4) （歡迎蒞臨紐約）

●預習 — *Sentences*

· Excuse me for interrupting.
· I wanted to greet our new neighbor.
· I'm in charge of Hispanic marketing.
· I've got to scoot.
· See you all at the Tech Center demo on Friday.

●*Vignette*

Owens: In the meantime, you'll have to come to Greenwich for some golf. It's only an hour by car and you can tie it in with weekend house hunting in Connecticut.

Sawasaki: Sounds great.

Owens: Oh, Maria. Hi. This is Maria Cortez.

Cortez: Excuse me for interrupting. I wanted to greet our new neighbor. I'm Maria. I'm in charge of Hispanic marketing— and I'm your unofficial welcome wagon.

Sawasaki: Shoichi Sawasaki. My pleasure.

Owens: I've got to scoot. See you all at the Tech Center demo on Friday. And, Shoichi, if you have any questions, my door's always open.

Cortez: Hank means it too. A nice guy to work with. Roz, do you mind if I borrow Shoichi for lunch today?

Weathers: That'd be great. I'm afraid he may get lonely by himself in that office.

Sawasaki: And hungry.

Weathers: Your orientation meetings start at 2:30, Shoichi. And Maria, please take Shoichi by Security, so he won't be stuck on the second floor.

　　漢克・歐文斯極力推薦澤崎一個打高爾夫球的好地方。而隔壁辦公室的瑪莉亞・古岱茲也加入了歡迎之列，她還主動要帶澤崎去吃午餐。大家都顯得很和藹可親，這也讓澤崎稍微放寬了心。

歐文斯： 另外，你一定要到格林威治去打打高爾夫球。開車只要一個小時就到了，而且你還可以順道在週末到康乃狄克去找房子。

澤崎： 聽起來不錯。

歐文斯： 哦，瑪莉亞。嗨！這是瑪莉亞・古岱茲。

古岱茲： 抱歉打斷你們的談話。我想跟我們的新鄰居打聲招呼。我是瑪莉亞，負責美籍拉丁人的市場拓展 —— 我要來充當一下你的新人歡迎車。

澤崎： 澤崎昭一。很榮幸能有妳為我作介紹。

歐文斯： 我得快點走了。我們星期五科技中心說明會見。還有，昭一，如果你有任何疑問，我的門永遠是開著的。

古岱茲： 漢克可是當真的，他是個好同事。羅絲，你介意我今天借一下昭一去吃午餐嗎？

威德斯： 那再好不過了。我還怕他自己一個人在那間辦公室會覺得孤單呢！

澤崎： 還會肚子餓哩！

威德斯： 昭一，你的新進人員講習兩點半開始。還有，瑪莉亞，請帶昭一過一下警衛的地方，這樣他才不會卡在二樓出不去。

Lesson 18　Welcome Wagon in New York (4)

Words and Phrases

in the meantime　於其時; 另一方面

Greenwich　[ˈgrɛnɪtʃ]　格林威治
　(康乃狄克州的一個城市)

an hour by car　車程一個小時

house hunting　找房子

Sounds great.　聽起來很好。

interrupt　打斷

greet　問候

neighbor　鄰居; 鄰近的人

My pleasure.　我的榮幸; 很樂意。

scoot　跑走; 逃掉

demo　(<demonstration)　展示
　(會); 說明(會)

guy　人; 傢伙

work with　一起工作; 共事

orientation meeting　新進人員講習

be stuck　陷住

Vocabulary Building

- **tie in with**　使與…連結
  The new logo ties in nicely with our effort to project a more contemporary image.
  (我們一直努力要營造出一個更具現代感的形象, 而這個新的公司標誌正好吻合了這樣的訴求。)

- **Hispanic marketing**　對美國境內講西班牙語或葡萄牙語的美籍拉丁人所進行的市場拓展。
  cf. The Hispanic market accounts for about ten percent of our domestic sales.
  (我們的國內銷售額中有百分之十是來自拉丁裔市場。)

- **welcome wagon**　「新人歡迎車」(為某地的新住戶或新來者帶來當地訊息或載來商店所提供樣品的車子)
  cf. They really rolled out the red carpet for the visitors from China.
  (他們的確是熱烈且隆重地歡迎了那些從中國大陸來的訪客。)

- **mean**　故意要…; 想要…
  I didn't mean to make fun of you when I corrected your pronunciation, but you do have trouble with your Ls and Rs.
  (我糾正你的發音並不是故意要取笑你, 但是你在發 L 和 R 的時候確實有問題。)

1. You'll have to come to Greenwich for some golf.

   a) it may be a good idea
   b) dinner

2. If you have any questions, my door's always open.

   a) you should speak up
   b) whenever

3. He may get lonely by himself in that office.

   a) doesn't like being
   b) without anyone to talk to

◆◆◆◆◆◆◆◆◆◆◆◆◆◆ 簡短對話 ◆◆◆◆◆◆◆◆◆◆◆◆◆◆

Sawasaki: Er, Maria, I have one request to make before we go to lunch.
Cortez: Sure, what is it?
Sawasaki: Could you direct me to the facilities, so to speak?
Cortez: The— oh, I read you. The washrooms on this floor are locked, but there's one you can use by the cafeteria. Remind Roz to get you a key this afternooon. She's well organized, but sometimes she forgets those little human details.

---

direct someone to   指引某人到…的路   **facilities**   設施   **I read you.**   我瞭解你說這話的意思。   **washroom**   洗手間   **cafeteria**   〔美〕員工餐廳
well organized   有條有理的; 整齊不紊的

Lesson 18

Welcome Wagon in New York — 總結

■ ■ ■

　　羅絲‧威德斯是澤崎的 administrative assistant，實際上就是他的「祕書」。近來由於辦公室自動化的結果，祕書的工作內容也大為改變。只會打字或做做雜務的祕書已跟不上時代了。

　　從另外一個角度來看，有能力的祕書也因此而有機會從昔日單調的工作中解放出來，擔負更為重大的責任。所以，像是 secretary 或 executive secretary 這種舊式職稱，正逐漸被 administrative assistant, personal assistant, executive assistant, staff assistant, staff coordinator, executive office manager, 或 executive coordinator 等所取代。

　　"I've heard many things about you." 是個經常使用的寒喧語，而對方的反應有時會像羅絲一樣，就是「你聽到的一定都是些不好的傳聞，可是只有一半是真的喔！」或是恰恰相反，"They're all true." 「風評不錯吧，全是真的喔！」不過，這些都是帶點玩笑性質的表達方式。

　　澤崎向羅絲打招呼時稱她為 "Ms. Weathers"。通常，在不清楚對方婚姻狀況時，"Ms." 是個相當管用的字。但要切記，由於 women's lib movement (婦女解放運動) 的關係，有些女性不喜歡別人用 "Ms." 來稱呼自己。而有些禮儀方面的書則建議讀者在類似情形最好選用 "Miss" 一字。至於到底該怎麼用，也只能靠事先的觀察，或 wing it (隨機應變) 了。

Lesson 19

Drug Testing and Screening

（毒品測試）

◆ Lesson 19 的內容 ◆

　　對剛到達美國的澤崎而言，第一件令他震驚的事，就是目睹了警察用手銬銬住犯人。在美國，大部分暴力犯罪的元兇都是「毒品」。聽說有二千萬的美國人經常性地吸食大麻，六百萬人經常使用古柯鹼，這令他非常驚訝。ABC 食品公司也有義務對前來應徵工作者作毒品測試。任何無法通過測試的人，公司都不予錄用。

You'll soon get used to that. People struggle to survive in New York and, unfortunately, violent crime is part of it.

Lesson 19

Drug Testing and Screening (1)（毒品測試）

●預習 — *Sentences*

- What's happening over there?
- I'm witnessing a crime scene for the first time.
- You'll soon get used to that.
- Dealing in drugs is a lucrative business.
- How does Japan keep drugs out?

●*Vignette*

[*Police car siren*]

Sawasaki: What's happening over there? I see a policeman hand-cuffing someone. Gee, I'm witnessing a crime scene for the first time.

Cortez: You'll soon get used to that. People struggle to survive in New York and, unfortunately, violent crime is part of it.

Sawasaki: Everything I read blames the violence on drugs. Why are drugs such a problem in America?

Cortez: Why? There are a lot of reasons for the current epidemic of drug abuse, but to my mind the prime cause is people's desire to escape from their problems and frustrations—or even from themselves. And dealing in drugs is a lucrative business.

Sawasaki: I understand some liberal Americans are saying drugs should be legalized.

Cortez: I don't see what good that would do.

Sawasaki: Well, for one thing, it would lower the price by a huge margin.

Cortez: Oh, I get it. Then the gangs won't fight over profits and the addicts won't mug little old ladies, right?

Sawasaki: That's the idea. Legalization would also reduce law-enforcement costs, and the tax revenue from selling drugs could go to treatment programs for addicts.

Cortez: But you can't say that drugs are bad at the same time you go and make them legal. Tell me, though, how does Japan keep drugs out?

Sawasaki: I'd say it's with a combination of strict laws and family discipline.

* * *

　　澤崎在和瑪莉亞出去吃中飯的途中，親眼目睹了警察逮捕罪犯。瑪莉亞已經習已為常了，她說，暴力犯罪在紐約簡直就是家常便飯。

[警笛聲]

澤崎：　那邊發生甚麼事了？有個人被警察戴上手銬了。哇，這是我第一次目擊犯罪現場耶！

古岱茲：　你很快就會習慣的。在紐約，人們掙扎著要求生存，不幸地，暴力犯罪也是其中的一部分。

澤崎：　我讀到的東西都將暴力歸咎於毒品。為甚麼毒品在美國造成的問題這麼嚴重？

古岱茲：　為甚麼？毒品近來如此氾濫的原因有很多。不過依我看，最主要是因為人們亟欲逃離他們所面臨的問題和沮喪的情緒 —— 他們甚至不願面對自己。而且，販賣毒品的利潤又這麼高。

澤崎：　我知道有些自由派的美國人在說毒品應予合法化。

古岱茲：　我可看不出這麼做能有甚麼好處。

澤崎：　這個嘛，一個是，毒品價格會因此而大大降低。

古岱茲：　噢，我懂了。然後那些幫派分子就不會為了利益而爭鬥，吸毒者也不會從背後襲擊可憐的老太婆了，是嗎？

澤崎：　就是這個意思。毒品合法化也能減少執法單位花在緝捕上的費用，而銷售毒品所得的稅收則可作為吸毒者的戒治計畫之用。

古岱茲：　可是，你不能一面說毒品不好，一面又要使它合法化。不過，告訴我，日本是如何杜絕毒品氾濫的？

澤崎：　我會說是由於嚴格的法律和家教二者結合所致。

＊　　＊　　＊

Lesson 19   Drug Testing and Screening (1)

Words and Phrases

handcuff *v.*	給…戴上手銬〈逮捕〉		有利可圖的
witness *v.*	目擊; 目睹	legalize	使合法化
struggle	掙扎; 奮鬥	by a huge margin	大幅地
violence	暴力	addict	有毒癮者
epidemic	流行	mug	〔美俗〕從背後襲擊勒住被害
frustration	挫折; 失敗		者的脖子
deal in	從事…	legalization	合法化
lucrative [ˈlukrətɪv] *adj.*	有利的;	tax revenue	稅收

Vocabulary Building

- **abuse**   濫用; 虐待

  cf. Thomas quit because he was tired of getting so much abuse from the boss.

  (湯瑪士受夠了老闆諸多的虐待, 所以他辭職了。)

- **to my mind**   依我看

  To my mind, doing the morale survey is a waste of time, because nothing will happen as a result.

  (依我看, 調查員工士氣是個浪費時間的作法, 因為根本不會有甚麼結果產生的。)

- **law-enforcement**   執法的〈警官、檢察官等〉

  Each year, many law-enforcement officers are killed while carrying out their official duties.

  (每年都有許多執法員警在執行任務的時候殉職。)

- **discipline** *n.* 紀律   *v.* 規律; 使受制於; 鍛鍊

  cf. If you want to be a professional writer, you have to discipline yourself to write every day, whether it's a personal letter or a diary.

  (如果你想成為一位專業作家, 你必須規定自己每天都寫點東西, 不管是私人信件或是日記都可以。)

1. People struggle to survive in New York.

   a) hustle
   b) the Big Apple

2. Some liberal Americans are saying drugs should be legalized.

   a) have been insisting
   b) radicals

3. I don't see what good that would do.

   a) it's not apparent to me
   b) why it should be done

◆◆◆◆◆◆◆◆◆◆◆◆◆ 簡短對話 ◆◆◆◆◆◆◆◆◆◆◆◆◆◆

Sawasaki: I've heard a lot about all the crime here in New York, but I've never actually encountered it myself before.
Cortez: Don't you have a crime problem in Tokyo?
Sawasaki: Well, it would be an exaggeration to say that the city's completely crime-free, but you certainly don't have to worry about your personal safety the way you do here.
Cortez: That must make life a lot simpler. Still, I wouldn't be too concerned if I were you. You should be OK just so long as you take a few reasonable precautions and stay alert to what's going on around you.

---

encounter 碰見　　**exaggeration** 誇張　　**crime-free** 零犯罪的　　**take precautions** 防備; 採行預防措施　　**stay alert** 保持警戒

Lesson 19

Drug Testing and Screening (2) （毒品測試）

●預習 —Sentences

- Your papers are all straightened out.
- I was talking about the physical examination.
- Will I be tested for drugs too?
- Are they a big problem at ABC Foods?
- We test all new job applicants.

●Vignette

[*Office of Felicity Chambers, Manager— International Human Resources*]

Chambers: Let's see, Shoichi, your papers are all straightened out. You'll get your Social Security number and you know about the physical . . .

Sawasaki: The "physical," Ms. Chambers?

Chambers: Oh, make that Felicity, please. I was talking about the physical examination that's standard for executives over 35. You know, X-rays, blood tests, specimens—gives the doctors kind of a baseline picture of your health.

Sawasaki: Will I be tested for drugs too?

Chambers: You won't be drug-tested, no. That's mandatory only for pre-employment applicants.

Sawasaki: Maria Cortez and I were just talking about drugs at lunch. Are they a big problem at ABC Foods?

Chambers: We're doing everything possible to keep them from turning into one.

Sawasaki: What's the policy on drug-testing?

Chambers: We test all new job applicants, whether they're exempt, non-exempt, or hourly. Nobody gets hired without being certified as drug-free.

　　國際人資處的經理全勃茲向澤崎說明，前來應徵工作的人都得作毒品測試。ABC 食品公司不錄用任何無法通過測試的人。

[國際人資處 ── 經理斐莉絲蒂・全勃茲的辦公室]

全勃茲：　我們來看一下，昭一，你的文件都弄好了，你有了社會保險號碼，你也知道健檢…

澤崎：　「健檢」？全勃茲女士？

全勃茲：　噢，請叫我斐莉絲蒂。我是在說健康檢查，規定是，凡年滿三十五歲以上的主管級人員都要作。你知道的，就是 X 光、血液檢查、尿液檢體等的 ── 好讓醫生能大概知道一下你的健康情形。

澤崎：　我也要作毒品測試嗎？

全勃茲：　你不用。只有尚未錄用的應徵者才得作。

澤崎：　午餐的時候，瑪莉亞・古岱茲才和我在談毒品的事。在 ABC 食品公司，毒品的問題大嗎？

全勃茲：　我們盡可能地不讓毒品成為大問題。

澤崎：　關於毒品測試，公司政策怎麼說呢？

全勃茲：　對於新來應徵工作的人，不管他是主管，一般員工，或是按時支薪的雇員，我們都要作毒品測試。任何人，在無法證實為非吸毒者之前，我們都不予錄用。

Lesson 19 Drug Testing and Screening (2)

Words and Phrases

International Human Resources
　　國際人資部門

Social Security　　社會安全福利

physical (examination)　健康檢查

standard　　標準的; 普通的

mandatory　　必須的; 強制的

pre-employment　　任聘之前的

job applicant　　應徵工作者

certify　　證實

drug-free　　不吸毒的

Vocabulary Building

- **straighten out**　　解決

  The problem in our accounting procedures has been straightened out.

  (公司會計流程上的問題已經解決了。)

- **specimen**　　(尿液)檢體; 樣品

  A tissue specimen taken from my father's stomach proved he has cancer.

  (我爸爸去做了胃部切片檢查, 結果證實, 他得了胃癌。)

- **baseline**　　基準線

  cf. The bottom line is our profit margin.

  (我們能有多少利潤才是最重要的問題。)

- **exempt, non-exempt, or hourly**　　美國在法令上對於勞動者的區分, 依其薪資和加班時數 (wage and overtime) 能否適用 Fair Labor Standards Act (公平勞動基準法)、及加班費應否免除 (exempt), 而分成 exempt employee, non-exempt employee。 exempt employee 指的是沒有資格領取加班費或假日勤務津貼 (overtime or premium time pay) 等的主管人員。 non-exempt employee 則指依此條款能領取加班費的一般員工。 hourly 是按時支薪的勞工。

  Exempt employees are not entitled to overtime, while non-exempt employees are. Hourly workers are paid wages in accordance with the actual hours worked during a week.

  (主管人員不能領加班費, 一般員工則可以。按時支薪的勞工是依其每週的實際工作時數支領薪水。)

▶ *Exercises*

請勿改變例句的句型, 用a)、b)詞組代換下列例句。　　(解答見 262頁)

1. That's mandatory only for pre-employment applicants.

   a) required
   b) the physical examination is

2. Maria Cortez and I were just talking about drugs at lunch.

   a) discussing
   b) over breakfast

3. Nobody gets hired without being certified as drug-free.

   a) no one
   b) drug-testing

◆◆◆◆◆◆◆◆◆◆◆◆◆◆ 簡短對話 ◆◆◆◆◆◆◆◆◆◆◆◆◆◆

Sawasaki: But I had a complete check-up, sponsored by the company, just before I left Tokyo, and they gave me a clean bill of health.

Chambers: Well, it may seem redundant to you, but company policy is for all employees taking posts at corporate headquarters to be examined at the clinic here.

Sawasaki: My physical in Tokyo was a two-day affair, including one night in the hospital. I don't think I can spare that amount of time now.

Chambers: Oh, this one'll be much shorter than that. It should only take two hours— three at the outside.

---

check-up 健康檢查　　**clean bill of health** 完全健康證明　　**redundant** 多餘的　　**take a post** 到任 (職位)　　**physical** 健康檢查　　**two-day affair** 要花掉兩天時間的事　　**spare** 撥出 (時間)　　**at the outside** 頂多

Drug Testing and Screening (3) (毒品測試)

●預習 —Sentences

- How do people use them in America?
- That's a good question.
- It's short but pretty informative.
- I can show it to you now.
- I'll come back afterwards to answer any questions.

●Vignette

Sawasaki: Drugs are so rare in Japan I wouldn't even know what to look for. How do people use them in America?

Chambers: That's a good question, Shoichi. Actually, we have a video if you're interested. It's short but pretty informative. I can show it to you now, if you'd like.

Sawasaki: It's no problem?

Chambers: Nope, the tape machine is always ready to go. I'll come back afterwards to answer any questions.

Sawasaki: Thanks, Felicity.

[*Sounds of a gun fight*]

Narrator: The drama of drugs in America is on television because the tragedy of drugs is now in our homes, our schools, and our businesses. Sixty billion dollars is lost each year by businesses alone through absenteeism, injury, theft, and poor productivity because of drugs—illegal drugs. The President's Commission on Organized Crime has reported that 20 million Americans regularly use marijuana, six million regularly use cocaine, and 500,000 are addicted to heroin . . .

*　　*　　*

全勃茲所放映的錄影帶，真實地描述了毒品所造成的悲劇，以及它給美國社會帶來的重大影響，相當地駭人聽聞。

澤崎：　毒品在日本很少見，我甚至不知道哪些才是。在美國，毒品是怎麼個用法？

全勃茲：　好問題，昭一。事實上，如果你有興趣的話，我們這兒有一卷錄影帶，很短，不過它能告訴你很多東西。如果你要的話，我現在就可以放給你看。

澤崎：　沒有問題嗎？

全勃茲：　沒有，放影機隨時待命。帶子放完後，我會再回來，如果你有任何問題，我到時候再回答你。

澤崎：　謝謝，斐莉絲蒂。

[槍戰聲]

敘述者：　現在放映的是美國的毒品劇場，現今毒品的悲劇在我們的家庭、學校、甚至是事業裡頭都在上演。每年，因著非法毒品所導致的曠職、傷害、竊盜以及生產力低下等問題，單是企業界就要損失六百億美元。根據總統諮詢委員會關於組織犯罪的報告指出，有二千萬的美國人經常性地吸食大麻，六百萬人經常使用古柯鹼，五十萬人吸食海洛因成癮…

＊　　＊　　＊

Lesson 19　Drug Testing and Screening (3)

Words and Phrases

informative *adj.*　提供知識的	organized crime　組織犯罪
nope　〔美俗〕=no	marijuana [ˌmærəˈwɑnə]　大麻
tragedy　悲劇; 慘事	cocaine [koˈken]　古柯鹼
theft　竊盜	be addicted to　染上…(毒癮)
productivity　生產力	

Vocabulary Building

- **if you'd like**　如果你要的話

  cf. If you don't mind, let's use Jim's office for the interview.

  (如果你不介意的話，我們用吉姆的辦公室來面談好了。)

- **no problem**　沒問題

  "Do you mind explaining to me the meaning of this passage?"— "No problem."

  (「你介意解釋一下這段話的意思給我聽嗎？」「沒問題。」)

- **absenteeism** [ˌæbsənˈtiɪzɪn]　長期缺席(不上班); 曠職

  Our corporate management is alarmed by rising absenteeism in the plant, since the peak production season is about to set in.

  (眼看著生產的高峰季就要來臨，可是工廠裡員工的曠職率卻一直升高，公司的管理階層可緊張了。)

- **commission**　諮詢委員會; 佣金

  cf. He earned a handsome commission on the sale.

  (他在這次的買賣中賺了一筆為數不小的佣金。)

1. Drugs are so rare in Japan I wouldn't even know what to look for.

    a) they look like
    b) uncommon

2. We have a video if you're interested.

    a) can show you
    b) you'd like to see it

3. I'll come back afterwards to answer any questions.

    a) return
    b) chat with you

◆◆◆◆◆◆◆◆◆◆◆◆◆◆ 簡短對話 ◆◆◆◆◆◆◆◆◆◆◆◆◆◆

Chambers: So you have no drug problem at all in Japan?

Sawasaki: Well, I wouldn't go so far as to say that there's no problem, but it's certainly quite minor compared with the States.

Chambers: Even so, I suppose you must at least have the "softer" drugs like marijuana.

Sawasaki: Even marijuana is rare. If anything, amphetamines are more of a problem for the police to control.

Chambers: Amphetamines? I don't think our police have the time to even think about them.

---

wouldn't go so far as to say 不至於過分到說…   **softer** 毒性較小的   **if anything** 如果有的話   **amphetamine** 安非他命

Lesson 19

Drug Testing and Screening (4) (毒品測試)

●預習 — *Sentences*

- Did the video answer your questions?
- Why is this program necessary?
- Most people just want to be let alone.
- What's wrong with taking any drug?
- You seem to have a sensitive job.

●*Vignette*

Chambers: Did the video answer your questions, Shoichi?

Sawasaki: Well, it helped. But tell me, Felicity, why is this program necessary?

Chambers: We have a responsibility to provide a safe and productive work environment for our employees.

Sawasaki: Don't some people consider all this testing an invasion of their privacy?

Chambers: Un-huh. Most people just want to be let alone. "What's wrong with taking any drug I want as long as I don't hurt anyone else by doing so?" Right? But it's difficult for an individual to do something to himself that has consequences on himself alone. To "drop out" via drugs means that the person becomes dependent upon the social structure. Someone has to pay the bill. In our own case, we make sure job applicants know they're going to be tested, so it's their choice to either take the tests or not be considered for employment.

Sawasaki: You seem to have a sensitive job, Felicity.

Chambers: You're right, Shoichi. And sometimes a tough one.

錄影帶放完後，全勃茲跟澤崎說明公司政策。毒品測試的目的，是為了給員工一個安全、有生產力的工作環境。

全勃茲： 昭一，這卷帶子解答了你的問題嗎？

澤崎： 嗯，是有幫助。不過，斐莉絲蒂，告訴我，為甚麼要有這種計畫？

全勃茲： 我們有責任要提供給員工一個安全、有生產力的工作環境。

澤崎： 不會有人認為這種測試侵犯了他們個人的隱私嗎？

全勃茲： 呃，大部分的人不願意有人來干預他們的私事。「只要我不傷害到別人，吸毒又有甚麼不對？」是嗎？可是，一個人若對自己做了些甚麼事，他也難保事情的後果不會禍及他人。藉由毒品來「逃避現實」的作法意味著這個人對社會結構已經有了依賴性。總得要有人付出代價。以公司的例子來看，我們會讓來應徵工作的人確實明白，他們得接受測試，所以他們可以選擇接受測試，或是放棄這個工作機會。

澤崎： 斐莉絲蒂，看來妳的工作相當敏感。

全勃茲： 昭一，你說的沒錯。而且，這工作有時還很不好做呢！

Lesson 19　Drug Testing and Screening (4)

Words and Phrases

responsibility 責任; 義務	consequence [ˈkɑnsə‚kwɛns] 結果
productive 有生產力的	via 經由…
work environment 工作環境	social structure 社會結構
invasion (權利的)侵犯; 入侵	sensitive *adj.* 神經質的; 敏感的
individual 個人	

Vocabulary Building

● **as long as** 只要…; 當…時候

As long as Mr. Johnson is here, why don't we go ahead and talk to him about our proposition?

(趁著強森先生在這裡, 我們何不上前去, 同他談談我們的提案?)

● **drop out** 退出; 不參與; 輟學

cf. The job market is tight for high-school dropouts.

(對於那些高中沒念完就輟學的人而言, 工作機會很有限。)

● **dependent upon** 依賴…

Our Christmas bonus this year is dependent upon exports, because the domestic market is sluggish.

(因為國內市場不景氣, 所以今年冬季的紅利就要視出口情形來決定了。)

● **pay the bill** 付帳

cf. Crime doesn't pay.

(犯罪是划不來的。)

Exercises　　請勿改變例句的句型, 用a)、
b)詞組代換下列例句。　　(解答見262頁)

1. Don't some people consider all this testing an invasion of their privacy?

    a) think
    b) a waste of time

2. Most people just want to be let alone.

    a) get away from it all
    b) only wish they could

3. Someone has to pay the bill.

    a) for it
    b) the person responsible

◆◆◆◆◆◆◆◆◆◆◆◆◆ 簡短對話 ◆◆◆◆◆◆◆◆◆◆◆◆◆

Chambers: By the way, you don't smoke, do you?
Sawasaki: Well, I used to, but I quit right after my first visit here.
Chambers: That's good.
Sawasaki: Any special reason you say that?
Chambers: We've just announced a no-smoking policy for the entire cor-
porate headquarters, to go into effect in six months. That's to give the
smokers time to wean themselves of their nicotine habit.
Sawasaki: Or to find themselves new jobs?
Chambers: Right.

---

go into effect　(法律或規則等)生效　　**wean oneself of**　(使自己)戒除(惡
習)　　**nicotine habit**　尼古丁的習慣(抽菸的習慣)

Lesson 19

Drug Testing and Screening — 總結

■　■　■

　　美國多數的一流企業對前來應徵工作者都有所謂的毒品測試。但對於其在職員工，則基於保護個人隱私的觀點，現已不再施行 random check 了。

　　第一次檢查（驗尿 urinalysis）的費用要 15 至 45 美元，所以也有人說毒品測試業是個有十億美元身價的產業。但員工因吸食毒品而衍生的曠職、傷害、竊盜、或是生產力低落等問題，卻要使美國的產業界每年蒙受六百至一千億美元的損失，其破壞力不可謂不大。

　　至於毒品測試的結果統計，並非每家公司都會公布出來。不過，根據 *IABC Communication World* 雜誌的報導，加州的運輸公司 Southern Pacific Co. 在 1984 年 8 月至 1986 年 10 月間，對其員工所進行約五千次的測試結果為：683 人呈陽性反應，其中 52% 吸食大麻，26% 使用古柯鹼。

　　呈陽性反應的員工，大部分都遵從公司指示接受治療，不久即回到工作崗位，而不願接受戒治計畫的 17 名員工則遭到解雇。報告顯示，在那兩年間，人為事故減少約 70%，傷害率則約 30%。

　　雖然也有 "Just Say No"「向毒品說不」的宣傳活動，但美國政府對於毒品這個社會之瘤仍無法提出有效的因應對策。於是，毒品合法化的論調又再度燃起。

　　贊成派的說法是，政府可以把現在用來取締毒品所花費的八十億美元拿來運用在教育或治療上，而幫派分子每年藉販賣大麻和古柯鹼所賺得的二百億美元進帳也會告終。相對地，反對派則認為，毒品若能便宜購得，則吸毒者的數量也會增加，而花在吸毒者身上的戒治費用也會從現在一年的六百億美元快速跳升。

　　有人說，美國多數暴力犯罪的動機都是為了要獲得金錢去購買毒品。如果說話的人能確實證明，毒品合法化之後，犯罪率就會大幅下降，那麼，合法化也就不得不成為時勢所趨了。

Personal Security

（個人安全）

◆ **Lesson 20** 的內容 ◆

　　《日本人與猶太人》一書的作者曾說：「日本人以為，水和安全都是不要錢的。」所以，這也難怪澤崎在赴紐約之前，從未認真思考過「安全」的問題。然而，一旦身處異鄉，再加上那些傳聞，澤崎又開始有種莫名的不安之感。不過，多餘的擔心有時也會適得其反。

I'm no John Wayne, but do you think I should own a gun?

Lesson 20

Personal Security (1)（個人安全）

●預習 — *Sentences*

- I'm here about my ID badge.
- Thanks for coming back.
- Something went wrong with the camera.
- Sorry for the trouble.
- I don't even know what that is.

●*Vignette*

[*Corporate Security Office*]

Sawasaki: Good afternoon. My name is Sawasaki. I'm here about my ID badge.

Healey: Mr. Shoichi Sawasaki, good. My name's Tom Healey. I'm the Corporate Security manager. Thanks for coming back. Something went wrong with the camera and computer goofed up your security number. Murphy's Law really works, you know.

Sawasaki: Sorry, whose law?

Healey: Murphy's Law. It's an administrative aphorism that whatever can go wrong will go wrong. Anyway, here's your new badge. Sorry for the trouble.

Sawasaki: Not at all.

Healey: Say, did you just move to the United States, Shoichi?

Sawasaki: Yes, that's right. I just moved into a nice comfortable apartment in Scarsdale over the weekend.

Healey: Did you get an ABC Foods security kit?

Sawasaki: No. What's that?

Healey: It's basically a checklist of ways to improve security in your home, your car, and when you're traveling. By the way, if you intend to buy a car, you might want to have a window etching done on it.

Sawasaki: I don't even know what that is.

Healey: It's sort of a psychological deterrent to car theft. You see, a thief who wants to resell a stolen car usually changes the license plates to conceal the car's proper identity.

46

[公司警衛處]

澤崎：　午安。我的名字是澤崎。我是為了我的身分識別章而來的。

希利：　澤崎昭一先生，很好。我是湯姆・希利，公司警衛處的負責人。謝謝你又回到這裡來。照相機出了點問題，而電腦又搞錯了你的安全號碼。你知道的，墨菲定律真的應驗了。

澤崎：　抱歉，你說誰的定律？

希利：　墨菲定律。那是一句管理上的格言：會出岔的事終歸要出岔。不管怎樣，這是你新的識別章。不好意思給你帶來麻煩。

澤崎：　不會、不會。

希利：　我說昭一啊，你剛搬到美國來嗎？

澤崎：　是啊。我上週末才搬到斯卡絲黛一間舒適宜人的公寓裡。

希利：　那你有拿一份 ABC 食品公司的安全手冊嗎？

澤崎：　沒有。那是甚麼東西？

希利：　基本上，那是一份清單，告訴你如何增進居家、用車以及旅行時的安全。順帶一提，如果你要買車，你可能會想在車窗上弄點蝕刻。

澤崎：　我甚至不知道那是甚麼。

希利：　那是對偷車賊的一種心理遏阻。你看，如果小偷想轉售贓車，通常會改變牌照，不叫人知道這車的真正來路。

Lesson 20 Personal Security (1)

Words and Phrases

administrative	行政管理上的	resell	轉售
etching	蝕刻	conceal	隱藏
thief	小偷；竊賊		

Vocabulary Building

- **go wrong**　不對勁；錯了
  cf. Nothing goes right for me when I'm tired.
  (我如果累了的話，甚麼事都會不對勁。)

- **goof up**　搞錯；弄錯
  cf. Stuart was fired because he was always goofing off at work.
  (史都華被開除了，因為他在工作上老是出錯。)

- **aphorism** [ˈæfəˌrɪzm̩]　格言；警句；金言
  Good managers know when to quote a pertinent aphorism or tell an interesting anecdote.
  (一個好經理會知道何時該引用恰當的格言或說個有趣的軼事。)

- **deterrent**　抑止；遏阻
  Is capital punishment an effective deterrent to vicious crime?
  (死刑能有效遏阻兇惡的罪行嗎？)

▶ **Exercises**　請勿改變例句的句型, 用a)、
b)詞組代換下列例句。　（解答見 262 頁）

1. It's an administrative aphorism that whatever can go wrong will go wrong.

   a) is least expected
   b) a rule of thumb

2. Say, did you just move to the United States, Shoichi?

   a) from Japan
   b) incidentally

3. It's basically a checklist of ways to improve security.

   a) maximize
   b) package of tools

◆◆◆◆◆◆◆◆◆◆◆◆◆ 簡短對話 ◆◆◆◆◆◆◆◆◆◆◆◆◆

Healey: Could I have that name again?
Sawasaki: Sure, it's Sawasaki, and my first name is Shoichi.
Healey: Do you mind spelling that for— no, wait, it's probably better if you write it down for me.
Sawasaki: Let's see, can I have a piece of paper?
Healey: Just put it on the back of this envelope.
Sawasaki: Here you go.
Healey: Thanks. Oh, and can I have your employee ID number?
Sawasaki: Uh-huh. It's 87-0327-9.

Could I have that name again? 可以再告訴我一次你的名字嗎？　**Here you go.** 在這裡; 這是你要的東西。

Lesson 20

Personal Security (2) (個人安全)

●預習 — *Sentences*

- Don't worry needlessly.
- I know some judo from my high school days.
- Risk your property, not your life.
- Do you think I should own a gun?
- Have you ever fired a gun?

●*Vignette*

Healey: But if you've etched the registration number on each car window, the thief will have to replace all the glass, which is an expensive and time-consuming business. Window etching won't prevent vandalism or the theft of valuables from the car, but it's an inexpensive way to discourage theft of the car itself.

Sawasaki: I see. Where should I take my car to get the windows etched?

Healey: You can buy a kit that contains the stencils and the stylus.

Sawasaki: To be honest with you, Tom, I've heard so many horror stories about crime in this country; I really worry for my family.

Healey: I appreciate exactly how you feel. But fear is not a useful weapon in self-defense. Don't worry needlessly. The unfortunate reality in this country dictates that you have to be always aware of potential danger.

Sawasaki: I know some judo from my high school days, but I . . .

Healey: Whatever you do, Shoichi, avoid confronting any intruder or attacker. Go the opposite direction and call the police. If you are confronted, give them your wallet, camera, rings, whatever — just don't put up a fight. Risk your property, not your life.

Sawasaki: I'm no John Wayne, but do you think I should own a gun?

Healey: Have you ever fired a gun?

Sawasaki: No.

　　希利給了初至美國的澤崎一個建議:「如果要買車, 可以在車窗上蝕刻車子的登記號碼」, 如此一來, 在偷車賊的心理上會有遏阻作用。

希利: 但是如果你在每個車窗上蝕刻車子的登記號碼, 小偷就得更換所有的玻璃, 而那是既昂貴又耗費時間的事。蝕刻窗戶沒有辦法避免他人的破壞行為, 而車內的貴重物品也還是有可能失竊, 但若要打消竊賊偷車的念頭, 這倒不失為一個廉價的方法。

澤崎: 我了解了。我應該把我的車送到哪裡去蝕刻窗戶呢?

希利: 你可以買一組工具, 裡面有鏤空型版和鐵筆。

澤崎: 湯姆, 坦白跟你說, 關於這個國家裡的犯罪行為, 我聽到很多怪恐怖的事, 我真替我家人擔心呢!

希利: 我非常了解你的感受。不過, 在自衛時, 恐懼可派不上用場。不要作無謂的擔心。這個國家中所存在的這些不幸事實, 就是要你隨時提高警覺, 留意周遭潛在的危險。

澤崎: 我在中學時學過一些柔道, 但是我…

希利: 昭一, 你做甚麼都好, 但就是要避免與任何侵入你家或襲擊你的人作正面衝突。要朝反方向跑, 打電話給警察。如果你正面碰上了, 就把你的皮夾、照相機、戒指, 管他其麼東西, 都給他們 —— 就是不要抵抗。拿你的財產去冒險, 不要用你的性命。

澤崎: 我不是約翰・韋恩, 可是你認為我該配把槍嗎?

希利: 你有沒有開過槍?

澤崎: 沒有。

Lesson 20 Personal Security (2)

Words and Phrases

vandalism	(野蠻的)破壞行為	dictate	命令；指揮
discourage	使…打消念頭	potential	潛在的；有潛力的
stencil	鏤空型版	confront v.	面對
stylus	尖筆；鐵筆	intruder	入侵者；闖入者
horror story	令人戰慄的言語	attacker	攻擊者
needlessly	不必要地	property	所有物；財產

Vocabulary Building

- **time-consuming**　耗費時間的

  The urban renewal project proved too time-consuming and capital intensive for the small firm.

  (事實證明，這個都市再開發計畫對小公司而言太耗時，而所需的資本更非他們所能負擔。)

- **to be honest with you**　坦白跟你說

  cf. Speaking quite frankly, I'm not sure if there's future for you in this company. You may be happier in a different corporate environment.

  (我很坦白地說，我不能確定你在這家公司會不會有前途。也許你在一個不同的企業環境會比較愉快吧！)

- **put up a fight**　(做出)抵抗；打架

  The company put up a good fight but couldn't stop the hostile takeover.

  (公司已盡力抗爭過了，但仍然無法阻止這個用意不善的購併事件。)

- **risk** *v.*　冒險

  Mary risked her savings by speculating on foreign exchange.

  (瑪莉冒著錢財損失的危險，將存款拿來炒作外匯。)

1. I appreciate exactly how you feel.

    a) what's going on in your mind
    b) understand

2. Fear is not a useful weapon in self-defense.

    a) overcoming the situation
    b) won't help you at all

3. Whatever you do, avoid confronting any intruder or attacker.

    a) don't antagonize
    b) by all means

◆◆◆◆◆◆◆◆◆◆◆◆◆◆ 簡短對話 ◆◆◆◆◆◆◆◆◆◆◆◆◆◆

Sawasaki: I understand some people hook up burglar alarms in their cars. Are they effective?

Healey: To some extent, sure, but you shouldn't set too much store by those things.

Sawasaki: Why? Don't they emit an ear-splitting noise if somebody breaks into the car?

Healey: They do, but your professional thief can probably disable the alarm in the space of less than a minute. And chances are that nobody'll interfere with him in the meantime.

---

hook up 安裝　　**burglar alarm** 防盜警報器　　**to some extent** 到某種程度　　**set store by** 重視…　　**emit** 放出; 發出　　**ear-splitting** 震耳欲聾的　　**break into** 侵入　　**disable** 使無能力; 弄壞　　**in the space of** 在…期間　　**chances are** 很可能…　　**interfere with** 介入…; 干擾…

Lesson 20

Personal Security (3) （個人安全）

●預習 — *Sentences*

- I would strongly recommend against it.
- I see your point.
- I guess they're part of the reality here.
- I've been used to being so trusting in Japan.
- You better look out.

●*Vignette*

Healey: Unless you're already fairly expert in the use of firearms, I would strongly recommend against it. You're more likely to have an accident than to deter a criminal. And if you display a gun when you're confronted, your chances of getting shot at are pretty high.

Sawasaki: I see your point. But let me tell you, one of the things that really depresses me about life in New York is seeing so many security devices on the door of my apartment. I guess they're part of the reality here.

Healey: You'll soon get used to them. Establish good habits. Always double- or triple-lock your doors even if you're leaving the apartment for just a few minutes. Doors should be double-locked or deadbolted when you're inside too.

Sawasaki: But I've been used to being so trusting in Japan.

Healey: In U.S. cities, you better look out. Scarsdale may have a Neighborhood Watch program. If so, you might do well to join it.

Sawasaki: What is it?

Healey: It's a community movement that started in the early '70s to combat the increasing wave of crime. It's proven to be quite effective in reducing burglaries, as well as street crime, auto crime, and vandalism.

澤崎在想是否該買把槍來自衛，但希利卻明確地告誡他：「萬萬不可。」因為有了槍枝就有發生意外的可能，而且一旦槍枝亮相，則遭射殺的可能性也會相對提高。

希利： 除非你對槍枝的使用已相當熟練，否則我會強烈奉勸你不要配槍。你因使用槍枝而發生意外的可能，會比你真正遏阻罪犯的可能要來得大。而且，在正面衝突時，如果他們看到你身上有槍，那你被射殺的可能性會相當高。

澤崎： 我瞭解你的意思了。不過，容我告訴你，在紐約的生活中，真正令我沮喪的事情之一是，我公寓的門上居然有那麼多安全裝置。我猜想，這也是此地現實面的一部分吧！

希利： 你很快就會習慣的。要養成好習慣，即使只離開公寓幾分鐘都要給門上個兩層或三層鎖。如果你人在屋內，也要上個兩層鎖，或是從裏面閂死。

澤崎： 可是我在日本已經很習慣信任別人了。

希利： 在美國都市，你最好還是提防點。斯卡絲黛可能會有一個鄰里的守望相助計畫。如果真是這樣，那你也加入會比較好。

澤崎： 那是甚麼東西？

希利： 那是一種從 70 年代早期就有的社區性活動，目的是要對抗日益增加的犯罪率。而事實證明，這不只減少了街頭犯罪、減少了與汽車相關的罪案、以及一些破壞行為，而且，它對於降低竊盜事件也相當有效。

Lesson 20 Personal Security (3)

Words and Phrases

firearm 輕型武器; 槍
recommend 建議; 勸告
deter 抑止; 妨礙
depress 使憂鬱; 使意氣下沈
security device 安全裝置

triple-lock *v.* 上三層鎖
deadbolt *v.* 閂死; 用門閂閂上
combat 對抗
burglary 竊案

Vocabulary Building

- **chances are high** 可能性高
  cf. The chances of the new design being marketable are slim.
  (這種新的圖案很有可能會賣不出去。)

- **I see your point.** 我瞭解你的意思了。
  cf. I must have missed your point. Are you for or against downsizing?
  (我一定是沒弄懂你的意思。你是贊成還是反對這個人事裁減計畫？)

- **habit** 習慣
  Tom had an annoying habit of doodling during important meetings.
  (湯姆有個惱人的習慣，就是他會在重要會議進行當中塗鴉。)

- **wave of crime** 犯罪率高漲
  cf. Washington D.C. has been suffering from a rash of drug-related crimes.
  (華府方面一直因著為數甚多的毒品罪案而困擾不已。)

1. You'll soon get used to them.

   a) to know the other staff
   b) gradually

2. It's a community movement that started in the early '70s.

   a) began
   b) social

3. It's proven to be quite effective.

   a) considered
   b) exceedingly

◆◆◆◆◆◆◆◆◆◆◆◆◆◆ 簡短對話 ◆◆◆◆◆◆◆◆◆◆◆◆◆◆◆

Sawasaki: Don't most people here own guns?

Healey: No, far from it. At least in this part of the country, the gun owners are definitely in the minority.

Sawasaki: But I suppose the criminals are all armed.

Healey: Not all of them, but if you should happen to run into a mugger or a burglar, it's best to act on the assumption that he's packing a gun. Even if he's not, he's probably got a knife, which can kill you just as dead as any bullet can.

Sawasaki: I'll keep that in mind.

Healey: Remember, it's better to part with your belongings than with your life.

Sawasaki: Right you are.

Far from it. 差遠了；才不是那樣。　　**in the minority** 佔少數的　　**happen to** 碰巧…　　**run into** 不期然碰到　　**mugger** 先襲擊人而後搶劫者；強盜 **burglar** 強盜；小偷　　**act on the assumption that** 假設…而行事　　**pack a gun** 配帶槍枝　　**keep in mind** 牢記　　**part with** 與…分離　　**belongings** 所有物

Lesson 20

Personal Security (4) (個人安全)

●預習 — Sentences

- You're expected to be on the lookout for crime.
- I once joined a neighborhood patrol in Japan.
- So that's what it was about.
- There are watchful eyes and ears.
- Thanks and see you later.

●Vignette

Healey: If you participate in the program, you're expected to be on the lookout for crime or for anyone suspicious watching your home or a neighbor's home.

Sawasaki: Oh, I once joined a neighborhood patrol in Japan looking for an arsonist.

Healey: Here you're not expected to patrol the streets. Nor should you become involved in any way with a suspected criminal. That's the job of the local police.

Sawasaki: Is this sort of program initiated by the police?

Healey: Sometimes by the residents and sometimes by both. In any case, the participants work in close cooperation with the local police force. Also, they encourage you to mark your property to deter burglars and help in identifying property that has been stolen.

Sawasaki: Yesterday, I saw a street sign that said "You are entering a Watch area." So that's what it was about.

Healey: Yes. The sign is supposed to deter the potential burglar, because he knows that in that area, there are watchful eyes and ears.

Sawasaki: I have to run now, but I must say this conversation has been very informative and useful. Thanks and see you later.

　　希利建議澤崎加入「守望相助」計畫。這是美國在 70 年代初期，為了對抗日益增加的犯罪，而聯合發起的區域性社會運動。據說不少城市在推行之後，成效都相當顯著。

希利：　如果你參與了這個計畫，就得隨時保持警戒，注意有無犯罪事件，或是留心任何在觀察你家或鄰舍屋子的可疑人物。

澤崎：　哦，我在日本曾參加過一個鄰里的巡邏，尋找縱火犯。

希利：　在這裡，沒有人要你去巡邏街道，而你也不該跟嫌疑犯在任何事上有所牽連。那是當地警方的責任。

澤崎：　像這種計畫是由警方發起的嗎？

希利：　有時是居民發起的，有時兩者都有。但不管是那一種狀況，參與者都必須與當地警力密切配合。此外，警方會鼓勵民眾在自己的所有物上做標記，這一方面可以遏阻竊賊，一方面也可以協助指認贓物。

澤崎：　昨天，我看到街道上有一個標示說「你現在進入警戒區了」。原來就是這麼回事。

希利：　沒錯。這個標示是用來遏阻潛藏的罪犯，因為他會因此知道，在那個地區，有人正放亮了眼睛，張大了耳朵，在注意他的一舉一動。

澤崎：　我得快點走了。不過，跟你談了這些，真的獲得了不少知識，有用得很。謝了，再見。

Words and Phrases

patrol 巡邏; 巡視	in any case 不管是甚麼情況
arsonist 縱火犯	encourage 鼓勵
suspected criminal 嫌疑犯	identify 確認
initiate *v.* 發起; 著手做…	watchful *adj.* 小心的; 警戒的

Vocabulary Building

● **be on the lookout for**   警戒…; 小心…

The strike is over but we'll be on the lookout in the future for any signs of employee unrest.

(罷工結束了，但是我們將來會小心注意員工是否有任何不滿的情緒。)

● **suspicious**   令人起疑的; 存疑的; 疑心的

My boss was suspicious of my motives for suddenly taking a week off.

(我老闆對於我突然要請假一個星期的動機感到懷疑。)

● **in cooperation with**   與…配合 (協力)

We have to seek ways to improve the quality of our products and lower prices in cooperation with our vendors.

(我們必須和我們的銷售商配合，想辦法改善產品的品質，並降低產品的價格。)

● **be supposed to**   被認為是用來…; 應該要…

I was supposed to drive the visitor to the airport but was too busy to.

(我應該要載訪客到機場的，可是我太忙了。)

請勿改變例句的句型, 用a)、
b) 詞組代換下列例句。

▶ **Exercises**   (解答見 263 頁)

1. I once joined a neighborhood patrol in Japan looking for an arsonist.

   a) a rapist
   b) at one time I

2. The participants work in close cooperation with the local police force.

   a) collaborate
   b) volunteers

3. The sign is supposed to deter the potential burglar.

   a) intended to discourage
   b) crime

◆◆◆◆◆◆◆◆◆◆◆◆◆◆ 簡短對話 ◆◆◆◆◆◆◆◆◆◆◆◆◆◆

Sawasaki: This may not have anything to do with crime per se, but one thing that really struck me compared to the last time I was in New York is the decrease of graffiti on the subway cars.

Healey: Yeah, they made a major effort to clean 'em up. And you know, I think it does make a difference crime-wise.

Sawasaki: Really? How so?

Healey: Well, when you put people in a clean, well-kept-up environment, they're less likely to act like animals than if they're in a place that looks like a zoo or a junkyard. Of course, no environment's going to stop the hard-core weirdos.

---

have to do with 與…有關係　　**per se** (=by itself)　本身　　**graffiti** 塗鴉
clean 'em up (=clean them up)　把那些東西清除掉　　**crime-wise** 與犯罪相關
聯地　　**well-kept-up** 維護得整整齊齊的　　**junkyard** 垃圾場　　**hard-core**
頑強的　　**weirdo** 怪人; 習性古怪的人

Lesson 20

Personal Security — 總結

在美國，據說每五秒鐘就會有一起暴力犯罪事件發生。 *U.S. News & World Report* 指出，美國的強盜、殺人等重大犯罪，平均一年雖達810萬件，但被逮捕的只有724,000人，其中被判刑的，也僅193,000人，因之入獄的有149,000人，而其中36,000人的刑期不滿一年。

澤崎來自素以低犯罪率著稱的日本，他在看到美國的現況之後，著實吃驚不已。湯姆‧希利也說，"The unfortunate reality in this country dictates that you have to be always aware of potential danger."

然而，如果過於恐懼，嚴重到不敢離開住處一步，那生活也未免太過悲慘。所以，重要的是隨時提高警覺，恐懼是幫不上忙的。

其實，一般到海外出差的人並不容易遇到像綁架之類的計畫性犯罪，反而他們所碰上的罪案，幾乎都是由於自己的疏忽，使歹徒有機可乘而造成的 (casual offense)。譬如像是長時間把車停放在路邊卻沒有上鎖、深夜一個人出入危險場所、將鑰匙藏在門口墊子或花盆底下、在地鐵打瞌睡、或是在大庭廣眾下打開錢包數錢等的。換句話說，出門在外一定要有危機意識，這也可以避免輕啟他人的犯罪之心。而且，若正值旅遊之際發生意外而掃了玩興，那才划不來。

總而言之，"Better safe than sorry." 「與其事後懊悔，不如早作預防。」

A Traffic Accident

（交通事故）

◆ Lesson 21 的內容 ◆

連日來的勞累，難免使人粗心大意。澤崎駕駛著租用汽車，和機車發生相撞事故。所幸對方只是受了點擦傷，但是澤崎卻必須上法庭。難道才剛來美國就要受審判了嗎？真是讓人意想不到啊！

Lesson 21

A Traffic Accident (1) (交通事故)

●預習 — *Sentences*

- How will you be paying, cash or credit card?
- Do you have any other identification?
- Here's my business card.
- Here's your contract and the keys.
- I'll call an ambulance.

●*Vignette*

[*At a rent-a-car office*]

Agent: Do you want the damage and collision coverage?

Sawasaki: Yes, I want maximum coverage.

Agent: All righty. How will you be paying, cash or credit card?

Sawasaki: Credit card.

Agent: Your driver's license, please. A Japanese driver's license, huh? I'm not sure . . . You'll have to help me read it. Do you have any other identification?

Sawasaki: Only my passport. I've moved here from Japan to work for ABC Foods. Here's my business card.

Agent: I guess it's OK. You'll need to get a New York license soon. Your credit has now been approved. Please sign here, here, and here. Here's your contract and the keys. It's that red convertible in the corner. Do you want a map?

Sawasaki: Yes, thank you.

*   *   *

[*A crash*]

Sawasaki: Oh, no.

[*Sound of car door opening and Sawasaki getting out of car*]

Sawasaki: Are you all right? I'm sorry. I didn't see you.

[*Sound of another car stopping*]

Driver: Is he OK? I have a cellular phone. I'll call an ambulance.

*   *   *

　　澤崎使用日本駕照和信用卡租了部車子。那是一部漂亮的紅色敞篷車。但才開沒多久，馬上就在哈特絲黛附近的一個十字路口，和輛機車撞上了。

[在租車辦公室]

代辦：你要保損失險和擦撞險嗎？

澤崎：要。我要保全險。

代辦：好的。那你要怎麼付款呢？付現還是刷卡？

澤崎：刷卡。

代辦：請把你的駕照給我。呃，日本駕照？這我不太清楚誒…你得要念給我聽才行。你有沒有甚麼別的證件？

澤崎：就只有護照了。我在這兒的 ABC 食品公司工作，才剛從日本搬來。這是我的名片。

代辦：我想這也可以，不過你得早點去辦你的紐約駕照。好了，你的信用也沒問題。請在這裡，這裡，還有這裡簽名。這是你的合約還有車鑰匙。車子就是那輛停在角落的紅色敞篷車。你需要地圖嗎？

澤崎：要，謝謝。

＊　　＊　　＊

[碰撞聲]

澤崎：噢，糟糕！

[車門打開的聲音，澤崎下車]

澤崎：你還好嗎？很抱歉，我沒看到你。

[另一輛車停下來的聲音]

駕駛：他還好嗎？我這兒有行動電話，我叫輛救護車來。

＊　　＊　　＊

Words and Phrases

collision	碰撞	convertible	敞篷車
All righty.	〔俗〕=All right.	cellular [ˈsɛljɔlɔ] phone	(蜂巢式
identification	身分證明	的) 行動電話	
contract	合約; 契約	ambulance	救護車

Vocabulary Building

- **damage**　　損害; 損失

  The collision has caused damages estimated at about $650.

  (這個碰撞估計約已造成 650 元的損失。)

- **coverage**　　(保險的) 賠償範圍; (報導的) 取材範圍

  cf. The Japanese mass media gave little coverage to the death of a one-time dictator of a Latin American country.

  (一位曾統有某拉丁美洲國家的獨裁者死了, 但日本媒體幾乎沒有報導此事。)

- **Cash or credit card?**　　付現還是刷卡?

  cf. "Is there anything else you need?" — "No, that's it." — "All right. Cash or credit?"

  (「你還需要甚麼嗎?」「沒有, 這樣就夠了。」「好的。付現還是刷卡?」)

- **approve**　　認可; 批准

  cf. You should get approval from your supervisor before you purchase computers or office furniture.

  (你在購買電腦或辦公家具之前, 應該先得到你上司的批准。)

▶ *Exercises*

請勿改變例句的句型, 用a)、
b) 詞組代換下列例句。　　　　（解答見 263 頁）

1. Do you want the collision coverage?

    a) insurance
    b) need

2. I've moved here from Japan to work for ABC Foods.

    a) be with
    b) been transferred

3. You'll need to get a New York license soon.

    a) it's imperative for you
    b) apply for

◆◆◆◆◆◆◆◆◆◆◆◆◆◆ 簡短對話 ◆◆◆◆◆◆◆◆◆◆◆◆◆◆

Sawasaki: Oh, one question: What type of gas does the car take?

Agent: Glad you mentioned that. All our cars take only unleaded.

Sawasaki: Anything else I need to know before I hit the road?

Agent: Let's see, you should bring the car back with the tank full. Oh, and will anybody besides you be driving it?

Sawasaki: No, just me.

Agent: Then you're all set to go.

Sawasaki: Thank you.

Agent: Have a nice day.

---

gas (=gasoline) 汽油　　**unleaded** 無鉛的　　**hit the road** 〔俗〕開始旅行; 上路　　**tank** 汽油箱　　**all set to go** 準備好可以出發了　　**Have a nice day.** 再見。（離別時的客套話）

A Traffic Accident (2) (交通事故)

●預習 — *Sentences*

- Can I see your driver's license?
- I'm afraid it's not valid here.
- How long have you been in the United States?
- I live in Scarsdale and work for ABC Foods.
- I was traveling north toward Hartsdale.

●*Vignette*

[*As the sound of a siren fades*]

Officer: You weren't injured, sir? Can I see your driver's license, registration, and insurance certificate, please?

Sawasaki: Yes, I'm all right. Here's my driver's license and the papers from the rental car company.

Officer: A Japanese driver's license. I'm afraid it's not valid here. Do you have a passport, sir?

Sawasaki: Yes, sir.

Officer: Mr. Sawasaki, how long have you been in the United States and where are you staying?

Sawasaki: Four weeks. And I live in Scarsdale and work for ABC Foods.

Officer: I see. While my partner checks the information through our computer, please tell me exactly what happened.

Sawasaki: I was traveling north toward Hartsdale and must have missed seeing the motorcycle coming from my left. Before I knew it, he collided with me right here.

Officer: How fast were you going at the time of the accident, sir?

Sawasaki: About 15 or 20 miles an hour.

Officer: In Japan, you drive on the left-hand side of the road, correct? Have you driven much in the U.S.?

Sawasaki: A little.

　　警官的語氣很客氣，但在看到澤崎的日本駕照後便問：「你在美國常開車嗎？」因為他知道日本和美國的交通規則不太一樣，日本是靠道路左側行駛的。

[警笛的聲音慢慢消失]

警官：　先生，你沒有受傷吧？可不可以請你出示一下你的駕照、登記證、還有保險憑證？

澤崎：　沒有，我沒怎樣。這是我的駕照還有租車公司的文件。

警官：　日本駕照。它在這裡恐怕不能用。先生，你有護照嗎？

澤崎：　有的，警官。

警官：　澤崎先生，你到美國來有多久了？還有，你住在哪裡？

澤崎：　四個禮拜了。我住在斯卡絲黛，服務於 ABC 食品公司。

警官：　我知道了。趁著我的夥伴還在經由我們的電腦調查一些資料，你可以確切地告訴我發生了甚麼事嗎？

澤崎：　我正朝北開，往哈特絲黛的方向，這輛摩托車是從我左邊上來的，我一定是沒看到他。我還不清楚發生了甚麼事，他就跟我撞上了，就是在這個地方。

警官：　先生，車禍當時你的車速是多少？

澤崎：　時速大概十五或二十英里吧！

警官：　在日本，你們都是靠左邊開車的，對不對？你在美國常開車嗎？

澤崎：　開過幾次。

Lesson 21　A Traffic Accident (2)

Words and Phrases

be injured　受傷	collide　*v.*　碰撞；衝突
registration　登記證	left-hand side　左側
insurance certificate　保險憑證	

Vocabulary Building

- **valid**　有效的；正當的
  I hope you have a valid reason for being late.
  (我希望你對於你的遲到能有一個正當的理由。)

- **partner**　搭檔；夥伴；合夥人
  You're a bright young lawyer. I'll be quite disappointed if you're not made a partner in this law firm in five years' time.
  (你是一位傑出的青年律師。如果在五年內，你無法成為這家法律事務所的合夥人，那我會相當失望。)

- **exactly**　正確地
  What exactly are you trying to tell me?
  (你究竟想要告訴我甚麼?)

- **before I knew it**　我還搞不清狀況 (就…)
  cf. When I came to, I found myself in a hospital bed.
  (我清醒時發現自己躺在醫院床上。)

1. I'm afraid it's not valid here.

   a) invalid
   b) I suspect

2. How long have you been in the United States?

   a) this country
   b) lived

3. While my partner checks the information through our computer, please tell me exactly what happened.

   a) describe to
   b) how this has

◆◆◆◆◆◆◆◆◆◆◆◆◆◆ 簡短對話 ◆◆◆◆◆◆◆◆◆◆◆◆◆◆◆

Officer: What's your local address?
Sawasaki: It's 120 Beverly Road, Apartment 10-G, Scarsdale.
Officer: Phone number?
Sawasaki: 723-0456.
Officer: Is that home or husiness?
Sawasaki: That's my home phone. Would you like my daytime number too?
Officer: Yeah.
Sawasaki: Let me check on my card to be sure . . . It's 543-2100.
Officer: That's for ABC Foods, right?
Sawasaki: Yes, their corporate headquarters in Westchester County.

---

daytime number 　　白天的電話號碼

Lesson 21

A Traffic Accident (3) （交通事故）

●預習 — *Sentences*

- Did you stop at the stop sign there?
- Don't worry too much.
- Now I'd like you to sign here.
- Is your vehicle operative?
- Drive carefully and have a nice day.

●*Vignette*

Officer: Did you stop at the stop sign there?

Sawasaki: A stop sign? No, I didn't see a stop sign.

Officer: Well, I see that the stop sign is somewhat hidden by that tree branch.

Sawasaki: That's right! I'll be darned. But how's the motorcyclist?

Officer: He'll be fine—a few bruises maybe, but he was wearing a good helmet. Perhaps made in Japan. Now, Mr. Sawasaki, you're going to have to appear in court sometime in the next seven days.

Sawasaki: Court? I never . . .

Officer: I'm sorry, sir, but the State requires vehicle operators involved in an accident resulting in more than $500 damage without proper licensing and insurance documentation to appear before a judge. We also have to cite you for not observing a stop sign. Don't worry too much, though. It's standard procedure. All the information is on the back of this citation. Now I'd like you to sign here. It indicates that you understand and promise to appear.

Sawasaki: Yes, of course.

Officer: Is your vehicle operative, Mr. Sawasaki?

Sawasaki: The door on the driver's side is all dented but the car runs OK.

Officer: All right. Drive carefully and have a nice day.

Sawasaki: I don't think it can get any worse.

*   *   *

所幸機車騎士只受了一點皮肉之傷，但是澤崎卻被告知要在七天內出庭。雖然警官說不需要太擔心，但是…

警官： 在那邊停車再開標誌的地方，你有沒有停車？

澤崎： 停車再開標誌？沒有啊，我沒有看到有停車再開標誌。

警官： 嗯，我看這個標誌有點被那棵樹的樹枝遮住了。

澤崎： 真的耶，怎麼會這樣！不過，那個摩托車騎士情況如何？

警官： 他會沒事的 —— 也許一點皮肉之傷吧，他戴的安全帽好得很。大概是日本製的。好了，澤崎先生，未來七天內，不確定是甚麼時候，你得上次法庭。

澤崎： 法庭？我從來沒有…

警官： 先生，我很抱歉，但本州法律要求，汽機車駕駛只要涉及任何損失逾五百美元的意外事件，又無法出示正確的駕照和保險文件，那該駕駛必須到法庭上把事情說明清楚。另外，因為你沒有在停車再開標誌前停車，我們也得開傳票給你。不過，別太擔心，這只是標準程序。這張傳票背面有一切說明。現在我要你在這裡簽名，表示你都瞭解了，並且也答應出庭。

澤崎： 好的，當然。

警官： 澤崎先生，你的車還能跑嗎？

澤崎： 駕駛座側面的車門都凹進去了，不過跑倒還沒問題。

警官： 好。小心開車，還有，祝你有個愉快的一天。

澤崎： 我可不認為還有甚麼更糟的事會發生。

$$* \quad * \quad *$$

Lesson 21　A Traffic Accident (3)

Words and Phrases

motorcyclist	摩托車騎士	cite	傳喚…（出庭到案）
bruise [bruz]	擦傷；皮肉輕傷	citation	傳票
documentation	文件	be dented	凹陷

Vocabulary Building

- **I'll be darned.**　　太突然了；怎麼會這樣。〈有 I'm very surprised. 之意〉
  cf. The darned computer is having problems again.
  （這可惡的電腦又出問題了。）

- **appear in court**　　出庭
  cf. That's just a pittance. No way will I accept it. See you in court.
  （才這麼一點錢？我絕對不會接受的。法庭見吧！）

- **standard procedure**　　標準程序
  Send us a bill before the 15th of each month, and we'll make payments by the end of the following month. That's standard procedure here.
  （帳單要在每個月十五號之前寄給我們，這樣我們才能在下個月月底之前把錢付清。這是這裡的標準程序。）

- **operative**　　生效的；運轉的
  The new assembly line will be operative in two weeks.
  （這條新的裝配線將在兩週後開始運作。）

1. The stop sign is somewhat hidden by that tree branch.

   a) partially
   b) isn't really visible because of

2. You're going to have to appear in court sometime in the next seven days.

   a) it may be necessary for you
   b) testify at the trial

3. We also have to cite you for not observing a stop sign.

   a) give you a ticket
   b) failing to observe

◆◆◆◆◆◆◆◆◆◆◆◆◆◆ 簡短對話 ◆◆◆◆◆◆◆◆◆◆◆◆◆◆◆

Officer: Oh, one more thing.
Sawasaki: Yes?
Officer: You realize that your Japanese license is not valid for driving here?
Sawasaki: I thought that I could use it temporarily till I got a New York license.
Officer: No, the only out-of-state licenses we recognize are ones from other U.S. states or from Canadian provinces.
Sawasaki: How about international driver's permits?
Officer: Those are good only for visitors.

---

valid 有效的　　**temporarily** 暫時地　　**out-of-state** 非本州的; 他州的
Canadian province 加拿大的省　　**permit** 許可證

Lesson 21

A Traffic Accident (4) （交通事故）

●預習 — *Sentences*

- I'd appreciate your assistance.
- Our legal representation won't be necessary.
- You just plead not guilty.
- Simply go to the table in front of the judge.
- Do you swear to tell the truth?

●*Vignette*

Grimes: Mr. Sawasaki, I'm Janice Grimes from Legal. I understand you've inquired about your court hearing tomorrow.

Sawasaki: Yes, I have and I'd appreciate your assistance.

Grimes: In my opinion, you have an excellent case and our legal representation won't be necessary. Your court appearance is really only necessary to uphold the letter of the law.

Sawasaki: But what about the traffic ticket— the stop sign I missed?

Grimes: The officer who cited you also noted that the stop sign at the intersection was out of sight— hidden by a tree, I believe. Don't worry, you just plead not guilty.

Sawasaki: How do I do it, specifically?

Grimes: When your name is called, simply go to the table in front of the judge, present your evidence to the clerk, and be sworn in by the bailiff.

Sawasaki: Wow!

Grimes: The bailiff is a police officer in court and he will ask you, "Do you swear to tell the truth, the whole truth, and nothing but the truth, so help you God?"

Sawasaki: Then what do I say?

Grimes: "I do." That's all you need to say.

法律部門的珍妮絲・格林姆告訴澤崎關於明天出庭要注意的事。開始時居然還要像梅森探案中的場景那樣舉起手宣誓，光是想像就令他忐忑不安。

格林姆： 澤崎先生，我是從法律部門來的珍妮絲・格林姆。我知道你在詢問關於你明天要出席法院聽證會的事。

澤崎： 是的，我是想瞭解一下情形，很感激有妳的協助。

格林姆： 依我看，你這個案子有利極了，我們沒有必要為你出庭辯護。你之所以要出庭到案只是因為州法條文上如此要求。

澤崎： 可是那張罰單怎麼辦 —— 我沒有在停車再開標誌前停車？

格林姆： 那個開傳票給你的警官也注意到了，路口那個停車再開標誌根本就看不到 —— 是被棵樹遮住了，我想。別擔心，你只要以無罪答辯就可以了。

澤崎： 我到底該怎麼做，可不可以請妳說得明確一點？

格林姆： 當你聽到有人叫你名字的時候，你就走到法官前面的桌子，把你的證詞交給書記官，然後庭吏會帶你宣誓。

澤崎： 哇！

格林姆： 庭吏是一種法院裡的警官，他會問你說，「你是否願意對著神發誓，你所說的都是事實，全部的事實，而且只有事實？」

澤崎： 那我該說甚麼？

格林姆： 你只要說，「我願意。」

Words and Phrases

inquire 詢問	intersection 交叉口; 十字路口
appreciate 感激	specifically 具體地 (說明)
representation 代理; 辯護	evidence 證據
appearance 到場; 出庭	bailiff ['belɪf] 庭吏

Vocabulary Building

● **uphold**　確認; 支持

The Supreme Court rejected the appeal and upheld the decision by the appeals court, thus putting an end to the extended product liability lawsuit.

(最高法院駁回了這件上訴, 並且確認了上訴法院的判決, 這件已經拖了一陣的產品責任訴訟案件終於告終了。)

● **letter of the law**　法律條文

cf. The company was following the spirit of the law in giving refunds for the defective product.

(這家公司秉著法律精神, 把貨款退還給買到瑕疵品的顧客。)

● **out of sight**　不在視線範圍內; 看不到

cf. Please tell me when their plane is in sight.

(看得到他們的飛機時, 請告訴我。)

● **plead not guilty**　不服罪; 以無罪答辯

cf. The jury came back with the verdict of "not guilty."

(陪審團帶回「無罪」的判決。)

▶ *Exercises*

請勿改變例句的句型, 用a)、
b)詞組代換下列例句。

(解答見264頁)

1. I understand you've inquired about your court hearing tomorrow.

   a) heard
   b) made an inquiry

2. You have an excellent case and our legal representation won't be necessary.

   a) should be unnecessary
   b) so a lawyer

3. The officer noted that the stop sign at the intersection was out of sight.

   a) partially hidden
   b) crossing

◆◆◆◆◆◆◆◆◆◆◆◆◆◆ 簡短對話 ◆◆◆◆◆◆◆◆◆◆◆◆◆◆

Sawasaki: Can't I just pay a fine instead of going to court?
Grimes: I'm afraid that New York state law makes it mandatory for the violator to appear in court in cases like this.
Sawasaki: Is there any chance that I'll get a jail sentence?
Grimes: Don't let your imagination run away with you. It's only a traffic violation, after all. At worst the judge'll slap you with a $50 fine.
Sawasaki: That's a relief, but I still can't help feeling jittery about the whole business.
Grimes: Relax, you've got nothing to worry about.

---

pay a fine 付罰金　　**go to court** 出庭　　**mandatory** 強制性的; 義務的　**violator** 違反者　　**get a jail sentence** 被判入獄　　**let one's imagination run away** 讓個人的想像力奔馳　　**at worst** 再糟 (也不過); 充其量　　**slap** 〔口〕分派　　**That's a relief.** 那就令人放心多了。　　**jittery** 〔口〕心神不定的; 急躁不安的

79

Lesson 21

A Traffic Accident —— 總結

■ ■ ■

　　在美國，大部分的州十六歲以上就可以取得駕駛執照，不需要去駕訓班學習，而考試也非常簡單。通過筆試後，只要旁邊坐著一位有駕照的人，就可以上路練習了。

　　筆者於 1972 年在俄亥俄州的 Columbus 取得駕照。費用只要五美元。筆試只有二十題左右，都是用記號就可以回答的題目，路考則是在超級市場的停車場以時速十英里左右行駛，還有 parallel parking (路邊停車)，可允許失敗兩次。

　　我用陪考朋友的車來考試，當場就拿到了駕照。歸途中買了一輛 Opel 中古車，直接就開回家了。

　　從俄亥俄州調到紐約時，只要再作一次筆試就可取得紐約州的駕照，我還留著當時的試卷，舉其中一題為例：

If you drive past your exit on an expressway, you should

(假設你在高速公路上錯過了出口站，你應該)

a. Drive to the next exit and get off the highway.

b. Pull onto the shoulder, then back up to the exit.

c. Make a U-turn at the nearest emergency turn area.

d. Make a U-turn at the next service area.

正確答案為 a。

　　我在美國取得駕照的一年內，就像這次的故事一樣，和機車發生擦撞，上了法庭。我雖然以 not guilty 答辯，仍被判了罰金十五美元，我的保險公司隔年大幅增加了我的保費。

Lesson 22

Baby Boomers

（嬰兒潮世代）

◆ Lesson 22 的內容 ◆

　　出生於二次大戰後嬰兒潮時期的人，在美國稱之為 "baby boomers"。這些 baby boomer 約占美國成人人口的半數，而且他們也是全美勞動人口的主力。據云，嬰兒潮世代是大眾行銷市場上成功的族群。他們勤勉、企圖心旺盛、有教養，但同時也兼具了不信任他人以及傲慢自大的缺點。在他們心中，到底有著甚麼樣的美國夢呢？

Brad, what can you tell me about "baby boomers"?

Lesson 22

Baby Boomers (1) (嬰兒潮世代)

● 預習 — *Sentences*

- I should treat you to dinner sometime.
- You said you were engaged to an international banker.
- Why do the two of you work so hard?
- We want to succeed at our jobs.
- But don't tell anybody at the office.

● *Vignette*

Sawasaki: It feels so good to be back doing early morning aerobics, Maria. Thanks for the push. I should treat you to dinner sometime.

Cortez: Only after you clear it with my boyfriend, the hulk. Only kidding, Shoichi.

Sawasaki: You said you were engaged to an international banker, right? Does he travel as much as you do?

Cortez: More. He's gone 75 percent of the time. Let's see, it's Monday today, so he must be in Buenos Aires. We have to schedule our time together by phone and E-mail. Now I'm so busy with a new Hispanic promotion event in Chicago I couldn't join him for the weekend even if he happened to be in town.

Sawasaki: Why do the two of you work so hard? What motivates you? Do you have a grand master plan for life?

Cortez: Come on, Shoichi, you make me feel like I'm back at last week's press conference. Anyway, I guess we both work hard because it's fun and we want to succeed at our jobs. We plan to get married next spring provided we can arrange a date, but we don't intend to start a family until we've started up our own business. But don't tell anybody at the office. OK?

Sawasaki: OK, but tell me—why does everyone in America dream of starting their own business? Especially somebody like you, who's working for a Fortune 500 company.

82

　　古岱茲的夢想是希望能跟未婚夫兩個人一起開創自己的事業。她甚至認為即使結了婚，也要等到有了自己的公司才要生小孩。

澤崎：　我現在又開始跳晨間有氧舞蹈了，瑪莉亞，那種感覺真棒。謝謝妳推我一把。我應該要找時間請妳吃頓飯才對。

古岱茲：　那你得要先得到我那大個兒男友的批准才行。昭一，跟你開玩笑的啦！

澤崎：　妳說過妳跟一個國際銀行家訂婚了，對不對？他也像妳一樣經常要旅行嗎？

古岱茲：　他比我還更常跑哩！他有百分之七十五的時間都是在外地度過的。我看一下，今天是星期一，所以他一定是在布宜諾斯艾利斯。我們必須藉由電話和電子郵件來排定我們的時間。而我現在正忙著芝加哥的一個新的拉丁裔市場銷售案，所以就算他正好在城裡，我週末也沒辦法跟他碰頭。

澤崎：　你們兩個為甚麼這麼賣力工作？是甚麼東西在驅策你們？你們有偉大的生涯規畫嗎？

古岱茲：　得了，昭一，你讓我覺得好像又回到上週的記者招待會似的。總之，我想我們都這麼拼命工作是因為覺得樂在其中，而且我們也都想在工作上有所成就。我們計畫明年春天結婚，如果排得出日子來的話。但是，除非我們有自己的事業了，否則我們不打算生小孩。不過，這些話你可別告訴辦公室裡其他的人喔，可以嗎？

澤崎：　當然，可是，告訴我 —— 為甚麼在美國每一個人都夢想著開創自己的事業呢？尤其是一個像妳這樣的人，現在的東家都已經是上榜財星雜誌前五百名的大公司了。

Lesson 22　Baby Boomers (1)

Words and Phrases

push　推; 推動	E-mail (electronic mail)　電子郵件
treat　請客	come on　得了; 拜託
clear *v.*　得到批准	press conference　記者招待會
hulk　大個子	Fortune 500 company　美國財星
Only kidding.　只是開玩笑的。	雜誌所列舉銷售前五百名的大公司

Vocabulary Building

● **motivate**　給與動機

How do you motivate a person who's not interested in financial rewards?

(你要如何驅策一個對金錢報酬不感興趣的人呢？)

● **master plan for life**　生涯規畫

According to his master plan for life, Terry intends to set up his own company by age 30.

(依照泰瑞的生涯規畫,他打算在三十歲之前成立自己的公司。)

● **provided**　假如…的話

I don't mind hard work, provided the pay is good.

(假如薪水不錯的話, 工作辛苦一點也沒關係。)

● **start a family**　生小孩

cf. I see that you're in a family way. When is the baby due?

(妳有喜了! 預產期是甚麼時候？)

（解答見 264 頁）

▶ **Exercises**   請勿改變例句的句型, 用a)、
b) 詞組代換下列例句。

1. You said you were engaged to an international banker.

   a) told me
   b) about to be married

2. We plan to get married next spring provided we can arrange a date.

   a) as soon as we manage to
   b) we're still interested in each other

3. We don't intend to start a family until we've started up our own business.

   a) have a baby
   b) made it

◆◆◆◆◆◆◆◆◆◆◆◆◆◆ 簡短對話 ◆◆◆◆◆◆◆◆◆◆◆◆◆◆◆

Sawasaki: I bet your parents will be happy when you get married.

Cortez: They want me to get married, yeah, but they're not too keen on Geoff.

Sawasaki: Why not? The way you describe him, he sounds like a good catch.

Cortez: Well *I* think so, but they were hoping I'd find myself a nice Puerto Rican boy or let them find one for me.

Sawasaki: So they don't like you marrying outside your own ethnic group.

Cortez: My mother's especially upset. "Maria," she says to me, "He's not even Catholic." She's pretty serious about her religion. To console her, we plan to be married by a priest.

---

get married 結婚   **be keen on** 熱中於…   **good catch** 好的結婚對象;
寶藏   **ethnic group** 種族團體   **be upset** 擔心; 煩惱   **console** 安慰
priest 神父; 牧師

Baby Boomers (2) (嬰兒潮世代)

●預習 — *Sentences*

- No bosses, no office politics, no rat race.
- What kind of business will you go into?
- But we're going to raise $650,000 to start up.
- We've seen it happen with our own eyes.
- Now it's worth well over $10 billion.

●*Vignette*

Sawasaki: Won't there be less resources to work with, longer work hours, and little security?

Cortez: Control, Shoichi, control. No bosses, no office politics, no rat race. And the results will speak for themselves. An experience like working for ABC Foods trains you to develop good business instincts and recognize opportunities.

Sawasaki: What kind of business will you go into?

Cortez: Sorry, Shoichi, I can't tell you that. But we're going to raise $650,000 to start up.

Sawasaki: Wow! That's a big number. But don't more than a quarter of new businesses in America fail within two years?

Cortez: Yes, but one successful shot as an entrepreneur and you've got it made.

Sawasaki: Why do you think being an entrepreneur is so appealing?

Cortez: We're the baby boomers and we've seen it happen with our own eyes. In the mid-'70s, the personal computer industry was created by two students working in a garage. Now it's worth well over $10 billion. It's the American dream.

*   *   *

古岱茲認為她在 ABC 食品公司的工作經驗，不僅能培養她在商業上的敏銳直覺，而且更是一種洞悉商機的訓練。

澤崎： 可是那樣一來，可運用的資源不就少了嗎？而且工作時間會加長，也沒有甚麼保障，不是嗎？

古岱茲： 不受轄制啊！昭一，不受轄制！沒有老闆，沒有公司內部的權力鬥爭，沒有同事之間的明爭暗鬥。而且，你付出了甚麼，馬上就能在結果上見真章。在 ABC 食品公司的工作經驗，可以培養你敏銳的商業直覺，並訓練你如何洞察商機。

澤崎： 你們打算走哪一行？

古岱茲： 抱歉，昭一，我不能告訴你。不過，一開始我們打算籌措到六十五萬美元的資金。

澤崎： 哇！那是一筆很大的數目耶！可是，在美國這些剛起步的事業當中，有超過四分之一的比例不是兩年內就無聲無息了嗎？

古岱茲： 是沒錯，可是只要有那麼一次以企業家姿態打出的漂亮出擊，那你就成功了。

澤崎： 你們為甚麼會這麼執著於要成為企業家呢？

古岱茲： 我們是嬰兒潮世代的一份子。我們親眼見到了事情的發生。在 70 年代中期，就因為兩個學生在車庫裡埋頭苦幹，個人電腦業於焉誕生，而它現在的價值已遠逾一百億美元了。這就是美國夢。

＊　　＊　　＊

Words and Phrases

resource	財源; 財力; 資產	start up	開始
work hours	工作時間	shot	嘗試
security	安全; 保障	you've got it made	你就成功了
business instinct	商業直覺	appealing	有吸引力的
raise	募集 (資金); 籌措	garage	車庫

Vocabulary Building

● **office politics**　辦公室內的權力鬥爭 (政治活動)
He did his best to avoid getting involved in office politics.
(他盡量避免跟公司內部的權力鬥爭有任何牽扯。)

● **rat race**　同事之間的競爭
My boss got tired of the rat race and decided to become a forest ranger.
(我老闆厭倦了同事之間的明爭暗鬥，決定去當森林警備隊員。)

● **entrepreneur** [ˌɑntrəprəˈnɝ]　企業家
cf. You don't have the entrepreneurial skills it takes to get a new business off the ground.
(新事業要能起步，得要有企業家的幹才，而這是你所欠缺的。)

● **American dream**　美國夢
For many people, life in Orange County, California epitomizes the American dream.
(對許多人來說，加州奧倫治郡的生活就是美國夢的縮影。)

▶**Exercises** 請勿改變例句的句型, 用a)、
b)詞組代換下列例句。 (解答見 264 頁)

1. What kind of business will you go into?

    a) type
    b) start

2. Why do you think being an entrepreneur is so appealing?

    a) could you explain why
    b) attractive

3. Now it's worth well over $10 billion.

    a) the annual sales come to
    b) something like

◆◆◆◆◆◆◆◆◆◆◆◆◆◆ 簡短對話 ◆◆◆◆◆◆◆◆◆◆◆◆◆◆

Sawasaki: How can you stand to face that level of risk?

Cortez: Well, I admit it's a little bit scary. But Geoff and I are pretty confident that we can make a go of our business.

Sawasaki: You have a product whose time has come?

Cortez: As I said, I can't go into the details. We're confident, but of course we can't be absolutely sure we'll succeed. That's why we plan to wait a bit before having kids.

Sawasaki: I must say I respect your drive.

---

stand to face 面對　　**scary** 恐怖的　　**make a go of** 在…上成功　　**time has come** 時候到了　　**go into the details** 描述細節　　**drive** 驅策力

Lesson 22

Baby Boomers (3) （嬰兒潮世代）

●預習 — *Sentences*

· What can you tell me about "baby boomers"?
· They're often skeptical, arrogant, and demanding.
· It means traditional husband and wife.
· Ozzie goes to work and Harriet stays home.
· They tend to have high aspirations.

●*Vignette*

Sawasaki: Brad, what can you tell me about "baby boomers"?

Winchell: Baby boomers? They're the "new breed" of Americans, born during the post-World War II baby boom, or, between 1946 and '65. They make up nearly half of the U.S. adult population and slightly more than half of the labor force.

Sawasaki: What would you say are their characteristics?

Winchell: Hardworking, ambitious, educated. On the downside, they are often skeptical, arrogant, and demanding. They're the former students of the '60s and '70s and their opinions have been shaped by the civil rights movement, Vietnam, and Watergate. In two-thirds of baby-boom families, both spouses are wage earners. Only about ten percent are Ozzie-and-Harriet families.

Sawasaki: Meaning what?

Winchell: Sorry, Shoichi, it means traditional husband and wife. Ozzie goes to work and Harriet stays home to take care of the perfect house and adorable kids. Comes from an old TV show. That kind of lifestyle is rare to find now. Besides, half of baby-boomer marriages end in divorce.

Sawasaki: They have so much to juggle in so little time, huh?

Winchell: Right. They tend to have high aspirations, which show up in their work and in the products they buy.

*　　*　　*

所謂的嬰兒潮世代在他們的學生時期，正好遭逢60、70年代的民權運動、越戰及水門事件，所以他們發展出來的思考模式也十分獨特。

澤崎： 布雷，關於「嬰兒潮世代」，你可以告訴我些甚麼嗎？

溫謝爾： 嬰兒潮世代？他們是「新品種」的美國人，出生於二次大戰後的嬰兒潮時期，或者說是 1946 到 65 年間。現在美國人口有將近一半都是在那個時期出生的，而他們也佔了時下勞動人口總數的一半還要多一點。

澤崎： 你覺得他們的特色是甚麼？

溫謝爾： 勤奮、企圖心旺盛、有教養。以負面而言，他們不太信任別人、自大傲慢，而且很會東要求西要求的。他們的學生時期正好是在 60、70 年代，所以當時的民權運動、越戰、和水門事件，對於他們信念的成形有相當的影響。而他們婚後的家庭中，有三分之二是雙薪家庭。只有大約百分之十是歐紀和哈麗特式的家庭。

澤崎： 那是甚麼意思？

溫謝爾： 對不起，昭一，那是指傳統的夫妻。歐紀去上班，而哈麗特則待在家裡照料他們美好的屋子和可愛的小孩。那是以前電視劇裡的人物。現在那種生活型態已經很少見了。此外，嬰兒潮世代的婚姻有一半都是以離婚收場。

澤崎： 他們沒有辦法在那麼有限的時間內把那麼多的事都搞好，對嗎？

溫謝爾： 沒錯。而且他們也傾向擁有崇高的抱負，這可以從他們的工作和他們所購買的東西上看得出來。

＊　　＊　　＊

Lesson 24 Baby Boomers (3)

Words and Phrases

baby boomer　即在二次大戰後，1946~65 年間的嬰兒潮中出生的人

breed　團體；群

characteristics　特徵；特色

hardworking　勤奮的

skeptical [ˈskɛptɪkl]　懷疑的；不信的

arrogant [ˈærəgənt]　傲慢的；自大的

civil rights movement　民權運動

Vietnam　越戰

Watergate　水門事件

spouse　配偶

Ozzie-and-Harriet family　對傳統夫妻的稱呼〈源自美國在 50、60 年間所播出過的一齣受歡迎的電視連續劇〉

traditional husband and wife　傳統夫妻

lifestyle　生活方式

juggle　處理得很好

Vocabulary Building

- **labor force**　勞動人口
  The educational level of the labor force has a major impact on productivity.
  (勞動者的教育程度對生產力有很大的影響。)

- **downside**　負面
  The downside of our company's expansion is the loss of the family-like atmosphere we had when we were smaller.
  (公司擴編的負面影響是，昔日公司較小時那種一家親的氣氛不再有了。)

- **wage earner**　薪水階級；上班族
  It's become hard for a single wage earner to support a middle-class family.
  (現在要以單單一個薪水階級的收入來維持一個中等階級家庭的開銷是很困難的。)

- **Meaning what?**　甚麼意思呢?
  cf. "You went to the general hospital to get a what?" — "A physical, I said. You know, a physical examination or check-up."
  (「你說你要到綜合醫院去做個甚麼?」「我是說健檢。你知道的，就是身體健康檢查。」)

1. They make up nearly half of the U.S. adult population.

   a) account for
   b) close to

2. What would you say are their characteristics?

   a) how would you describe
   b) special qualities

3. Harriet stays home to take care of the perfect house and adorable kids.

   a) look after
   b) is the typical housewife

◆◆◆◆◆◆◆◆◆◆◆◆◆ 簡短對話 ◆◆◆◆◆◆◆◆◆◆◆◆◆

Winchell: Why do you want to know about baby boomers?
Sawasaki: It was something Maria said to me.
Winchell: What?
Sawasaki: You see, she and her boyfriend are—um, anyway, she used the word when she was explaining why some people her age are so hardworking.
Winchell: I see. Well, that's one of the traits of the baby boom generation. It's partly because there are so many of them competing for the same limited number of jobs.

---

hardworking 勤奮的　　**trait** 特徵; 特質　　**partly** 部分地

Baby Boomers (4) （嬰兒潮世代）

●預習 — *Sentences*

- These baby-boom managers in their 30s were so busy.
- This was the only evening we could get them together.
- I thought the facilitator was excellent.
- They seemed pretty restless and demanding.
- Not easy for most companies to provide these days.

●*Vignette*

Turner: Mike, I'm glad you were finally able to organize this focus group discussion. We wanted to find out more about them, and if we can address any of their issues and concerns through our corporate advertising and social action campaigns.

McCabe: These baby-boom managers in their 30s were so busy. This was the only evening we could get them together, Eric.

Sawasaki: It was fascinating listening to their comments from behind this two-way mirror. And I thought the facilitator was excellent.

Owens: Yeah, he kept the conversation on target, but he gave people plenty of room to express their honest feelings.

Cortez: Overall, they seemed pretty restless and demanding.

Winchell: They all wanted good pay, meaningful work, and satisfying careers. Not easy for most companies to provide these days.

Turner: After they agreed how busy, rushed, and tired they all were, it really sparked the discussion. Why do you think they work so hard?

Sawasaki: Competition, several said.

Cortez: Recognition. They wanted to stand out as excellent performers among their peers.

Owens: The man with the glasses said something interesting, remember? He said that the loosening of ties within the family, church, and small communities made interacting at work more important. Not that work can provide an adequate substitute.

Turner: They said that their jobs force them to neglect their personal relationships.

Sawasaki: Maybe work comes before family for this generation.

嬰兒潮世代的最大特徵或許就是他們把工作看得比家庭重要吧!

透納: 麥可,我很高興你終於能把這個小組討論會議辦起來了。我們一直想要多瞭解一下他們,也想知道我們能否透過公司的宣傳廣告和社會活動來解決他們所關切的問題。

馬可伯: 這些三十來歲的嬰兒潮世代經理一直都好忙。艾瑞克,這是我們唯一可以把他們都聚在一起的一個晚上。

澤崎: 能在玻璃帷幕後面傾聽他們所發表的意見,這真的是很有趣。而且我認為會議主持人表現得好極了。

歐文斯: 是啊,他使所有的談話都能正對著議題發展,但卻沒有剝奪大家發表真實感想的空間。

古岱茲: 整體而言,他們看起來都相當不滿,而且要求個沒完。

溫謝爾: 他們都想要有好的薪水,重要的職務,還要有令人滿意的事業。近來可沒有多少公司提供得了這些東西。

透納: 而在他們都承認了自己有多忙碌、老是在趕場、又常是疲憊不堪之後,整個的討論都熱烈起來了。你覺得他們為甚麼要工作得這麼辛苦?

澤崎: 競爭啊!有些人是這麼說的。

古岱茲: 認同。他們想要在同儕中成為出類拔萃的人物。

歐文斯: 記得嗎?那個戴眼鏡的人說了點有意思的話。他說,由於家庭、教堂和小社區中人群關係的日益淡薄,就愈形突顯了工作上互動關係的重要性。並不是說工作足以取代一切。

透納: 他們說工作迫使他們疏忽了人際關係。

澤崎: 也許對這個世代而言,工作比家庭要來得重要吧!

Lesson 22　Baby Boomers (4)

Words and Phrases

focus group discussion　　小組討論
會議〈通常用作消費者意見調查〉
corporate advertising　　企業廣告
social action campaign　　社會活動
fascinating ['fæsə,netɪŋ]　　令人著
迷的；吸引人的
two-way mirrorr　　（鏡後人可見鏡
前人，而鏡前人看不見鏡後人的）單
向透明玻璃鏡；玻璃帷幕

restless　　不安的；急忙的
demanding　　要求過多的
rushed　　匆忙的
spark　　使…熱烈起來
performer　　實行者
interacting　　互動；相互影響
neglect　　忽視；忽略
personal relationships　　人際關係

Vocabulary Building

- **issue**　　問題所在
  The major issues and concerns for retirees are quite different from those of working-age people.
  （退休的人與正值勞動年齡的人所著重關心的問題有很大的不同。）

- **facilitator**　　會議主持人；領會者
  cf. Her knowledge of Spanish greatly facilitated her work.
  （懂得西班牙文對她的工作而言十分有助益。）

- **on target**　　不偏離正題；正對目標進行
  cf. You are way off base with your criticism of Nancy. She's one of the most conscientious employees in this firm.
  （你那樣子批評南西簡直是大錯特錯。她可是這公司裡最盡責的員工之一。）

- **substitute**　　替代品 (者)
  cf. A lot of people substitute margarine for butter.
  （很多人用瑪其琳來取代奶油。）

▶ *Exercises*

請勿改變例句的句型, 用a)、
b)詞組代換下列例句。

(解答見 265 頁)

1. He gave people plenty of room to express their honest feelings.

   a) encouraged the participants
   b) feel free to state

2. They wanted to stand out as excellent performers among their peers.

   a) be counted
   b) top players

3. Their jobs force them to neglect their personal relationships.

   a) they can't afford
   b) hobbies

◆◆◆◆◆◆◆◆◆◆◆◆◆ 簡短對話 ◆◆◆◆◆◆◆◆◆◆◆◆◆

Group member A: I remember when I was growing up, my father was always home for supper. I'm lucky if I can eat with my kids twice during the week.

Group member B: Same here. I'm not married, but my girlfriend and I are both so tied up with work, we can almost never get together during the week.

Group member C: Then the weekends are so exhausting, because you have to make up for that lost time.

Group member D: You guys think you have it bad—you should try being a working mother sometime. I mean, sure, my husband helps around the house, but he's so bad at it that I end up doing practically all the housework myself.

---

be tied up with 忙於⋯ 　　**exhausting** 令人疲憊的 　　**make up for** 償回;
補回　　**have it bad** 狀況惡劣; 情況糟 　　**help around the house** 幫忙家務
end up 結果是⋯　　**housework** 家事

97

Lesson 22

Baby Boomers —— 總結

　　■　　■　　■

　　說起美國傳統的白領階級，「白朗黛」漫畫中的 Dagwood Bumstead 就是一個絕佳的範例。

　　Dagwood Bumstead 的角色定位為公司裡一個不受重視的上班族，他總是動輒得咎，常令得暴君般的老闆對他大吼 "You're fired." 而且總有帳單追著他跑。即使是在家裡，他的地位也不如他美麗的妻子 Blondie，更別提那一雙也不怎麼敬重老爸的兒女了。

　　可是，像那樣的家庭在今日的美國已不多見了。代之而起的是出生於戰後嬰兒潮 (1946～1965) 的 baby boomers。

　　嬰兒潮世代平均每三人就有兩人是薪水階級，而且都有 workaholic (工作狂) 般的勤奮，一般都富有 entrepreneurship「企業家精神」及 competitiveness「進取心」。

　　他們非常勤勉、企圖心旺盛、有教養，但同時也兼具不信任他人以及自大傲慢的特徵，而且他們的婚姻有半數都是以離婚收場。據估計，現在出生的小孩當中，有高達百分之六十的比例將來會面臨到單親家庭 (single-parent household) 的問題。

　　嬰兒潮世代常常強調自我權利，也會要求較高的薪資以及能令他們滿意的工作條件。因為他們是在 60、70 年代受的教育，所以深受當時民權運動、越戰、和水門事件的影響，自我更加高漲。

　　這種姿態也可說是 "Neither flatter wealth, nor cringe before power." 「不拜金，不屈權」吧!

　　嬰兒潮世代的父母們所處的時代是個較混亂的局面，他們還經歷過 the Great Depression「大蕭條」時期，所以一般而言較為溫順、質樸，且以節儉為美德。

　　兩代如此的不同，使得 old-line management 與 baby boomers 之間的摩擦不斷，常有內部告發或下屬控告上司的情事，而社會上的控訴事件更是屢見不鮮。如何去瞭解嬰兒潮世代的想法以及管理方式也成了美國現代經營者所必須面對的課題。

Lesson 23

Sense of Humor

（幽默感）

◆ Lesson 23 的內容 ◆

　　常令澤崎感到困擾的是 —— 他有時實在搞不懂，到底這個美國人是在說笑，抑或該把他的話當真。雖說在商業社會裡，人們已經逐漸失去了幽默感，但是，看來美國人的幽默手法卻是越來越高明。一個好的笑話不僅能使聽眾精神振奮，順利切入演說主題，也能提高會議的氣氛。不過，澤崎今天差點又把透納說的笑話當真了。

Shoichi, can you tell us a typical Japanese joke?

Sense of Humor (1) (幽默感)

●預習 —*Sentences*

- How are the interviews coming along?
- I asked him what he was good at.
- Eric must have just gotten it from some TV comedian.
- Humor's been the last thing on my mind.
- The Japanese actually don't use much humor in business.

●*Vignette*

Sawasaki: Eric, how are the interviews coming along? Do you have any strong candidates for staff additions?

Turner: They're mostly all right, but this last person was awful.

Sawasaki: Oh? How so?

Turner: I asked him what he <u>was good</u> at and he said, "Nothing." Of course, I wouldn't hire him. If there's one thing I hate, it's somebody who's after my job.

Sawasaki: Er, after your job? I thought he was . . .

Cortez: Look, Shoichi, it was meant to be a joke. It didn't work on either of us, but Eric must have just gotten it from some TV comedian.

Sawasaki: Oh, I get it now. [*Laughs*]

Turner: [*Laughing*] You looked so serious, Shoichi.

Sawasaki: You're right. I've been so busy with work, humor's been the last thing on my mind.

Cortez: We all tend to take ourselves a bit too seriously. Humor seems to be a lost <u>commodity</u> in today's <u>hectic</u> business world. Maybe we need to wait for the Japanese to start exporting it to us.

Sawasaki: But the Japanese actually don't use much humor in business. Americans may hold up a business conference to tell the latest jokes, but a Japanese doing that would be considered frivolous. It's not that they don't appreciate humor, but a businessman who cracks a lot of jokes doesn't <u>fit in with</u> other people's expectations.

澤崎： 艾瑞克，面試的情況怎樣？應徵者當中有沒有甚麼特別好，可資增聘的人選？

透納： 大部分的人都還好，不過，最後這一個人糟透了。

澤崎： 哦，怎麼會這樣？

透納： 我問說他擅長甚麼，他回答：「沒有甚麼。」當然了，我是不會用他的。如果有甚麼東西是我所恨惡的，那就是某個覬覦我工作的人了。

澤崎： 呃，覬覦你工作？我以為他是…

古岱茲： 嘿，昭一，這是一個笑話。我們兩個都沒聽懂。艾瑞克一定是剛從某個電視喜劇演員身上學來的。

澤崎： 哦，我現在懂了。[笑了起來]

透納： [笑著] 昭一，你剛剛看起來好認真哦！

澤崎： 你說得沒錯。我工作太忙了，很少會去想到幽默。

古岱茲： 我們都很容易把自己弄得過於嚴肅。在今日繁忙的商業世界中，幽默是一項消失了的商品。也許我們得要等日本人向我們進口幽默了。

澤崎： 可是實際上，日本人在商場上也沒多少幽默的。美國人可以中途打斷一場商務會議，就為了講些最新的笑話，可是如果有日本人那麼做的話，大家會認為他很輕浮。並不是說日本人不瞭解幽默的好處，只是，一個常說笑話的企業家可不是別人所期望看到的樣子。

Words and Phrases

interview	面試	take oneself too seriously	把自
candidate	候選人; 應徵者	己弄得太嚴肅	
hire	錄用	business world	商場; 商業界
meant	視作…; 意指…	hold up	打斷
work on	對…發生作用	frivolous [ˈfrɪvələs]	輕浮的; 膚淺的
last thing	萬萬想不到的事	crack a joke	說笑話

Vocabulary Building

- **be good at**　擅長於…
  Bob's no good at defusing conflicts.
  (鮑伯不太會平息紛爭。)

- **commodity**　商品; 日用品
  XYZ company treats its workers like a disposable commodity.
  (XYZ公司對待員工猶如隨手可丟的用品般。)

- **hectic**　十分忙亂的
  I had such a hectic day at the office that I clean forgot about lunch.
  (我曾有一天在辦公室忙得昏天黑地, 連中飯都忘得一乾二淨。)

- **fit in with**　適合; 符合
  David's pushy style didn't fit in with the low-key mood of the division as a whole.
  (大衛那種咄咄逼人的強悍風格與部門整體的低調作風無法合拍。)

（解答見 265 頁）

► **Exercises**　　請勿改變例句的句型，用a)、
　　　　　　　　　　b)詞組代換下列例句。

1. Do you have any strong candidates for staff additions?

   a) did you find
   b) to fill the vacancies

2. I asked him what he was good at.

   a) questioned
   b) his strengths are

3. Americans may hold up a business conference to tell the latest jokes.

   a) delay
   b) exchange

◆◆◆◆◆◆◆◆◆◆◆◆◆ 簡短對話 ◆◆◆◆◆◆◆◆◆◆◆◆◆◆

Sawasaki: You know, though, there's one situation where humor is really out of place.

Turner: At a funeral, right?

Sawasaki: Well, that too, of course, but what I was thinking of was something different.

Turner: Yeah?

Sawasaki: It's when you're speaking through an interpreter. Many jokes really lose a lot in translation.

Turner: I can understand that. Puns must be especially difficult.

Sawasaki: Actually, puns aren't difficult to translate— they're *impossible* to translate.

---

out of place 不適宜的；不合當時狀況的　　**speak through an interpreter** 透過翻譯來講話　　**pun** 雙關語

Lesson 23

Sense of Humor (2)（幽默感）

●預習 ── Sentences

- Laughter is often rejected as inappropriate.
- Is that a cultural difference?
- The idea was that laughing made them look undignified.
- It's been tested scientifically.
- What's the endorphin level?

●Vignette

Sawasaki: Laughter is often rejected as inappropriate in a business context.

Turner: Yeah, I've noticed the Japanese businessmen I've come into contact with in the past have tended to be pretty humorless. Is that a cultural difference?

Sawasaki: Maybe so. You'll find them perfectly ready to joke and laugh if you go out drinking with them after work, but they're not accustomed to accepting humor in certain situations. Part of it may come from the tradition of the samurai, who were taught that they should only flex the muscles of one cheek every three years. The idea was that laughing made them look undignified, so the less they did it, the better.

Turner: I see. But did you know, Shoichi, that a person with a good sense of humor has better healing qualities? Honestly. It's been tested scientifically. There's evidence that laughter increases circulation, respiration, and the endorphin level in the blood.

Sawasaki: Pardon me, what's the endorphin level?

Turner: Endorphin is like opium. It's a natural painkiller that your body produces when you chuckle.

Cortez: Humor also can stimulate creativity and promote relaxation to a great degree. When you're relaxed, your vista broadens and you may see things you were missing before.

Turner: Yeah, that's right.

104

日本人經常被認為是比較緊張，缺乏幽默感的民族。但是澤崎卻辯稱，「他們只是在某些情況下不習慣接受幽默。」

澤崎： 在商業場合，大家通常不太常笑，因為覺得那樣不合適。

透納： 是啊，我過去接觸過一些日本商人，我注意到他們常常都很沒幽默感。這是文化差異嗎？

澤崎： 也許吧！但你如果在下班後跟他們一道去喝酒，你會發現他們也很會開玩笑、嘻嘻哈哈的。他們只是在某些情況下不習慣接受幽默。這有些可能是源自於武士的傳統。武士所受的教導是，每三年只能動到半邊的臉部肌肉。他們的想法是，笑使得他們看起來不夠威嚴，所以愈少笑愈好。

透納： 我懂了。不過，昭一，你知道嗎？一個幽默感不錯的人，他本身會有較佳的疾病治癒力。這話可一點不假，有科學證實過的。有證據說，笑能增進血液循環、呼吸作用、以及血液中的腦啡比數。

澤崎： 對不起，甚麼是腦啡比數？

透納： 腦啡就像鴉片一樣。它是一種天然的止痛劑。當你在咯咯笑的時候，你的身體就會製造出腦啡來。

古岱茲： 幽默也可以激發創造力，使人得到相當的放鬆。你人一放鬆，視界就會擴大，你可能會因此看到一些以前不曾注意到的事。

透納： 是啊，沒錯。

Lesson 23 Sense of Humor (2)

Words and Phrases

reject	拒絕	circulation	(血液的) 循環
inappropriate	不適當的	respiration	呼吸 (作用)
flex the muscles	伸縮肌肉; 活動	opium [ˈopɪəm]	鴉片
肌肉		painkiller	止痛劑
undignified	有損威嚴的	chuckle	咯咯笑
healing	治療的	stimulate	刺激
Honestly.	真的。	relaxation	放鬆; 舒緩
evidence	證明; 證據	to a great degree	大幅地; 大大地

Vocabulary Building

● **in a [business] context**   在 [商業] 場合 (情況) 中
You shouldn't impose on your friends in a professional context.
(在工作上, 你不應該利用你的朋友。)

● **come into contact with**   接觸; 遇到
Roger's easily the most persuasive sales rep I've ever come into contact with.
(羅傑當然是我所接觸過最有說服力的業務代表了。)

● **endorphin**   腦內啡; 恩多芬〈跟鎮定劑一樣具有止痛作用〉
I miss the endorphin high I used to get from jogging every day.
(我懷念以前每天慢跑時那種身上腦內啡成分升高的感覺。)

● **vista**   眼界; 視野
Living in a foreign country has opened new vistas for me.
(在國外的生活給我開啟了新的視野。)

1. Laughter is often rejected as inappropriate in a business context.

   a) some types of language are
   b) on formal occasions

2. The idea was that laughing made them look undignified.

   a) everybody thought
   b) silly

3. You may see things you were missing before.

   a) can develop abilities
   b) when you were younger

◆◆◆◆◆◆◆◆◆◆◆◆◆◆ 簡短對話 ◆◆◆◆◆◆◆◆◆◆◆◆◆◆

Sawasaki: Speaking of cultural differences, there's one thing about humor in America that's really hard for me to adjust to.

Turner: What's that?

Sawasaki: It's the way people sometimes groan or say "boo" when they hear a joke.

Turner: Oh yeah, we do that a lot, especially when somebody tells a bad pun.

Sawasaki: Because it's not funny?

Turner: No, because it is funny but we don't want to laugh at it. Maybe because it would seem too unsophisticated.

---

speaking of 說到⋯   **adjust** 調整; 適應   **groan** 呻吟   **say "boo"**
發出(憤怒、責備或不滿)之聲   **unsophisticated** 未經世故的; 天真的; 純潔的

107

Sense of Humor (3) (幽默感)

●預習 — *Sentences*

- Your sense of humor deteriorates.
- I got two parking tickets in Manhattan in a single week.
- Because first you have to find a place to park.
- Have you heard any New York jokes?
- And you know what the first prize was?

●*Vignette*

Turner: When you're depressed or nervous, your sense of humor deteriorates. But if you use humor, you may be able to switch yourself back into a more upbeat mood.

Sawasaki: That reminds me. Not long ago, I got two parking tickets in Manhattan in a single week. I was quite upset but when I told Brad about it his reaction was, "That's amazing. Most people have a hard time getting even one parking ticket in Manhattan." "Why's that?" I asked, and he said, "Because first you have to find a place to park." [*Everybody laughs*] He helped me snap out of my bad mood.

Cortez: Life in New York can be tough at times, so we often joke about it. Have you heard any New York jokes, Shoichi?

Sawasaki: Not that I can remember.

Cortez: Well, there's the one about the company that offered incentive prizes for its top two sales people during a special campaign period. Second prize was an all-expense-paid trip to New York for one week. And you know what the first prize was?

Sawasaki: No, what?

Cortez: Same deal, but for one day.

Sawasaki: [*Laughing*] I like that.

Turner: That's an old one and the trip is sometimes to Philadelphia or Detroit.

美國人就算遭遇困境，也不忘要來點笑話，給彼此打打氣。
有許多笑話就是為了要幽環境一默而產生的。

透納： 在你沮喪或緊張的時候，幽默感會比較糟糕。但如果你用點幽默，就
有可能使自己的心情重又快活起來。

澤崎： 這倒使我想起，不久前，我在曼哈頓單單一週內就收到兩張違規停車
罰單。我心情很不好。可是當我把這事告訴布雷，他的反應卻是，「真令人
震驚耶，大多數的人在曼哈頓連一張違規停車罰單也不容易收得到呢！」
「怎麼說？」我就問了。他回答，「因為你得先要找到地方停車才行。」
[每個人都笑了] 他使我甩掉了不愉快的心情。

古岱茲： 在紐約，生活有時是相當辛苦的，所以我們也常拿它來開玩笑。昭
一，你有沒有聽過甚麼紐約的笑話？

澤崎： 不記得有過。

古岱茲： 嗯，有個笑話是說，某家公司在一個特別活動期間，要提供獎勵品
給兩位最佳銷售員。第二名是免費紐約一週行，你知道第一名是甚麼嗎？

澤崎： 不知道。是甚麼？

古岱茲： 同樣的內容，不過，時間只有一天。

澤崎： [笑著] 我喜歡這個笑話。

透納： 這是個老笑話，而且有時候去的地方會變成費城或底特律。

Lesson 23　Sense of Humor (3)

Words and Phrases

be depressed	沮喪	be upset	不高興; 心情不好
nervous	緊張的; 焦急的	amazing	令人吃驚的
deteriorate [dɪˈtɪrɪəˌret]	惡化; 降低	tough	困難的
switch oneself back into	把自己轉	at times	有時候
換至…		incentive prize	獎勵品
not long ago	不久前	campaign period	活動期間
parking ticket	違規停車罰單	deal	對待; 待遇

Vocabulary Building

- **upbeat**　樂觀的; 開朗的
  The enthusiasm of Anne's upbeat presentation was contagious.
  (安作了一個前景看好的簡報, 其熱切之情感染了在座的人。)

- **That reminds me.**　那倒提醒我了。
  cf. Di reminds me of a woman I used to work with.
  (黛令我想起了一個以前共事過的女子。)

- **Not that I can remember.**　我不記得有過 (這麼一回事)。
  cf. Not that I can think of offhand.
  (我一時也想不出來。)

- **all-expense-paid**　全額免費的; 免費招待的
  He won an all-expense-paid trip for two to Hawaii.
  (他贏得了兩人免費同遊夏威夷的獎項。)

▶ Exercises

請勿改變例句的句型, 用a)、
b)詞組代換下列例句。

(解答見 265頁)

1. When you're depressed or nervous, your sense of humor deteriorates.

   a) if you don't get enough sleep
   b) is likely to be lost

2. I got two parking tickets in Manhattan in a single week.

   a) was ticketed twice
   b) as soon as I bought a car

3. Life in New York can be tough at times.

   a) is a real pain
   b) for all of us

◆◆◆◆◆◆◆◆◆◆◆◆◆◆ 簡短對話 ◆◆◆◆◆◆◆◆◆◆◆◆◆◆

Cortez: You know the saying: "Laughter is the best medicine."
Sawasaki: Well, I do now.
Cortez: There's something else I read not long ago about laughter— or smiling rather.
Sawasaki: It gives you premature wrinkles in your face.
Cortez: Oh, Shoichi! No, apparently they've found that the physical act of forming a smile actually makes a person feel happier.
Sawasaki: Somebody should tell that to the sourpuss at the cash register in the cafeteria.

"Laughter is the best medicine." 「笑是最佳藥方。」   **premature** 提早
(出現)的   **wrinkle** 皺紋   **sourpuss** 討厭鬼; 脾氣古怪的人

111

Sense of Humor (4) (幽默感)

●預習 — *Sentences*

- We also joke a lot about computers.
- Have you heard about the ultimate computer hacker?
- Finally, he types in the question.
- The shopowner was suspicious.
- The merchant was still unimpressed.

●*Vignette*

Turner: We also joke a lot about computers. Maybe it's because we feel insecure about them. I just heard a funny one. It's about an artificial intelligence program that takes over an MIT computer. It holds valuable files hostage and threatens to delete one file per hour until its demands are met.

Cortez: Have you heard about the ultimate computer hacker? He hocks everything he owns to build his home computer into the world's most powerful machine. Then he plugs it into every database, lets it invade every library in the nation and has it read every book. Finally, he types in *the* question: "Computer, is there a God?" The computer flashes, the screen flickers, and at last the machine responds: "THERE IS NOW!" [*Laughs*]

Turner: Shoichi, can you tell us a typical Japanese joke?

Sawasaki: Well, one of my favorites is the story from the Edo era about a masterless samurai who enters a sake shop and makes a weak excuse about not paying his bill. The shopowner was suspicious. "If you don't believe me," the samurai said, "I'll have to perform *harakiri*." The merchant only sneered at him. So the samurai took out his sword, stabbed it in his belly, and drew it toward his navel. The merchant was still unimpressed and asked coldly, "Why not all the way?" The samurai replied feebly, "I must cut the other half at the rice shop."

透納： 我們也常拿電腦開玩笑。這也許是因為我們對電腦沒有安全感吧！我剛剛才聽到一個有趣的笑話，是說一個具有人工智慧的電腦程式，它控制了一部麻省理工學院的電腦，挾持了那些極具價值的檔案，並威脅說，如果它的要求不遂，那它每小時就要殺掉一個檔案。

古岱茲： 你們聽過終極電腦侵入者嗎？他把他所有的東西都當掉了，為的就是要使他的家用電腦成為全世界最厲害的機器。然後，他把電腦連接上每一個資料庫，讓它侵入全國每一間圖書館，讀遍所有的書。最後，他打進這個問題：「電腦，有神嗎？」這部電腦開始閃爍，螢幕明滅不定，終於，這個機器回答：「現在有了！」[笑了出來]

透納： 昭一，你可以說個典型的日本笑話給我們聽嗎？

澤崎： 好的，我最喜歡的是個關於江戶時代浪人(註：無主的武士)的故事。話說這個浪人進了一家酒店，找了個很爛的藉口說明他為何無法付帳。店主很懷疑。這位武士就說，「如果你不相信我，那我只好切腹了。」店主只是嘲笑他。於是武士就拔出刀子，往自己肚子刺下去，直切到肚臍的地方。店主仍然不為所動，冷冷地問他，「為甚麼不切到底呢？」武士虛弱地回答：「另一半我得留到米店切才行。」

Lesson 23　Sense of Humor (4)

Words and Phrases

artificial intelligence	人工智慧	hock	典當
take over	取得掌控權；接管	flash	閃爍
MIT (Massachusetts Institute of Technology)	麻省理工學院	flicker	閃爍；明滅不定
hold hostage	挾持人質	favorite	最喜歡的
threaten	威脅；要脅	masterless	沒有主子的；沒有主人的
ultimate	終極的	shopowner	店主；老闆
computer hacker	電腦玩家；電腦侵入者	suspicious	起疑的；奇怪的
		sneer	嘲笑
		belly	肚子

Vocabulary Building

● **insecure**　不安全的；擔心的
Many people felt insecure about their jobs after the company was acquired by an industrial giant.
(在公司被大企業購併之後，公司裡許多人就開始擔心起他們的工作來了。)

● **delete**　刪除；消去
Ronald deleted a whole page from the computer document by mistake.
(隆納德不小心把電腦檔案文件中的一整頁給刪除了。)

● **plug into**　插入；連接
Marie plugged a brand new word processor into an outlet under her desk.
(瑪莉把全新的文書處理機的插頭插到她桌子底下的插座。)

● **database**　資料庫
The contents of the encyclopedia are now available through a database.
(現在整部百科全書的內容都在資料庫裡頭，隨時可得。)

請勿改變例句的句型，用a)、
b)詞組代換下列例句。   （解答見266頁）

1. We also joke a lot about computers.

   a) have a great deal of experience with
   b) ourselves

2. Have you heard about the ultimate computer hacker?

   a) do you know the one
   b) entrepreneur

3. One of my favorites is a story from the Edo era.

   a) a joke that goes back to
   b) I like

◆◆◆◆◆◆◆◆◆◆◆◆◆ **簡短對話** ◆◆◆◆◆◆◆◆◆◆◆◆◆

Sawasaki: Americans really seem to like ethnic jokes too.
Cortez: That's one of the benefits of our melting-pot society, I guess. We can make fun of all sorts of people.
Sawasaki: Can you tell me any good ones?
Cortez: I'd rather not. The ones I could tell you about Puerto Ricans are pretty derogatory, and I don't want to dig into any other ethnic groups. After all, for all I know, Eric here could be Polish or something.
Sawasaki: With a name like Turner?
Cortez: Could have been changed from Turnakowski.

---

ethnic joke 關於種族的笑話　　**melting-pot society** 人種混雜的社會　　**make fun of** 開…的玩笑　　**derogatory** 有損顏面的；輕蔑的　　**dig into** 鑽研…

Sense of Humor ── 總結

■　■　■

本課的各個段落都有幾個笑話，你明白其中的奧妙了嗎？

其一。透納說，"If there's one thing I hate, it's somebody who's after my job." 若我們依著以下的模式來思考，應不難理解這個笑話。〈面試中，有位回答「沒甚麼專長」的求職者〉── 〈透納自己本身，事實上，也沒啥專長〉── 〈這麼一來，新的求職者也能勝任透納的工作，搞不好會搶了他飯碗也說不定〉── 〈所以，這樣一號人物絕對不採用〉

其二。有關 parking ticket 的笑話，在曼哈頓島上，違規停放的車輛都密密麻麻地擠在道路兩側，想要加入違規之列，還不是那麼容易的一件事。在這樣的情況下，收到兩張違規停車罰單，豈不表示他居然還幸運得找到了停車位，而且還在一週內找到過兩次，可說是「運氣奇佳」！

其三。有關紐約的笑話。「第二名的獎勵是為期一週的紐約之旅，但第一名的獎勵只有一天。」其意在諷刺，紐約之旅一天都嫌多了，更何況是一週。所以，一週之旅無法成為首獎，也是想當然爾。

其四。人工智慧已能自行操控，居然侵佔了 MIT 的電腦，還挾持了裡面的檔案。現實社會裡的恐怖分子常以每小時殺一名人質來要脅，而人工智慧也有樣學樣，以「每小時殺掉一個檔案」相恫嚇。

其五。瘋狂電腦玩家的笑話。他讓電腦連結所有的資料庫，並使之讀遍全美圖書館裡的每一本書。之後，他鍵入一個問題，「有神嗎？」答案卻是，"THERE IS NOW." 這個已經吸收了所有知識，成為「全知全能」的電腦，它的意思是說，「有的，那就是我。」

最後，澤崎也講了一個江戶時代的笑話。在美國，相處融洽的同事們若在辦公室以外的地方聚會聊天，一定會講個笑話。為了融入這樣的生活，最好下工夫把本國的笑話練習到能以英文說出，會比較好哦！

Lesson 24

Consumer Response System

（消費者申訴制度）

◆ Lesson 24 的內容 ◆

　　像 ABC 這樣龐大的食品公司，如何能夠迅速有效地處理消費者申訴，這是個極為重要的課題。早在數年前， ABC 食品公司就設有消費者免付費服務專線（在美國是 800 開頭的電話號碼）。號碼就印在所有食品包裝上面，消費者可藉此與公司的申訴部門聯絡。澤崎為了瞭解在美國申訴事件的處理方式，將陪同申訴部門的強森去拜訪某消費者。這位仁兄來電申訴說，他在所購買的冰淇淋中發現了異物。

Lesson 24

Consumer Response System (1)（消費者申訴制度）

●預習 — *Sentences*

- I want to know what you're going to do about it.
- Sir, what kind of ice cream was it?
- Let me get my glasses and I'll read the label to you.
- It's a nut like in nuts and bolts.
- Where did you buy the ice cream, sir?

●*Vignette*

Customer: Listen, I bought a carton of your ice cream and it had a nut in it. I found it when I took a bite of it, and the nut cracked my dentures. Now, I want to know what you're going to do about it.

Johnson: Sir, what kind of ice cream was it?

Customer: Wait a minute. Let me get my glasses and I'll read the label to you. [*Pause*] Nuts 'n' Stuff ice cream produced by ABC Foods in Tarrytown, New York.

Johnson: Sir, the nuts in Nuts 'n' Stuff are cashews and pecans. Both are usually fairly soft . . .

Customer: Not that kind of nut! It's a nut like in nuts and bolts. Looks like about 3/16 of an inch or so.

Johnson: Oh, now I understand. Sir, next to our address on the back of the package is a code number and on the front of the package you'll find the weight of the product. Could you read those to me, please?

Customer: Let's see, the code number here is X95G20A and it's a half-gallon carton.

Johnson: Where did you buy the ice cream, sir?

Customer: I bought it at Murphy's down the street from me. Been doing all my grocery shopping there for the past 25 years. Never found metal in anything before.

Johnson: Sir, let me take down your name and address . . .

*　　*　　*

　　消費者申訴部門接到了一通申訴電話，來電者抱怨說買到的冰淇淋中竟然有金屬的「螺帽」，害他把假牙都弄壞了。

顧客：　聽著，我買了一盒你們的冰淇淋，裏面有一個 nut (註： nut 有二意：螺帽或核果)。我吃了一口才發現，而且那個 nut 把我的假牙都弄壞了。好了，我想知道你們打算怎麼辦？

強森：　先生，請問是哪種冰淇淋？

顧客：　等一下，我戴個眼鏡，把標籤唸給你聽。[停頓]是紐約州，泰瑞鎮，ABC 食品公司製造的 Nuts 'n' Stuff 冰淇淋。

強森：　先生， Nuts 'n' Stuff 裡頭的 nut 是腰果和胡桃，通常都是很軟的…

顧客：　不是那種 nut！我吃到的是用來旋螺絲釘用的 nut。大約有 3/16 英寸大小。

強森：　哦，我現在瞭解您的意思了。先生，在包裝盒背面，我們公司地址的旁邊有個代碼，還有，在包裝盒正面標有產品重量，可以請您把這兩項唸給我嗎？

顧客：　我看一下，這上面的代碼是 X95G20A，還有，這盒冰淇淋是半加侖裝的。

強森：　先生，您這盒冰淇淋是在哪兒買的？

顧客：　我在「墨菲的店」買的，從我住的這條街直走下去就是。二十五年來，我日常的生活用品都是在那裡買的，可是我從來沒有發現過貨品裡頭會有金屬。

強森：　先生，我記一下您的姓名住址…

＊　　＊　　＊

119

Lesson 24　Consumer Response System (1)

Words and Phrases

carton	紙板盒; 盒	glasses	眼鏡
crack	使破裂	cashew [ˈkæʃu]	腰果
denture [ˈdɛntʃɚ]	假牙	half-gallon	半加侖 (的)

Vocabulary Building

- **take a bite**　咬一口
  You don't have to eat all your spinach, but at least take a bite of it.
  (你不必把你盤裡的菠菜都吃掉, 可是, 你至少得吃吃一口。)

- **label**　*n.* 標籤　　*v.* 在⋯上貼標籤; 予以分類
  cf. The bottle was clearly labeled "poisonous if swallowed."
  (這瓶子上清楚標示著「有毒, 請勿飲用」。)

- **nuts and bolts**　螺帽和螺絲釘; 實際作用的部分; 實務
  cf. He's strong on theory but weak on the nuts and bolts of manufacturing.
  (他在理論方面是很強, 可是對於製造實務就不太行了。)

- **grocery shopping**　日用品的採買
  Prices are so high in Japan that I'm tempted to do my grocery shopping in San Francisco before heading back to Tokyo.
  (日本的物價太高了, 我有點想先在舊金山把日用品都買齊了, 再回東京去。)

▶ **Exercises**

請勿改變例句的句型, 用a)、
b)詞組代換下列例句。　　　　　　　　　　(解答見266頁)

1. I bought a carton of your ice cream and it had a nut in it.

   a) purchased
   b) metal piece

2. I want to know what you're going to do about it.

   a) let me ask you
   b) how you will handle

3. On the front of the package you'll find the weight of the product.

   a) date of manufacture
   b) it shows

◆◆◆◆◆◆◆◆◆◆◆◆◆ 簡短對話 ◆◆◆◆◆◆◆◆◆◆◆◆◆

Johnson: Sir, would it be convenient for you if I came by your home sometime today or tomorrow to give you a replacement?

Customer: Oh, you don't have to do that. I guess I was feeling a little cross
about that nut, and I just wanted to get it off my chest. Now if you could
send me a coupon for a new carton of ice cream, that would take care of it.

Johnson: Still, if you don't mind, I'd like to go in person. How about, say,
3 o'clock or so this afternoon? Would that be all right?

Customer: Well, sure.

Johnson: Oh, and could you please hold on to that carton? I'd like to take
it back with me to help us pinpoint the source of the problem and make
sure it doesn't happen again.

---

replacement 替換品　　**cross** 生氣的　　**get something off one's chest** 卸
掉心中的某件事　　**take care of** 處理…　　**in person** 親自　　**say** 舉例;
大概　　**hold on to** 保留不要丟掉　　**pinpoint** 找出真正的原因或出處

121

Lesson 24

Consumer Response System (2) （消費者申訴制度）

●預習 — *Sentences*

- What's the complaint about?
- I've made an appointment to visit him at 3 this afternoon.
- You move pretty fast.
- It's important with this kind of complaint.
- I got the customer to give me the necessary information.

●*Vignette*

Weathers: Shoichi, Dennis Johnson from Complaint Response is here to see you.

Sawasaki: OK. Hi, Dennis. What can I do for you?

Johnson: Well, I was just in Eric's office and he suggested I invite you along on a complaint response visit I'm making this afternoon.

Sawasaki: Yeah, I'd really be interested in seeing how that sort of thing is handled in this country. What's the complaint about?

Johnson: It's a call that came in this morning from a man who found a nut—a metal nut, that is—in our ice cream. He lives in White Plains, and I've made an appointment to visit him at 3 this afternoon.

Sawasaki: You move pretty fast.

Johnson: It's important with this kind of complaint. Here's a copy of the consumer response report.

Sawasaki: [*Glances at report*] You took the call personally?

Johnson: Yes, I try to handle at least one complaint call myself every day. It keeps me in better touch with customers' feelings and it also helps me stay on the same wavelength as the complaint handlers that I supervise.

Sawasaki: So what transpired between you and the customer on the telephone?

Johnson: Basically, just what's on that sheet. I got the customer to give me the necessary information, set up the appointment, and let him know that we do everything possible to ensure the quality and wholesomeness of our products.

接到這通電話的丹尼斯‧強森，要儘速處理此事，所以他決定下午就去拜訪這位申訴者。而強森也接受了透納的建議，前來邀澤崎同去。

威德斯： 昭一，消費者申訴部門的丹尼斯‧強森在這兒，他要見你。

澤崎： 好的。嗨，丹尼斯，有甚麼可以效勞的嗎？

強森： 嗯，我今天下午要去做個消費者申訴回訪，剛剛我去找過艾瑞克，他建議我可以邀你一道去。

澤崎： 是了，我是對這個國家如何處理這類事件的方式蠻感興趣的。這是個有關甚麼的申訴呢？

強森： 是這樣的，今天早上我接到一通電話，有位先生說他在我們公司的冰淇淋裡發現了一個nut —— 就是那種金屬的螺帽。他住在懷特潘連恩。我跟他約好了下午三點去拜訪他。

澤崎： 你動作倒蠻快的。

強森： 我們很看重像這類的申訴。這裡是一份消費者回應報告的影本。

澤崎： [看了一下報告]你親自接了這通電話？

強森： 是啊，我每天都會盡可能地，至少親自處理一通消費者申訴來電。如此一來，我比較能夠瞭解消費者實際的感覺，而且，這也有助於我跟我底下所管理的人之間的溝通。

澤崎： 那你跟這位先生在電話上談了些甚麼？

強森： 基本上就是那張紙上所寫的東西。我從客戶身上得知了一些必要的資料，跟他約了時間見面，並且，我也讓他明白，我們會盡一切的可能來確保公司產品的品質和衛生。

Lesson 24 Consumer Response System (2)

Words and Phrases

complaint response visit 消費者 申訴回訪	glance at 約略看了一下…
	supervise 監督
handle 處理	wholesomeness 健全
appointment 約會	

Vocabulary Building

- **that is** 也就是; 即是

  I want to buy a new pen—a fountain pen, that is.

  (我想要買支新筆 —— 也就是, 一支自來水筆。)

- **keep in touch with** 與…保持聯絡; 取得…的近況

  Shoichi tried to keep in touch with what's going on in the Tokyo office.

  (昭一試著保持與東京分公司的聯繫, 以便得知他們的消息。)

- **on the same wavelength** 有相同的波長〈喻興趣、思想相同〉

  cf. He and his son are on totally different wavelengths.

  (他跟他兒子完全無法溝通。)

- **transpire** 發生

  It now transpires that the advertising manager demanded kickbacks from the ad agency.

  (現在發生的是, 廣告部經理跟廣告代理商要求回扣。)

請勿改變例句的句型,用a)、b)詞組代換下列例句。

▶*Exercises*

(解答見266頁)

1. Eric suggested I invite you along on a complaint response visit.

   a) take
   b) you should come

2. I've made an appointment to visit him at 3 this afternoon.

   a) on my way to the office
   b) Dennis promised

3. It keeps me in better touch with customers' feelings.

   a) competitors' moves
   b) one should stay

◆◆◆◆◆◆◆◆◆◆◆◆◆◆ 簡短對話 ◆◆◆◆◆◆◆◆◆◆◆◆◆◆◆

Sawasaki: Does the new quality veep know about this?

Johnson: Not yet. We report the quality-related problem that we find in the course of our work to him in weekly batches, so he'll be reading about this next Monday morning.

Sawasaki: I bet he'll be upset.

Johnson: I'm sure he will, especially since this is the third time we've had this sort of complaint in the past month.

Sawasaki: Christ, what do you think's going on?

Johnson: I dunno. But whatever the source of the problem is, I sure hope they fix it fast.

---

veep (=vice president) 副總裁   **in the course of** 在…的過程中   **batch** 一束; 一團   **be upset** 生氣   **I dunno.** (=I don't know.) 我不知道。 **fix** 修理; 解決

Lesson 24

Consumer Response System (3) （消費者申訴制度）

●預習 —*Sentences*

· So what do you hope to accomplish by the visit?
· Then we'll have to pay his medical bills.
· So you want to come along?
· Is there anything I should be careful of saying?
· Do we get many complaints like this?

●*Vignette*

Sawasaki: So what do you hope to accomplish by the visit?

Johnson: The aim is to come to a <u>preliminary</u> agreement with the customer on a fair <u>settlement</u> and to try and restore his faith in our company and our products. If it turns out that he decided to get medical treatment, then we'll have to pay his medical bills. We'll also give him a generous quantity of the product—with no foreign objects in it this time. So you want to come along?

Sawasaki: Er, sure. Of course, I'll let you do the talking, but just in case I do open my mouth, is there anything I should be careful of saying?

Johnson: The main points to remember are not to assume <u>liability</u>, to discuss only this situation and not any other complaints we've received, and to avoid guessing or talking about the cause of the problem.

Sawasaki: Do we get many complaints like this?

Johnson: Most of the complaints we receive are the result of a product not being properly stored by the customer or the grocer. For example, it's common for calls or letters to come in about food that's already gone past its <u>shelf life</u>. We also get complaints about prices, food quality, contamination by mold, or as in this case, foreign particles.

在拜訪之前，強森說明了一些注意事項。譬如說，別一味把責任往身上攬、不要提及其他申訴事件、避免去臆測事因等等。

澤崎：　今天這個訪問有甚麼預期的目標嗎？

強森：　我們的目標是，要在公平和解的原則下，與顧客達成初步的協議，我們也要試著恢復他對我們公司和公司產品的信心。假如事情演變成他要去做治療，那我們也得幫他付醫藥費。我們還會慷慨地送他不少那種冰淇淋——這次不能有異物。那麼，你要一道去嗎？

澤崎：　呃，當然。我會盡量不開口，讓你來跟他說，不過，萬一我開了口的話，有沒有甚麼是我不該提的？

強森：　要記住的重點是，別把責任一味往自己身上攬，也不要提及我們所接到的其它申訴，只要就事論事就好。還有，要避免去臆測或是談論問題的成因。

澤崎：　我們常接到類似的申訴嗎？

強森：　我們大部分的申訴案件都是因為顧客本身或是雜貨商貨品儲存不當所致。舉例來說，我們常接到電話或信件，抱怨食品已經過期了。也會有人抱怨價格太貴、食品品質不良、東西長黴了、或者是像這次的情形，產品內有異物。

Lesson 24 Consumer Response System (3)

Words and Phrases

accomplish	達成; 成就	foreign object	異物
aim	目的	assume	承當
restore	重拾; 回復	contamination	污染
medical treatment	治療; 醫療	mold	黴菌
generous	寬大的; 豐富的	foreign particle	異物

Vocabulary Building

- **preliminary** 初步的; 在前的
  This is only a preliminary report, to be supplemented by additional studies.
  (這只是份初步的報告，之後還會有另外的研究報告來予以補足。)

- **settlement** 和解
  The drivers involved in the accident reached an out-of-court settlement.
  (那場車禍中涉案的司機已經庭外和解了。)

- **liability** 責任
  The liability of shareholders is limited to the amount they have invested in the corporation.
  (股東所承擔的責任是有限的，要視他們在公司投資數額的多寡而定。)

- **shelf life** 保存期限
  Perishables have a short shelf life. Don't stock them up too much.
  (生鮮食品的保存期限很短。不要囤積太多。)

▶ *Exercises*

請勿改變例句的句型, 用a)、b)詞組代換下列例句。

(解答見266頁)

1. The aim is to come to a preliminary agreement with the customer on a fair settlement.

    a) Dennis managed
    b) sign an

2. Is there anything I should be careful of saying?

    a) not say
    b) can you think of

3. We also get complaints about prices.

    a) ABC Foods receives many
    b) letters from customers complaining

◆◆◆◆◆◆◆◆◆◆◆◆◆◆ 簡短對話 ◆◆◆◆◆◆◆◆◆◆◆◆◆◆

Sawasaki: The customer must have been absolutely furious.

Johnson: Well, he was kind of keyed up when he called, but he calmed down after a couple of minutes.

Sawasaki: It must be really tough on the nerves dealing with disgruntled customers like that.

Johnson: It's not the easiest job in the world, I admit. But most people are like this guy in White Plains. They're upset, but when they realize that somebody is seriously listening to their gripe, it makes them feel a lot better.

---

furious 發怒的　　**be keyed up** 激動　　**calm down** 鎮定　　**tough on the nerves** 令人頭痛的　　**disgruntled** 惱怒的　　**gripe** 不滿; 抱怨

Lesson 24

Consumer Response System (4)（消費者申訴制度）

●預習 — *Sentences*

- In addition, we sometimes get negative feedback.
- Nutrition is still a key issue among American consumers.
- They let them know it loud and clear.
- A mishandled complaint can undo years of goodwill.
- I'll come by to get you on my way out.

●*Vignette*

Johnson: In addition, we sometimes get negative feedback about the nutritive value of our products or the amount of sugar, fat, or salt they contain.

Sawasaki: Haven't those kinds of complaints decreased now that we're making such an effort to use fewer preservatives and to prepare the food as nutritiously as possible?

Johnson: Yes, somewhat, but nutrition is still a key issue among American consumers, and that's kept the calls coming in. In fact, now when someone calls to complain about, say, the use of white flour in a product instead of whole wheat flour, they often make a point of saying that we aren't living up to our reputation. When American consumers think a company has broken a promise or produced an inferior product, they let them know it loud and clear. No ifs, ands, buts, or maybes.

Sawasaki: I know a mishandled complaint can undo years of goodwill we have built up with a customer. Do you ever get people who can't be satisfied no matter what you do?

Johnson: Oh, sure, there are some. Occasionally, we've had to go to court because of suits initiated by disgruntled customers. But most cases are settled by simply giving the customer a generous supply of the product, plus reimbursing them for minor medical bills, if any.

Sawasaki: So when do we leave?

Johnson: In about half an hour. I'll come by to get you on my way out.

130

強森：　除此之外，對於我們在產品上標示的營養價值表，或是關於糖分、脂
　　　　肪或鹽的含量，有時候顧客也會有一些負面的反應。

澤崎：　可是我們不是也很努力要少用點防腐劑，在製作過程中也盡可能地不
　　　　使營養流失了嗎？難道這些都無法使抱怨減少嗎？

強森：　是有一些。不過，對美國消費者而言，食品營養與否仍是個大問題，
　　　　很多消費者來電都是為了這個原因。事實上，現在假如有個人打電話來抱
　　　　怨，就說是某產品為何用白麵粉而不用全麥麵粉好了，他們一定都會說，我
　　　　們不夠名至實歸。如果美國消費者覺得某家公司沒有履行承諾，或是該公
　　　　司生產劣等品，那他們會放大了音量，明確地告訴這家公司他們的不滿。
　　　　一點都不通融的。

澤崎：　我瞭解，只要有件申訴案件沒處理好，那麼公司長久以來營造的信譽
　　　　就有可能毀於一旦。你有沒有碰到過一些怎麼都擺不平的顧客？

強森：　噢，當然會有一些。偶爾，有些憤怒的顧客會跑去告我們，那我們也
　　　　只好上法庭了。不過，大部分的案件都不會這樣。我們只要多送一些該項
　　　　商品，如果要就醫的話，我們也負擔一些小額的醫藥費，那他們的氣大概
　　　　也消了。

澤崎：　那我們甚麼時候走？

強森：　大約再半小時。我要去的時候會順道來找你。

Words and Phrases

negative feedback 負面回饋	的申訴
nutritive value 營養價值	undo 破壞
fat *n.* 脂肪	years of goodwill 長年的良好信用
preservative 防腐劑	go to court 上法庭
inferior 劣質的	suit 訴訟
loud and clear 清清楚楚的	initiate 發起；開始
mishandled complaint 處理不當	disgruntled 不滿的

Vocabulary Building

- **make a point of** 照例；必定

  The new CEO made a point of eating in the cafeteria with regular employees.

  （這位新任總裁照例都會在員工餐廳跟一般員工一同進餐。）

- **live up to one's reputation** 夠得上某人所得到的名聲

  Leslie found it hard to live up to his reputation as a brilliant marketer.

  （大家總認為萊斯利是位出色的市場行銷家，不過他卻發現自己難以匹配如此美譽。）

- **no ifs, ands, buts, or maybes** 沒有「如果」、「而且」、「但是」、「也許」；不講條件；不容情

  cf. I want the evaluation report by 9 o'clock Monday morning— no ifs, ands, or buts about it, please.

  （這份評估報告，我星期一早上九點以前就要 —— 拜託，別跟我講任何理由。）

- **reimburse** 退款；付還

  You will be fully reimbursed for the cost of the move.

  （你這次搬家的費用會全數償清。）

▶ *Exercises*

請勿改變例句的句型, 用a)、
b)詞組代換下列例句。

(解答見 266頁)

1. We sometimes get negative feedback about the nutritive value of our products.

   a) actively solicit
   b) comments from our customers

2. Nutrition is still a key issue among American consumers.

   a) value for money
   b) the biggest concern of

3. Do you ever get people who can't be satisfied no matter what you do?

   a) won't forgive
   b) what do you say to

◆◆◆◆◆◆◆◆◆◆◆◆◆ 簡短對話 ◆◆◆◆◆◆◆◆◆◆◆◆◆◆

Sawasaki: I was really surprised to discover how concerned Americans are about the contents of the food they eat.

Johnson: It's true. I'd say the tendency has become much more pronounced in the last ten years or so.

Sawasaki: Sometimes I get the impression that they're more interested in what's in the food than they are in how it tastes.

Johnson: Well, that may be a slight exaggeration, but you've got a point there.

---

tendency 傾向　　**pronounced** 顯著的　　**get the impression** 得到⋯的印象
exaggeration 誇張　　**You've got a point there.** 你那樣說也有理。

Consumer Response System — 總結

　　凡經營像是食品之類的民生企業，他們為處理消費者申訴，一般都會印製一本載有應對方法的手冊。而且，關於回函和回訪所用的報告，也都有樣本可供參考。

　　以下是某家大食品廠的手冊中，一些關於處理電話申訴案件的注意事項：

- 在電話中，語氣態度要溫和友善(warm and friendly manner)。
- 注意傾聽對方所說的話，並記下重點。
- 詢問購買地點。若有必要，隨後和該商店取得聯絡，檢查庫存貨品是否有相同問題。
- 不要牽扯到申訴以外的話題，尤其不要提及其它申訴案件。
- 不要去臆測或論斷問題的成因。
- 不要承擔 product liability (產品製造責任。即製造商因生產出劣質產品而使消費者蒙受損害，為此所應承擔的損害責任和賠償義務。)
- 不要給與任何承諾。如果問題很大的話，可先和主管洽商，再決定下一步行動。在電話中，只要告訴對方一些可直接檢討回覆的事就行了。

若有必要拜訪對方時：

- 先好好研究一下從電話中所獲得的資料。
- 事先想好適當的解決方法，以及如何重拾該消費者對公司和公司產品的信心。方法之一是：免費提供該項商品。
- 如果有必要以「損害賠償」的方式來解決問題，要先跟主管談好才可以。

　　手冊中還提到「只要免費提供豐富的該項商品 (generous supply of the product)，或是在負責出面之人的權限內應允負擔小額的醫藥費，問題通常就會得到解決。」

Respected CEO

（受尊敬的CEO）

◆ Lesson 25 的內容 ◆

　　雷‧威斯敦率真和藹的個性，以及他重視團體默契的踏實經營，替他贏得了許多員工的愛戴。每天早上，威斯敦都是輕鬆自在地開著自己的車到公司上班，而且他並沒有私人停車位，這對於大企業的領導者而言是相當難能可貴的。此外，他還擁有驚人的活力和記憶力。有些人，就算他只見過一、兩次面，他也能叫出他們的名字，而與之攀談。最近，威斯敦獲選為「全美最受愛戴的十大執行長」。這證實了他不只是位經營者，更是個不折不扣的領導者。

Thanks, Shoichi.
Winning that
award was a
team effort.

Lesson 25

Respected CEO (1) (受尊敬的 CEO)

●預習 — *Sentences*

- How was the trip to Tokyo?
- I accomplished a lot in the week I was there.
- Winning that award was a team effort.
- Thanks for the congratulatory message you sent me.
- Business seems to be a lot better over there.

●*Vignette*

[*In front of elevators*]

Weston: Greetings! How was the trip to Tokyo, Shoichi? Did they remember who you are?

Sawasaki: Oh, good morning, Ray. Yes, thank you, not only did they remember me, but I felt that I accomplished a lot in the week I was there. And congratulations on making the list of American's most admired CEOs. Everybody at the office in Tokyo was really thrilled.

Weston: Thanks, Shoichi. Winning that award was a team effort. I appreciate the contribution you've made in the frozen foods area. Oh, and thanks for the congratulatory message you sent me from Tokyo. That was very thoughtful of you.

Sawasaki: Not at all.

Weston: You know, you marketing people have played a very important role in helping us move up from where we were five years ago. I think the frozen food line really gives the customers what they want, and that's what it's all about. Keep up the good work.

*   *   *

[*At the cafeteria*]

Compton: Welcome back, Shoichi.

Sawasaki: Thanks.

Owens: How was Tokyo?

Sawasaki: Well, actually business seems to be a lot better over there. Unlike here, where sales have been so flat recently, the operation in Japan has expanded so much since I left that I could hardly believe it.

136

正在等電梯的澤崎，被突然開口跟他打招呼的雷‧威斯敦嚇了一大跳。威斯敦不但記得澤崎的名字，還知道澤崎才從東京出差回來。

[在電梯前面]

威斯敦： 你好啊！東京之行如何，昭一？他們還記得你是誰嗎？

澤崎： 噢，早安，雷。是啊，謝謝你，他們不僅還記得我，而且我覺得我在那兒的一個禮拜內做了好多事。還有，我要恭禧你入選為全美最受愛戴的執行長。在東京辦公室，大家聽到這消息都很感動。

威斯敦： 謝謝你，昭一。這個獎是我們共同努力贏來的。我很感謝你在冷凍食品界所做的貢獻。噢，我還要謝謝你從東京發給我的賀函。你真的是很體貼。

澤崎： 那算不得甚麼。

威斯敦： 你可知道，這五年來我們之所以能進步，你們行銷部門人員所扮演的角色極其重要，幫了我們很大的忙。我認為，我們冷凍食品這個事業真的滿足了顧客的需求，而這正是我們唯一的目標。你們都做得很好，繼續保持下去。

*　　*　　*

[在員工餐廳]

坎普敦： 昭一，歡迎歸來。

澤崎： 謝了。

歐文斯： 東京那邊怎麼樣？

澤崎： 呃，事實上，那裡的生意好像比這裡要好太多了。我們這兒近來的銷售市場一直不景氣，可是在日本那邊，自我離開以來，他們事業擴展的速度簡直快得令人難以置信。

Lesson 25　Respected CEO (1)

Words and Phrases

Greetings!　你好！

accomplish　達成；成就

admire　欽佩

CEO (chief executive officer)

　最高責任主管；執行長；總裁

contribution　貢獻

frozen foods　冷凍食品

congratulatory　祝賀的

thoughtful　體貼的

cafeteria　員工餐廳

flat　不景氣的

operation　事業

Vocabulary Building

● **make the list of**　入選為…

The chairman's wife made the list of America's best dressed women.

(董事長夫人入選為全美衣著最佳的女士之一。)

● **be thrilled**　心情激動；興奮

He was so thrilled by his promotion that he let out a big yell.

(他知道自己升官的消息之後簡直樂歪了，還怪叫了一聲。)

● **that's what it's all about**　那就是唯一要緊的事

cf. Winning the customer's confidence is what it's all about in our business.

(在我們這一行，贏得顧客的信心是唯一要緊的事。)

● **Keep up the good work.**　幹得好，繼續保持下去。

cf. You've been doing a great job. Keep it up.

(你一直以來都做得很好。繼續保持下去。)

(解答見 267 頁)

▶ *Exercises*

請勿改變例句的句型，用a)、
b)詞組代換下列例句。

1. Everybody at the office in Tokyo was really thrilled.

   a) is easy to get along with
   b) I know

2. I appreciate the contribution you've made in the frozen foods area.

   a) Ray is grateful for
   b) sent to the magazine

3. Business seems to be a lot better over there.

   a) the most important consideration
   b) customer service

◆◆◆◆◆◆◆◆◆◆◆◆◆ 簡短對話 ◆◆◆◆◆◆◆◆◆◆◆◆◆

Sawasaki: You'll never guess who I just had a conversation with.
Weathers: Somebody I know?
Sawasaki: Not personally, maybe, but you certainly know *of* him.
Weathers: The pope.
Sawasaki: You're close. Actually it was Ray Weston.
Weathers: Ray Weston? What did he talk to you about?
Sawasaki: He asked me how my trip to Tokyo was.
Weathers: How did he know you had been to Tokyo?
Sawasaki: Beats me.

---

know *of* 聽過或是知道有⋯   **pope** 教宗   **Beats me.** 難倒我了。

Lesson 25

Respected CEO (2) （受尊敬的 CEO）

●預習 — *Sentences*

- I've missed a lot of excitement.
- I don't think he cares much about being in the limelight.
- Ray announced that Shirley is expecting a baby.
- It was after he lost his first wife to cancer.
- A lot of top executives have exceptionally good memories.

●*Vignette*

Sawasaki: But I suppose I've missed a lot of excitement with Ray Weston making *Business Review*'s list of the top ten CEOs for the first time.

Cortez: Well, he seemed to enjoy the party the employees threw in his honor. Generally, though, I don't think he cares much about being in the limelight.

Owens: He's probably a bit preoccupied with his wife now. At the party, Shoichi, Ray announced that Shirley is expecting a baby.

Sawasaki: Is that right? Ray is 55 and Shirley is . . .

Owens: Twenty-eight. You probably didn't know, Chris, but Ray re-married a couple of years ago. It was after he lost his first wife to cancer. Shirley, his new wife, used to be his secretary. The new baby will be younger than his grandchildren. I admire his vitality.

Sawasaki: I admire his memory. Ray greeted me by name this morning and he was asking about my trip to Tokyo. I only met him a couple of times and it never occurred to me that he'd remember who I was.

Owens: He does have an exceptional memory. Legend has it that Ray not only remembers what he ate for lunch at a restaurant a year ago but can recite the whole menu. Be that as it may, it does seem that a lot of top executives have exceptionally good memories.

Compton: My impression of Ray Weston is that he's very unpretentious, unlike some of the CEOs I met at my old job at the Drachman Institute.

澤崎： 不過，我猜當雷·威斯敦首次入選為商務論評雜誌所列的十大執行長時，這裡一定興奮得很，我大概錯過那些場面了。

古岱茲： 嗯，員工們為了祝賀他，給他辦了一場宴會，雷看來似乎很喜歡。不過，大體上，我想他並不是太愛出風頭的人。

歐文斯： 他的心思現在可能有點被他太太佔滿了。昭一，在那個宴會上，他向大家宣布說，雪莉懷孕了。

澤崎： 你說的是真的嗎？雷都五十五歲了，而雪莉…

歐文斯： 二十八。克莉絲，妳可能不知道，雷幾年前再婚了。那是在他第一任太太死於癌症之後的事。他現在的太太，雪莉，以前是他的祕書。而他們將要迎接的這個新生兒，年紀會比雷的孫子還小。我欽佩他的活力。

澤崎： 我欽佩他的記憶力。今天早上雷跟我打招呼時，他叫的是我的名字，而且他還問到我的東京之行。我跟他才打過幾次照面，想都沒想過他還會記得我是誰。

歐文斯： 他的記憶力是相當特出沒錯。人家說，雷不只能夠記得一年前在某家餐廳吃的午餐是甚麼，而且，他還能把整份菜單都背給你聽。不管怎樣，記憶力像他這麼驚人的高層主管似乎仍是大有人在。

坎普敦： 我對雷·威斯敦印象最深刻的是，他一點也不自高自大，不像我以前在達奇蒙協會工作時碰到過的一些 CEO。

Words and Phrases

throw a party 開辦宴會	greet someone by name 以名字
be in the limelight 成為眾所注目	(不帶姓) 跟某人打招呼
的焦點; 出風頭	occur to someone 使某人想到
be expecting a baby 懷孕	exceptional 格外的; 異常的
remarry 再婚	recite 背誦
lose someone to 某親屬死於…	unpretentious [ˌʌnprɪˈtɛnʃəs]
vitality 活力	謙遜的; 不好炫耀的

Vocabulary Building

● **in someone's honor**　向某人表示敬意; 為紀念某人

We put up a big banner in the visitor's honor.

(為了向來訪者表示敬意, 我們豎起了很大的歡迎布條。)

● **be preoccupied with**　(心思) 被…佔滿

James was so preoccupied with the new project he forgot his wedding anniversary.

(詹姆士一心想的都是那個新的企劃案, 以至他連結婚紀念日都給忘了。)

● **legend has it that**　傳聞說…

Legend has it that Ray remembers the name of every person he ever met.

(傳聞說, 只要是雷見過的人, 他都記得他們的名字。)

● **be that as it may**　不管怎樣; 無論如何

"We're sorry we missed the deadline by an hour, but there was a terrible traffic jam on the way here." — "Be that as it may, the bidding is closed and you're disqualified."

「抱歉我們比截止時間晚到了一個小時, 可是在我們來的路上, 交通堵塞得很嚴重。」「不管怎樣, 投標業已結束, 你們競標的資格取消了。」

▶ *Exercises*

請勿改變例句的句型, 用a)、b)詞組代換下列例句。　　(解答見 267 頁)

1. I don't think he cares much about being in the limelight.

   a) interviewed by reporters
   b) am not sure if

2. It never occurred to me that he'd remember who I was.

   a) my name
   b) I didn't expect

3. Ray remembers what he ate for lunch at a restaurant a year ago.

   a) never forgets
   b) who he met

◆◆◆◆◆◆◆◆◆◆◆◆◆◆ 簡短對話 ◆◆◆◆◆◆◆◆◆◆◆◆◆◆

Sawasaki: I get the impression that a lot of CEOs in this country are married to women much younger than themselves.
Owens: It's true. But Ray's case is a bit different from the norm.
Sawasaki: Oh? How so?
Owens: Well, a lot of those guys have ditched their first wives after they reached the top. Seems they think they deserve somebody younger and prettier to match their lifestyle.
Sawasaki: But Ray was a widower when he remarried.
Owens: Yeah, I don't think he's the divorcing type.

---

get the impression 得到⋯的印象　　**norm** 標準　　**How so?** 怎麼會這樣?
ditch 甩掉; 拋棄　　**deserve** 配得上　　**match** 配合; 符合　　**widower** 鰥夫

Respected CEO (3) (受尊敬的 CEO)

預習 ─ *Sentences*

- He drives his own car, a 1991 model, to work.
- Ray's different from the standard Japanese company president.
- He was pouring coffee for council members.
- A Japanese executive would never do that.
- Did you know that he doesn't have a college degree?

Vignette

Compton: What I heard is that he could draw a much higher salary at ABC Foods but he prefers to have the company plow the money back into R&D.

Cortez: That's true, and he also obviously has little interest in the perks that come with corporate power. He drives his own car, a 1991 model, to work and he doesn't even have a reserved parking place, so he has to leave his car at the far end of the parking lot when he comes in late.

Sawasaki: Ray's certainly different from the standard Japanese company president. When I gave that presentation on the changes in Japanese eating habits to the Executive Council, he was pouring coffee for council members as they walked in the door. A Japanese executive would never do that.

Cortez: Ray's very down-to-earth and knows how to recognize and motivate employees. He's paid his dues. Did you know that he doesn't have a college degree? He started at the bottom— in the mailroom— and worked his way up.

Owens: Remember what Shoichi said about being greeted by name? That's typical of Ray. He makes it a point to speak personally to as many employees as he possibly can and to make them see the importance of the work they do for the company.

　　從威斯敦身上看不到一絲一毫的官架子，他每天早上開自己的車到公司，連個私人停車位也沒有。這對大企業的領導者而言，實屬難能可貴。

坎普敦： 我聽到的消息是說，他在 ABC 食品公司本來可以多領很多薪水的，可是他寧願讓公司把那些錢投資到研發上。

古岱茲： 沒錯。而且，對於公司內權大位高者所坐擁的那些特權，他顯然也沒甚麼興趣。他每天上下班，開的是自己的車，91 年型的。此外，他也沒有自己的停車位，所以如果有時來晚了點，就只得把車停在停車場遠遠的一角。

澤崎： 雷當然也跟一般日本公司的總裁不同。有一回我跟執行委員會作簡報，講說關於日本人飲食習慣的改變，那次，我看到他為每位進門的委員倒咖啡。日本籍的主管絕對不做那種事。

古岱茲： 雷相當地實際，他知道如何去認識底下的員工，如何使他們有做事的動機。他之所以有今天，可不是平白得來的。你們知道嗎，他連大學文憑都沒有。他是從基層做起的 —— 從收發室開始 —— 然後一步步地做上來。

歐文斯： 記得昭一說雷跟他打招呼時叫他名字的事嗎？那是雷典型的作法。照例，他總是會盡可能地親自跟每一位員工都說說話，同時也讓他們瞭解到，他們每一位的工作對公司而言都是很重要的。

Lesson 25　Respected CEO (3)

Words and Phrases

draw a salary	支薪	pour coffee	倒咖啡
plow the money into	把錢投資在…	recognize	認得
R&D (<research and develop-		motivate	使有做事的動機
ment)	研究開發	college degree	大學學位
model	(車子的)年型	start at the bottom	從基層做起
standard	標準的	make it a point to	照例要; 一定會
Executive Council	執行委員會		

Vocabulary Building

● **perks** *pl.*　(員工的)特權　〈 perquisites 的縮寫〉

Use of the executive dining room is one of the most coveted perks in this organization.

(公司裡大家最想得到的特權之一, 就是能夠使用主管餐室。)

● **down-to-earth**　現實的; 實際的

In spite of his lofty position, Mark is actually a very down-to-earth person.

(雖然馬可的地位很崇高, 但事實上, 他是個相當實際的人。)

● **pay one's dues**　辛辛苦苦才掙來今天的地位; 付出過才得到

Henry paid his dues as a worker on the plant floor before succeeding his father as president of the company.

(亨利在繼承他父親當上公司總裁之前, 他也是先待過基層, 辛苦過來的。)

● **work one's way up**　一路做上來

It took Rob about 30 years to work his way up to the top of the corporate ladder.

(羅伯花了約三十年的時間才在公司從基層一路爬升至今日高高在上的地位。)

(解答見 267頁)

▶ **Exercises**   請勿改變例句的句型, 用a)、
b)詞組代換下列例句。

1. He prefers to have the company plow the money back into R&D.

   a) would rather
   b) invest in

2. Ray's certainly different from the standard Japanese company president.

   a) Ray isn't the same as
   b) superior to

3. He started at the bottom and worked his way up.

   a) climbed the ladder
   b) in the mailroom

◆◆◆◆◆◆◆◆◆◆◆◆◆◆ 簡短對話 ◆◆◆◆◆◆◆◆◆◆◆◆◆◆◆◆

Cortez: What are CEOs like in Japan, Shoichi? Are they like dictators?

Sawasaki: Well, there are some like that, but for the most part they leave a lot of the policy-making functions up to people at lower levels, and then they give the go-ahead after a consensus has been achieved among the departments concerned.

Cortez: Sounds more democratic than the usual system in this country.

Sawasaki: In a way, I guess it is. But you have to be very formal with them.

Cortez: So no first names?

Sawasaki: No last names, either. You call senior people by their titles instead.

---

dictator 獨裁者   **for the most part** 大部份地   **policy-making** 決定政策的   **give the go-ahead** 示意要下面的人開始執行某計畫   **consensus** 共識   **in a way** 在某方面

Lesson 25

Respected CEO (4) (受尊敬的 CEO)

●預習 — *Sentences*

- It's one of the things that separates him from the pack.
- Now it takes less time to get things going.
- Weston is the antithesis of empire-building managers.
- His predecessor ran his empire largely by the numbers.
- By contrast, Ray is low-key, a listener.

●*Vignette*

Owens: Ray has a real talent for doing that. It's one of the things that separates him from the pack.

Cortez: His skill in handling employees is one of the main reasons for his success. He not only makes the employees want to do a good job but empowers them to do it. Early on, he pushed decision making down to the level that really worked with the problem at hand. Now it takes less time to get things going.

Owens: In a lot of ways, Weston is the antithesis of conglomerate-era empire-building managers. His predecessor ran his empire largely by numbers and he treated the people working for him with all the finesse of a feudal lord. By contrast, Ray is low-key, a listener. He's an operations guy who's willing to roll up his shirt sleeves and get his hands dirty.

Sawasaki: The thing I like about Ray is that he doesn't talk about goals in terms of market share or sales revenues but rather in terms of our level of commitment to the customer and the quality of our work. You know how he says that an effective employee should strive to reach for the best in himself on a daily basis? I like that.

Owens: The thing about Ray is that he isn't just a manager; he's a real leader. That's what's put him where he is today.

Cortez: These days a lot of companies give lip service to concepts like worker empowerment, team building, and getting closer to the customer, but Ray's already put all that into practice in his own way.

　　與前任「封建領主」型的 CEO 相比，威斯敦是完全不同的典型。他重視每一位員工，知道如何使員工有做事的動機。

歐文斯： 雷在那方面真的很有天份，這是使他跟大多數的人不一樣的原因之一。

古岱茲： 他之所以成功，有一個原因是他善於管理底下的員工。他不只使員工會想要把工作做好，同時，他也授與當事者相當的權限。之前，他就把決策的權限移轉到那些實際在承辦業務的人手中了。所以，現在我們處理事情就省了不少時間。

古岱茲： 在很多方面，比起在這個複合企業時代中，那些只在意建立自己王國的經營者，雷簡直是個鮮明的對比。雷前任的那位 CEO，他經營自己王國的重點，只在於旗下人員數目的多寡，而他也用封建領主那種手腕來對待下屬。與之相對的，雷採取的是低姿態，他是個傾聽者。雷是一個做事的人，他會願意捲起衣袖，把雙手弄髒。

澤崎： 我喜歡雷的一點是，當他談到工作目標時，他不會用些像是市場占有率或是營業收入等的字眼，他講求的是，我們對顧客承諾了多少，以及我們的工作品質。你們也知道他是怎麼說的，一個工作有力的員工應該以當日為原則，不管怎樣都盡力而為。我喜歡那樣。

歐文斯： 雷的特點是，他不只是個經營者，還是個真正的領導者。這就是他為甚麼會有今日的原因。

古岱茲： 最近這些日子，對於像是員工權限委讓，建立小組責任制，以及拉近與顧客間距離的這些概念，有很多公司都嚷著要實行，卻影兒都沒有，但雷卻用他自己的方式，把這些都一一落實了。

Words and Phrases

separate someone from the pack
　使某人與大多數人有所差別

empower　　權限委讓

antithesis [æn`tɪθəsɪs]　　對比; 正好
　相反的東西

conglomerate-era　　複合 (集團) 企
　業的時代

predecessor　　前任

feudal lord　　封建領主

by contrast　　相對之下

low-key　　低調的; 不顯眼的

operations guy　　做事的人〈不是只
　有嘴巴講講而已〉

get one's hands dirty　　把手弄髒

sales revenue　　銷售收益

worker empowerment　　員工的權
　限委讓

Vocabulary Building

● **empire-building**　　建立自己王國的〈讓自己底下的人手愈來愈多〉
cf. I'm not an empire builder but I need more workers in my unit to get the job done.
(我並不熱中於建立自己的小王國，可是我這個組裡頭真的得多增加些人手，才能把事情做完。)

● **finesse** [fə`nɛs]　　手腕
It takes a lot of finesse to balance the demands of shareholders, customers, and employees.
(要能在股東、顧客和員工這三者的需要上取得平衡，是需要不少手腕。)

● **roll up one's shirt sleeves**　　捲起衣袖; 實際參與行動
Let's roll up our shirt sleeves and get to work before it's too late.
(趁著時候還不太遲，我們捲起衣袖來工作吧!)

● **give lip service to**　　只有口惠，沒有實際行動
The company gives lip service to equal opportunity, but it has no women managers.
(對於機會均等的論調，這家公司在口頭上頗為支持，但卻不見有甚麼女性經理出現。)

Exercises　　請勿改變例句的句型, 用a)、
　　　　　　　　　　b)詞組代換下列例句。　　　　　（解答見267頁）

1. It's one of the things that separates him from the pack.

   a) makes him stand out
   b) his true sense of devotion is

2. His skill in handling employees is one of the main reasons for his success.

   a) knowledge of marketing
   b) rise in the company

3. He's an operations guy who's willing to get his hands dirty.

   a) a hands-on manager
   b) roll up his shirt sleeves

◆◆◆◆◆◆◆◆◆◆◆◆◆ 簡短對話 ◆◆◆◆◆◆◆◆◆◆◆◆◆

Sawasaki: I must say, though, it's a big ego-booster when the CEO remembers your name.

Owens: Don't let it go to your head now, Shoichi.

Sawasaki: I know. But I can't help feeling kind of flattered.

Owens: Well, that's the idea, of course. It's bound to make an employee feel good when he knows top management is taking a personal interest in what he's doing.

Sawasaki: In a way, it's even more satisfying than getting a raise.

Owens: Ray realizes that people crave attention as well as money, and he's real master at satisfying that need.

---

ego-booster 令自尊心大為提高的東西　　**go to one's head** 使某人興奮　　**feel flattered** 受寵若驚　　**take a personal interest in** 對於…有個人的興趣　　**get a raise** 得到加薪　　**crave** 渴望

Lesson 25

Respected CEO ——總結

■　■　■

　　故事最後，歐文斯說，「雷的特點是，他不只是個經營者，還是個真正的領導者。」所謂真正的領導者，不僅能在處事上展現其領導能力，而且其「領導能力」也必須獲得下屬及同事的認同。在歐美，大家都說「現今企業需要的不是老闆而是領導者」(What industry needs now is not bosses but leaders.) (出自 John Adair 所著之 *Not Bosses But Leaders*)。

　　經營者與領導者之間的一大差別是，經營者重視形式與過程 (style and process)，而領導者則重視實體與現實 (substance and reality)。意即經營者所關心的是決策的經過和溝通的過程 (how decisions get made and how communication flows)，而領導者則關心決策的結果和溝通的內容 (what decisions get made and what he or she communicates)。

　　此外，經營者注重數字、定則和既定的流程 (numbers, formulas, and established processes)。相對的，領導者則扮演給與動機者的角色，藉此激勵他人，使之朝向目標工作 (motivators who inspire others to work toward a goal)。

　　一般人都不喜歡被管，但卻能接受他人的領導或調教。有人說領導者必須具備以下六項能力：

　　1) 透過溝通產生「價值」的能力。

　　2) 超脫一般上司與下屬的關係，給與下屬權限，並栽培出願意獻身工作的下屬(committed followers)的能力。

　　3) 設定高標準的能力。

　　4) 以身作則的能力。

　　5) 把工作重心擺在真正重要的事情 (what is really important) 上的能力。

　　6) 將下屬與外界結合的能力。

Lesson 26

Rumors

（謠言）

◆ Lesson 26 的內容 ◆

　　最近，ABC食品公司內部謠言四起。溫謝爾聽說，總公司近日將大量裁員，並解散行銷部門，而透納則要調到墨西哥。如此一來，公司內部的人事會有很大的變動，人心因此惶惶不定。這樣的謠言之所以會產生，恐怕是受到近來業績不振的影響。雖然透納認為「這不過是個謠言」而將此事輕鬆帶過，但「無風不起浪」，真相到底如何…。

No, all I'm saying is that it's going around on the grapevine.

Lesson 26

Rumors (1) (謠言)

●預習 — *Sentences*

- Are you sure that's true, Brad?
- It's going around on the grapevine.
- I'll check it out with him then.
- I heard a disturbing rumor this morning.
- There's going to be a massive staff cutback.

●*Vignette*

Sawasaki: Are you sure that's true, Brad?

Winchell: No, all I'm saying is that it's going around on the grapevine.

Sawasaki: Have you talked to Eric about this?

Winchell: No, he's not coming in till this afternoon.

Sawasaki: Well, I've got a meeting with him at 2 about a new advertising campaign. I'll check it out with him then.

Winchell: Let me know what he says.

Sawasaki: Will do.

*   *   *

Turner: I think that's an excellent angle. I'd say let's go ahead and see what kind of response it yields in the copy test.

Sawasaki: Fine. I'll call the agency today.

Turner: Got anything else?

Sawasaki: Well, it's not about the campaign but, er, I heard a disturbing rumor this morning.

Turner: Oh?

Sawasaki: They say that there's going to be a massive staff cutback here at headquarters, and Corporate Marketing will be disbanded. And you're being reassigned to Mexico.

Turner: That's considerably better than the previous rumor about an across-the-board pay cut and my being transferred to Siberia.

溫謝爾聽說總公司將大量裁員，並解散行銷部門。這個謠言著實給澤崎帶來不小的衝擊。澤崎下午正好與透納有約，他認為屆時有必要確認一下。

澤崎： 布雷，你確定這是真的嗎？

溫謝爾： 不確定，我只是在說，公司裡有這樣的謠言。

澤崎： 你跟艾瑞克談過這事了嗎？

溫謝爾： 沒有，他今天下午才會進辦公室。

澤崎： 嗯，今天下午兩點我跟他有個關於新廣告活動的會議要開。到時我再跟他問明是否真有此事。

溫謝爾： 要告訴我他說了些什麼哦！

澤崎： 會的。

＊　　　＊　　　＊

透納： 我覺得這個角度好極了。我看我們就著手進行，看看廣告文案的測試會得到什麼反應。

澤崎： 好的。我今天會打電話給廣告代理商。

透納： 還有別的事嗎？

澤崎： 嗯，這跟廣告活動無關，不過，呃，我今天早上聽到一則擾人的謠言。

透納： 哦？

澤崎： 他們說總公司這裡將會有個大裁員，公司行銷部門會解散，而你要調到墨西哥去。

透納： 比起上個謠言來，這個可好太多了。先前有人說，公司將全面調降員工的薪水，而我則要調到西伯利亞去。

Words and Phrases

go around on the grapevine 謠傳	disturbing 困擾的；令人不安的
advertising campaign 廣告活動	massive 大量的
angle 觀點；角度	staff cutback 人員裁減；裁員
copy test 廣告文案測試（在開始某	reassign 重新分派
一廣告活動之前，先對該廣告的文案	pay cut 薪水調降；減薪
內容所作的印象調查）	transfer 調任

Vocabulary Building

- **check out**   調查

  Be sure to check out the alternatives before you make a final decision.

  （在你做出最後決定之前，一定要先調查過其他的替代方案。）

- **yield** *v.*   產出；產生

  The myth of ever-increasing land prices has been destroyed in Japan. If you invest in real estate, it may not necessarily yield a positive return in the future.

  （日本地價飆漲不已的神話已然毀滅。如果你要投資房地產，未來的收益可不見得樂觀。）

- **disband**   解體；解散

  The task force disbanded after completing the cost-reduction project.

  （這個委員會在完成該削減成本的計畫之後就解散了。）

- **across-the-board**   全面的；整個公司的

  Just like most Japanese companies, Westin International gives across-the-board wage hikes to its employees once a year.

  （就像多數的日本企業一樣，韋斯亭國際公司給員工一年全面調薪一次。）

1. All I'm saying is that it's going around on the grapevine.

    a) telling you
    b) in the office

2. I've got a meeting with him at 2 about a new advertising campaign.

    a) I have to see him
    b) to discuss next year's budget

3. They say that there's going to be a massive staff cutback here at head-quarters.

    a) heard some rumors about
    b) severe downsizing program

◆◆◆◆◆◆◆◆◆◆◆◆◆◆ 簡短對話 ◆◆◆◆◆◆◆◆◆◆◆◆◆◆◆◆

Sawasaki: So who told you this, Brad?

Winchell: Now, don't try to make me reveal my sources. I don't want to get anybody into trouble on account of my loose mouth.

Sawasaki: Sorry, I didn't mean to . . .

Winchell: Oh, don't worry about it. It's only natural that you'd want to know. I would have asked exactly the same question myself. It's just that this time I'd rather not go into it. Hope I didn't offend you.

Sawasaki: No, not at all. And when I talk to Eric, I won't tell him I heard it from you.

---

reveal 揭露　　**source** 消息來源　　**get someone into trouble** 使某人陷入
麻煩之中　　**on account of** 由於…　　**loose mouth** 口風不緊　　**offend**
冒犯; 得罪

Lesson 26

Rumors (2) (謠言)

●預習 —*Sentences*

- We're under pressure to cut costs everywhere.
- We're already very lean, in my opinion.
- Where do you think it started?
- Rumors can start at any level in a firm.
- Some rumors can cost a company money.

●*Vignette*

Sawasaki: Then it isn't true?

Turner: Not to my knowledge. As you know, we're under tremendous pressure to cut costs everywhere because sales have been lagging in some product lines, but the company isn't thinking of staff reduction at headquarters. We're already very lean, in my opinion. But this kind of gossip hits the rumor mill every now and then.

Sawasaki: Where do you think it started?

Turner: Who knows? Rumors can start at any level in a firm and the target can be an employee, a department or the whole company. Some rumors can cost a company money and a damaged reputation. Others can hinder someone's career or sabotage a project.

Sawasaki: Are you going to do anything about this one?

Turner: Well, it certainly isn't going to sink ABC Foods but it could cause anxiety in some people. I'll set the record straight at our weekly staff meeting tomorrow. Thanks for bringing it to my attention, Shoichi.

Sawasaki: Not at all.

Turner: I sincerely appreciate your candor, though. You see, I believe that one of my prime responsibilities as a manager is to keep my staff informed. But if I don't hear a rumor, it's hard for me to counter it. Still, I always try to use the staff meeting as an opportunity to share factual work-related news. That in itself helps limit the rumors in my experience.

透納說那是毫無根據的謠言，公司雖然一直要縮減經費，但並沒有考慮裁員。在明天的員工週會中，透納將釐清此事。

澤崎： 那麼這不是真的囉？

透納： 我是沒聽過有這麼一回事。就像你所知道的，由於一些產品部門的銷售狀況遲滯，所以公司到處都有削減成本的壓力，不過公司可沒有在考慮要裁減總部的人事。在我看來，我們已經很精簡了，但像這種閒言閒語還是三不五時地就要來流傳一下。

澤崎： 你想這謠言起自何處？

透納： 誰曉得？在一家公司，謠言可以起自任何階層，而目標可以是員工、部門、或整個公司。有些流言會造成公司在金錢上的損失，並毀及公司的聲譽。而其他的則有可能會妨害到某人事業上的出路或致使某項計畫遭殃。

澤崎： 對於這個謠言，你打算採取什麼行動嗎？

透納： 嗯，這件事當然是不會使 ABC 食品公司因此而關門，但有些人卻會因此而憂慮不安。我會在明天的員工週會上把事情說明清楚。昭一，謝謝你把這事告訴我。

澤崎： 這算不得什麼。

透納： 不過我真的很欣賞你的坦誠。你知道的，我相信身為經理的主要職責之一就是要使我底下的員工知道他們該知道的事。但假使有事情在謠傳，而我卻不曉得，那我就很難與之相抗。而且，我總是會設法藉員工會議的機會來把與工作相關的確實消息告訴大家。就我以往的經驗，這麼做本身會有助於限制謠言的產生。

Lesson 26   Rumors (2)

Words and Phrases

under pressure	承受壓力		hinder	妨礙
lag	落後；減退		sabotage [ˈsæbə‚tɑʒ]	破壞
staff reduction	人事裁減；裁員		anxiety	不安
lean	(人事)精簡		candor [ˈkændə]	坦白；率直
every now and then	偶爾；有時		prime	最主要的
Who knows?	誰知道?		factual	實際的
target	目標			

Vocabulary Building

- **not to my knowledge**　　不在我所知的範圍以內
  cf. To the best of my knowledge, that rumor is false.
  (就我所知，那個謠言是錯誤的。)

- **hit the rumor mill**　　謠傳開來
  The securities firm quickly terminated a trader who was involved in shady deals before the scandal hit the rumor mill.
  (該證券公司在醜聞還沒傳開之前，很快就把那個涉及非法交易的業者開除了。)

- **set the record straight**　　把事情作個準確的傳達
  The CEO will hold a press conference this afternoon to set the record straight.
  (總裁今天下午會召開一場記者招待會，把事情原委說明清楚。)

- **bring something to someone's attention**　　把某事告知某人；叫某人注意某事
  cf. I'd like to call your attention to the last page in the proposals. That's the budget section.
  (我想要你注意一下這個企劃案的最後一頁。那是預算的部分。)

▶ **Exercises**   請勿改變例句的句型, 用a)、
b)詞組代換下列例句。

1. We're under tremendous pressure to cut costs everywhere.

   a) economize
   b) increase profits

2. We're already very lean, in my opinion.

   a) agile
   b) if you care for my opinion

3. Are you going to do anything about this one?

   a) will you
   b) to keep it from spreading

◆◆◆◆◆◆◆◆◆◆◆◆◆ 簡短對話 ◆◆◆◆◆◆◆◆◆◆◆◆◆◆◆

Turner: You know, Shoichi, it's kind of discouraging sometimes. I really do my best to be above board with the people who work for me, but still these wild stories keep going around from time to time. Often, I'm the last to know.

Sawasaki: Well, it seems to me that everybody in the office likes and trusts you, but you always seem so busy that people may be reluctant to bother you with idle gossip.

Turner: So what do you suggest?

Sawasaki: Maybe if you could take a bit of time every now and then for a non-working lunch or a couple of drinks after work, people might talk more freely.

---

kind of 〔俗〕有點兒   **above board** 光明正大地   **wild story** 荒誕無稽的話   **from time to time** 偶爾   **reluctant to** 不願意…   **idle gossip** 沒有根據的閒話; 閒聊

Lesson 26

Rumors (3) (謠言)

● 預習 —Sentences

- A hush-hush attitude breeds unneeded speculation.
- Does the company have a policy on dealing with rumors?
- It's best to stay above the whole thing.
- That's typical of an office rumor.
- I'm glad to hear it's just a lot of hot air.

●Vignette

Sawasaki: But don't you need to keep a lid on some things?

Turner: I don't do that unless it's really necessary— and possible. Employees feel betrayed when they find out management has been keeping secrets from them. A hush-hush attitude breeds unneeded speculation and suspicion.

Sawasaki: Does the company have a policy on dealing with rumors?

Turner: At the corporate level, rumors are never denied or confirmed as a matter of principle. Also, managers are strictly warned against using gossip as a tactic for getting things done. Using the grapevine as a tool can really backfire on a manager and cause him to lose credibility with his staff. It's best to stay above the whole thing and set a good example for the staff.

Sawasaki: Well, I hate to tell you but I think this one about you has made the rounds pretty quickly.

Turner: That's typical of an office ruomor.

Sawasaki: Anyway, I'm glad to hear it's just a lot of hot air.

*　　*　　*

■狀況

　　公司對於謠言基本是採中立的態度，不過透納將調任墨西哥的謠言，幾乎傳遍公司。

澤崎：　但有些事情你不需要保守祕密嗎？

透納：　除非是真的有必要 —— 而且也要做得到才行，否則我不會封鎖消息。員工若得知管理當局有事情瞞著不讓他們知道，那他們會有被出賣的感覺。神祕兮兮的態度會引起不必要的推測和懷疑。

澤崎：　公司有沒有什麼處理謠言的政策？

透納：　站在公司的立場，原則上，我們不會去否定或是證實某項傳言。而且，經理們還受到嚴厲警告，不准利用閒言閒語作為遂己目的的手段。作經理的若把流言當作一種工具，這事實上可能會造成反作用，令他在下屬面前失去信譽。最好還是對整件事保持超然立場，也給下屬做個好榜樣。

澤崎：　嗯，我很不願意告訴你，不過，我覺得這個關於你的謠言很快就已傳遍公司了。

透納：　辦公室裡的謠言都是這樣。

澤崎：　不管怎麼說，我很高興知道這事不過是空穴來風。

＊　　　＊　　　＊

Words and Phrases

keep a lid on　保守祕密; 控制情勢　　deny　　否定

betray　　背叛; 出賣　　　　　　　confirm　　確認

breed　　引起　　　　　　　　　　as a matter of principle　　原則上

unneeded　　不必要的　　　　　　warn against　　警告不得…

speculation　　推測　　　　　　　tactic　　戰術

suspicion　　懷疑　　　　　　　　credibility　　可信度; 信用

Vocabulary Building

- **hush-hush**　　祕密的; 機密的

  His hush-hush attitude left the staff members puzzled and concerned.

  (他那種神祕兮兮的態度使得員工們既困惑又擔心。)

- **backfire**　　招致與預期相反的結果; 適得其反

  The company's attempt to cover up the accident backfired.

  (公司意圖封鎖意外事故的消息, 但卻得到了反效果。)

- **make the rounds**　　巡視; 巡迴

  The president likes to make the rounds of the firm's overseas offices.

  (總裁喜歡來回巡視公司在海外的辦事處。)

- **hot air**　　大言大話; 吹牛

  Don't pay any attention to Reggie's claims. They're just a lot of hot air.

  (你可不要把雷濟那些振振有詞的話聽進去, 那些都不過是在放空氣罷了。)

請勿改變例句的句型,用a)、
b)詞組代換下列例句。　　　　　（解答見268頁）

1. I don't do that unless it's really necessary— and possible.

　　a) recommend against secrecy
　　b) except in cases where

2. A hush-hush attitude breeds unneeded speculation and suspicion.

　　a) mistrust among employees
　　b) withholding information

3. I'm glad to hear it's just a lot of hot air.

　　a) it's a relief
　　b) find out

◆◆◆◆◆◆◆◆◆◆◆◆◆ 簡短對話 ◆◆◆◆◆◆◆◆◆◆◆◆◆

Turner: Besides, if you stop and think about it, the very idea of closing down Corporate Marketing is ludicrous. I wouldn't want to say that marketing is the most important part of our entire operation, but it certainly ranks right up near the top.
Sawasaki: That's a load off my mind. I would have hated to see this department broken up just when I was starting to feel at home here.
Turner: Rest easy, Shoichi. Anyway, I'm glad you came to me about this.
Sawasaki: So am I.

---

ludicrous　可笑的; 滑稽的　　**rank** *v.*　位居　　**That's load off my mind.**
那我就放心多了。

Lesson 26

Rumors (4) (謠言)

●預習 — *Sentences*

- I thought we were ready to sign the papers.
- Now they're suddenly wanting to hold off.
- I doubt that ever made it out of here.
- They're not talking about us, are they?
- She said that there's been a rash of sudden meetings.

●*Vignette*

[In Brad's office some days later]

Sawasaki: Brad, I just had a strange conversation with Columbus Food Service Co. We've been negotiating a tie-up that will put ABC Foods' frozen foods into every hospital they service. I thought we were ready to sign the papers and get the show on the road. Now they're suddenly wanting to hold off. I just can't figure it out. Do you suppose they heard that rumor about the disbanding of Corporate Marketing?

Winchell: I doubt that ever made it out of here. No, I think they may have heard something else.

Sawasaki: What's that?

Winchell: Let me close the door, Shoichi. *[Pause, door closes]* Did you read Ken Bulow's "Today's Business" column this morning?

Sawasaki: No, I didn't. What's in it?

Winchell: Based on some rumors, he speculates that there's a good possibility that, quote, a large New York-based food company will be taken over, unquote.

Sawasaki: Gee. They're not talking about us, are they? If it's us, taken over by whom?

Winchell: I don't know but it's been on the grapevine that a takeover may be in the offing. Maria just left my office and she said that there's been a rash of sudden meetings between members of the Executive Council and the board of directors.

Sawasaki: I wonder what steps Ray Weston is going to take.

Winchell: I've been sitting here wondering what steps Brad Winchell is going to take.

　　澤崎得知了 ABC 食品公司即將被併購的傳聞，而公司內部近來的運作又似暗藏玄機。今後到底會發生什麼事呢？澤崎心中充滿不安。

[數日後在布雷的辦公室]

澤崎：　布雷，我剛剛跟哥倫布食品業務公司有個奇怪的談話。我們兩家公司一直在商討一項合作計畫，要用 ABC 食品公司的冷凍食品供應給跟他們有業務往來的每一家醫院。我還以為我們已經準備好簽約，要開始這個計畫了。但現在他們突然想要把計畫延後。我真是想不通。你想，他們是不是聽到我們公司行銷部門要解散的傳聞了？

溫謝爾：　我不相信那些話曾經傳出去過。不對，我認為他們是聽到一些別的事了。

澤崎：　是甚麼？

溫謝爾：　昭一，我關個門。[談話暫停，門關上] 你今天早上看過肯‧布洛的「今日商業」專欄沒有？

澤崎：　沒有，我沒看。他寫了甚麼？

溫謝爾：　根據一些謠言，他推測道，話是這麼說的，有家以紐約為據點的大食品公司很有可能會被購併。

澤崎：　啊！那不會是在說我們吧？假使是的話，要買我們公司的是誰呢？

溫謝爾：　我不知道，不過是有謠傳說，即將會有購併事件發生。瑪莉亞才剛離開我辦公室，她說近來執行委員會和董事會接二連三地召開臨時會議。

澤崎：　不知道雷‧威斯敦下一步會怎麼做？

溫謝爾：　我倒是一直地坐在這兒，想著不知道布雷‧溫謝爾下一步要怎麼走。

Words and Phrases

tie-up	合作	take over	接管
hold off	延期	rash	頻頻發生
figure out	瞭解	board of directors	董事會
speculate	推測		

Vocabulary Building

- **negotiate**　交涉

  The special envoy negotiated the release of the hostages.

  (那個特使交涉釋放人質的事。)

- **sign the papers**　簽約

  They just signed the papers setting up the joint venture in California.

  (他們剛簽下合約，要在加州成立合資事業公司。)

- **get the show on the road**　開始進行計畫

  Enough of these preliminaries. It's time we got this show on the road!

  (準備動作已經夠了，我們該要開始計畫的進行了。)

- **in the offing**　即將發生

  Management denies it, but substantial pay cuts are in the offing.

  (雖然資方否認有這樣的事，但即將到來的卻是可觀的減薪。)

（解答見 268 頁）

▶ **Exercises**　請勿改變例句的句型，用a)、b)詞組代換下列例句。

1. I thought we were ready to sign the papers.

    a) get official authorization
    b) was positive

2. It's been on the grapevine that a takeover may be in the offing.

    a) likely this month
    b) rumor has it

3. I wonder what steps Ray Weston is going to take.

    a) nobody can be sure
    b) how much money the project

◆◆◆◆◆◆◆◆◆◆◆◆◆ 簡短對話 ◆◆◆◆◆◆◆◆◆◆◆◆◆◆

Winchell: Ever lived through a takeover before?

Sawasaki: No. What's it like?

Winchell: Well, one thing you can be pretty sure of is that the new owners are going to want to squeeze more profits out of the operation. That's one reason why they're so eager to maximize the cash flow.

Sawasaki: I suppose that means staff cutbacks.

Winchell: Often it does. Also they may be less inclined to invest in plant and equipment that's not going to pay off in the short term.

---

live through 經歷過… **squeeze** 榨取 **maximize** 使達到最大 **staff cutback** 人事裁減；裁員 **be less inclined to** 比較不傾向… **invest in plant and equipment** 在設備上投資 **pay off** 合算；產生預期成果 **in the short term** 短期內

169

Lesson 26

Rumors — 總結

英文中常說 "If your ear tingles (or burns), someone is talking of you." 換句話說, 就是謠言中的主角「耳朵會痛或發熱」。

謠言是一種口耳相傳的傳播型態。根據大眾傳播學者的研究顯示, 那種具迫切性危機的謠言, 最容易在極短的時間內迅速散播開來。像是組織改革, 經營者的更換, 新的行銷策略等類似的變動, 除給人帶來不安外, 也會引起謠言。這種不安常成為壓力源, 導致生產力低落。

若有上述事件發生時, 該如何應變呢? 在美國某大企業所使用的管理者 Trouble-Shooting Guide (問題解決指南) 中, 有以下幾點建議:

- 要求自己的下屬 (direct reports) 報告所耳聞的謠言。
- 其中只要有一部分是事實, 在情況允許下, 應悉數公開。即使是「惡耗」(如工廠倒閉、大量裁員等的), 對於當事者而言, 與其被矇在鼓裡, 倒不如讓他們瞭解真相, 反而能有心理準備, 並為將來作打算。
- 對於下屬, 要絕對地開誠布公, 若真不知道就坦承不知, 並允諾若有可公開的消息, 就會即刻告知。
- 不可加入散布謠言的行列。參與傳播之列便等於表明自身的不安, 更會加深下屬的疑慮。

過去曾有過某公司企圖購併 ABC 食品公司的傳聞, 並迅速在華爾街流傳。當時威斯敦即寫信向全體員工聲明, 「本公司對於謠言既不否認也不證實, 這是一向的政策。但是, 保有公司的自主權, 才是對公司最有利的事 (it is in our best interest to remain independent)。」然而, 面對此次繪聲繪影的傳聞, ABC 食品公司是否能繼續保有其自主權呢? 我們且拭目以待。

Lesson 27

Takeover

（企業購併）

◆ Lesson 27 的內容 ◆

　　購併的傳聞果然是真的。美國大菸草製造商，A.C.勞雷，將買下 ABC 食品公司。由於正值業績低落之際，所以 ABC 食品公司也苦無對策。這實在是件令人遺憾的事。雖然雷·威斯敦要透過衛星對全美員工發表談話，但這整件事仍造成大家的不安。一般預料，公司在轉手不久後，有不少員工就要丟掉飯碗了。

Takeover (1) （企業購併）

●預習 — *Sentences*

- Ray Weston will address the employees at 1 o'clock.
- That's terrible news.
- Didn't the company try to counter it?
- Our financial health has been failing in recent months.
- What exactly did the management consider as options?

●*Vignette*

Turner: I have a very important message to share with you this morning. No doubt you have all heard rumors over the past several weeks about the impending ownership change here at ABC Foods. Well, it's official now: A.C. Raleigh, one of America's most profitable cigarette companies, has just bought this corporation. Ray Weston will address the employees at 1 o'clock today via satellite, but he has requested that all managers immediately inform their key team members of the situation.

Owens: That's terrible news. It's a hostile takeover, right? Didn't the company try to counter it?

Turner: The Executive Council and the board looked into a number of options, but it appeared we had no choice. Unfortunately, our financial health has been failing in recent months and we were caught with our guard down.

Cortez: What exactly did the management consider as options?

Turner: Obviously, the first thought was to find a merger partner, but we weren't able to find a suitable counterpart at this stage. Our only other possibility was to find a more compatible buyer and, unfortunately, that just didn't pan out.

Cortez: So we had to be taken over one way or another.

艾瑞克・透納面色凝重地召集了公司的主要成員。因為ABC
食品公司被大菸草製造商A.C.勞雷購併了。

透納: 今天早上,我有一件非常重要的事情要告訴你們。無疑的,過去幾個
　　　禮拜來,你們應該都聽到謠言說,我們ABC食品公司的老闆要換人了。
　　　嗯,現在公司已正式易手: A.C.勞雷,美國最賺錢的菸草公司,剛剛買下
　　　了這家公司。雷・威斯敦今天下午一點會透過衛星向全體員工發表談話,
　　　但他要求所有經理主管立即把公司目前狀況告知組內重要成員。

歐文斯: 這消息糟透了。這是一個非善意的購併,對不對?難道公司沒有試
　　　過找出反擊的辦法嗎?

透納: 先前,執行委員和董事會調查了一些可能的選擇,但情況顯示,我們
　　　別無選擇。不幸的是,最近幾個月來,我們的財務狀況持續衰退,在沒有
　　　防備能力的情形下,我們著了別人一道。

古岱茲: 到底管理階層所認為的可能選擇是甚麼?

透納: 很明顯的,第一個想到的是找個可以合夥的公司。可是,在目前這個
　　　階段,找不到合適的對等公司。剩下的唯一可能就是找個更合適的買主。
　　　不幸地,也沒有。

古岱茲: 所以,不管怎樣,我們的老闆鐵定要換人了。

Lesson 27 Takeover (1)

Words and Phrases

no doubt	無疑地	option	選擇
impending	迫近的；逼近的	have no choice	別無選擇
ownership	所有權	financial health	財務狀況
address	向…說話	merger	合併
via satellite	透過衛星	counterpart	對等人物
takeover	購併；接管	compatible	[kəmˈpætəbl] 相容
counter	對抗		的；符合一致的
look into	調查		

Vocabulary Building

- **hostile takeover**　懷有敵意的購併
  cf. Unfriendly takeovers are very rare in the world of Japanese business.
  (在日本商業界裏，用意不善的購併是相當少有的。)

- **be caught with one's guard down**　在沒有防備的狀態下被打中
  cf. In today's dog-eat-dog environment, you can never afford to let your guard down.
  (在今天狗咬狗的現實環境中，永遠要保持戒備，因為你損失不起的。)

- **pan out**　(計畫)成功
  The plan to establish a joint venture to manufacture VCRs just didn't pan out.
  (原先打算與人合資生產錄影機的計畫沒能成功。)

- **one way or another**　無論如何；不管怎樣
  One way or another, I'm going to get the message across to Shirley.
  (無論如何，我一定要把這封信送到雪莉手中。)

1. I have a very important message to share with you this morning.

   a) several announcements
   b) convey to

2. The Executive Council and the board looked into a number of options.

   a) carefully considered
   b) ways to survive

3. So we had to be taken over one way or another.

   a) it seemed that the company
   b) in spite of all our efforts

◆◆◆◆◆◆◆◆◆◆◆◆◆◆ 簡短對話 ◆◆◆◆◆◆◆◆◆◆◆◆◆◆◆

Winchell: Eric, I'm curious what your personal reaction is to this.
Turner: The takeover?
Winchell: Yeah.
Turner: Well, I can't say I'm overjoyed, but there's not much I can do about it, is there?
Winchell: Are you going to stay on?
Turner: I'd like to. Of course, a lot will depend on Raleigh's plans. They may decide they can do without my services.
Winchell: I guess the same goes for all of us. Time to update those résumés, huh?
Turner: Afraid so.

---

curious 好奇的　　**be overjoyed** 欣喜萬分　　**stay on** 留下來　　**do without**
沒有…也可以　　**go for** 適用於…　　**update** 使成為最新　　**résumé** 履歷
表　　**Afraid so.** (=I'm afraid so.) 恐怕就是這樣了。

Takeover (2) （企業購併）

● 預習 — *Sentences*

- They would have meant selling off our crown jewels.
- At least we would have held on to our independence.
- So we'll be working for a tobacco company.
- Judging from ACR's recent history, I very much doubt it.
- Why would a tobacco company want to acquire us?

● *Vignette*

Winchell: Did Ray look at "scorched earth" or other defense mechanisms?

Turner: I understand that our investment bankers advised against tactics of that sort. They would have meant selling off our crown jewels and then taking drastic cuts to economize.

Winchell: But at least we would have held on to our independence.

Turner: True, but other companies' track records show that a strategy like that often results in a permanent impairment of earning power and equity value.

Owens: So we'll be working for a tobacco company. I guess those "No smoking" signs will have to go.

Sawasaki: Will our management remain independent?

Turner: Judging from ACR's recent history, I very much doubt it. My hunch is that we'll be merged with Nelson Food & Beverages, which they acquired two years ago. Incidentally, Ray is expected to announce his retirement today.

Cortez: Is that right? It's too bad for him, but I supposed he'll be entitled to a golden parachute.

Winchell: But why would a tobacco company want to acquire us?

Turner: That's a good question, Brad. ACR is one of the 20 largest companies in the United States but for many years they've depended on a single cigarette brand, Greensboro, for more than half of their profits. They always wanted to diversify as a consumer products company but it's been difficult for them to get away from the cigarette business, since it's so profitable. But they know that their cigarette profits won't last forever.

澤崎最擔心的是，ABC食品公司能否繼續保有獨立經營權。透納的看法是，「這大概是不可能的事吧！」

溫謝爾：　雷有沒有研究過「焦土作戰」或是其他的防禦手法？

透納：　據我所知，我們的投資銀行勸過我們不要採取那樣的戰術。因為那意味著我們得把公司最具價值的資產賣掉，之後，為求更有效率地運用現有資源，再來個劇烈的裁減。

溫謝爾：　可是，我們至少可以繼續保有我們的自主權。

透納：　是沒錯，但是其他公司過去的紀錄顯示，那樣的戰略常會永久性地損害公司的收益力和資產值。

歐文斯：　那就是說，我們將為一家菸草公司效力了。我想，那些「禁止吸菸」的牌子得要撤掉了。

澤崎：　我們的經營管理還能維持獨立嗎？

透納：　根據ACR公司近來的作風研判，我很懷疑。我的預感是，我們將會與尼爾森食品飲料公司合併，那是一家他們在兩年前兼併的公司。順帶說一下，雷應該會在今天宣布退休。

古岱茲：　真的嗎？那對他而言真是太糟糕了。不過我想他應該可以拿到一筆豐厚的離職金。

溫謝爾：　只是為甚麼一家菸草公司會想要買我們這家公司呢？

透納：好問題，布雷。ACR是美國排行前二十名的大企業，可是，多年來他們的收入有一半以上是來自一個菸草品牌，格林斯布洛；他們一直想使產品多元化而成為一個消費財製造商，可是他們又難以脫離菸草事業，因為這一行的利潤實在太大了。不過他們也瞭解，菸草事業的春天會過去的。

Words and Phrases

"scorched earth"　「焦土作戰」
〈對抗企業購併的對策之一，就是被購併的一方將所謂的 "crown jew-els"，即公司最具資產價值的東西賣掉，故意使公司的價值貶低，以減少敵對企業想要購併的念頭〉

investment banker　投資銀行 (家)
tactics of that sort　那樣的戰術
crown jewels　最重要資產
impairment　損害；減低價值
earning power　收益力
equity value　資產值
hunch　直覺；預感

be entitled to　有…的權利；有權利…

golden parachute　黃金降落傘；高級職員去職補償費〈這是一筆為數不少的預留金，若該公司被他人購併，內部的高級主管可能會因被對方公司的高階層取代，而面臨去職一途，此一 golden parachute 即在此時作用，高級主管必須離開，但有優渥的離職金〉

consumer products company　消費財製造商

Vocabulary Building

● **advise against**　勸告不要…
I advised Joan against investing in the new wonder drug, but she ignored my advice and got burned.
(我勸告過瓊恩不要把錢投資在那種新的特效藥上，但她無視於我的忠告，結果把自己搞得灰頭土臉。)

● **economize**　節約
Economizing is fine, but don't scrimp on essential maintenance.
(節約是很好，但不要在基本的生活開支上太小氣了。)

● **track record**　實績；業績紀錄
Give XYZ company's track record for innovation, I'm surprised their production facilities are so antiquated.
(看到 XYZ 公司如此富於技術革新的業績紀錄，我實在是很驚訝他們的生產設備居然如此老舊。)

● **diversify**　多樣化；多元化
The cosmetics company has decided to diversify into the night club business.
(那家化妝品公司決定採多元化發展，將觸角伸至夜總會事業。)

請勿改變例句的句型, 用a)、
b)詞組代換下列例句。

(解答見 269 頁)

1. Our investment bankers advised against tactics of that sort.

   a) said we should avoid
   b) doing anything hasty

2. Ray is expected to announce his retirement today.

   a) slated
   b) step down

3. They know that their cigarette profits won't last forever.

   a) the business upswing
   b) they're reminded

◆◆◆◆◆◆◆◆◆◆◆◆◆◆ 簡短對話 ◆◆◆◆◆◆◆◆◆◆◆◆◆◆

Cortez: You know, I really feel sorry for Ray.

Owens: For Ray? Even with his golden parachute?

Cortez: Yeah. You know, he's really devoted the best years of his life to building ABC Foods into what it is today.

Owens: I know what you mean. He's not like some of those MBA-type executive who flit from one company to the next.

Cortez: I wonder what he'll do.

Owens: Don't lose any sleep over him, Maria. I bet he'll have plenty of offers to choose from.

Cortez: Still, it won't be like running a company he's been with his whole working life.

I know what you mean. 我瞭解你的意思。　　**MBA** (master of business administration)　企管碩士　　**flit from one company to the next**　跑過一家公司又一家公司; 不斷地換工作　　**lose sleep over**　為…擔心到失眠　　**offer**　願意聘用的表示　　**run a company**　經營一家公司

Lesson 27

Takeover (3) (企業購併)

●預習 — Sentences

- Hatchet men will be coming in to cut out jobs.
- The bottom line is all that counts in M&A situations.
- It doesn't do any good to bury your head in the sand.
- Not everybody will be kept on after the transition.
- When will they let us know the details of what's going on?

●Vignette

Turner: Domestic cigarette consumption is declining and they face the threat of product liability suits.

Owens: If ACR wants to make money in a slow-growing business like ours, they're going to have to slash costs. I can see it already. Hatchet men will be coming in to cut out jobs and even whole departments. The bottom line is all that counts in M&A situations. What really makes me angry is that there's so little concern for the people who get thrown out onto the street.

Turner: Well, it doesn't do any good to bury your head in the sand. I mean, we all fear change to one degree or another. But it's inevitable, just like death and taxes. And I think we should remember that the ability to face and accommodate change is one of the pillars on which our country's prosperity has been built. Granted not everybody will be kept on after the transition, but there will be a package for employees who are made redundant, including severance pay, special stock buyouts for stock-holding employees, and outplacement service.

Cortez: When will they let us know the details of what's going on?

Turner: In his speech this afternoon, Ray will basically go over what I've just said and report any new developments.

透納：　國內香菸消費一直在下降，而且他們還面臨到產品責任訴訟的威脅。

歐文斯：　假如 ACR 想要在像我們這種成長率低的食品業賺錢的話，那他們勢必要大幅削減成本。我已經可以預見了，會有裁員殺手進來，砍掉我們的工作，甚至殺掉整個部門。在企業購併的情形中，有沒有利益是唯一考量的要點。真正令我生氣的是，他們根本不在乎那些工作被裁、前途茫茫的人。

透納：　所以，逃避現實一點好處都沒有。我的意思是，我們或多或少都會害怕面臨一些改變。但就像死亡和納稅一樣，這是無可避免的。我想，要記得的是，我國之所以繁榮，其下的支柱之一，就是國人善於處變的能力。就算是這次變動後，必須有人走路，但為顧及這些因成為冗員而得要裁撤的員工，會有一套方案公布，其中包括資遣金、為持股員工設計的特別買進方案和安排新工作的服務。

古岱茲：　對於目前發生的一些事，他們甚麼時候會讓我們知道細節？

透納：　在雷今天下午要發表的談話中，甚本上，他會複述我剛剛所說的話，並報告任何的新發展。

Words and Phrases

consumption	消費	prosperity	繁榮
decline	下降	granted	即使;姑認
product liability suit	產品責任訴訟	transition	變遷;轉變
slash	大幅削減	be made redundant	成為冗員
bottom line	帳本底行 (顯示公司	severance pay	資遣費
的盈虧)		stock buyout	將股權全部買下
M&A	企業購併	outplacement service	為解聘員工
inevitable	無可避免的	安排新工作的服務	
pillar	柱子	go over	反覆;重覆

Vocabulary Building

- **hatchet man**　　裁員殺手
  Neil's too soft-hearted to be used as a hatchet man.
  (奈爾心太軟了,沒辦法做一個裁員殺手。)

- **all that counts**　　唯一有份量的東西
  All that counts in George's mind is making money.
  (喬治滿腦子想的都是賺錢。)

- **get thrown out onto the street**　　丟掉工作,前途茫茫
  It's especially tough on older employees when they get thrown out onto th street.
  (對於年紀較大的職員而言,被公司裁撤而無路可去是件格外殘酷的事。)

- **bury one's head in the sand**　　逃避現實〈像駝鳥 (ostrich) 一樣,遇到危險,就把頭藏到沙子裡頭,以為看不到就沒事了〉
  cf. He took an ostrich-like approach, pretending that the problem didn't exist.
  (他採取了像駝鳥一樣的逃避方式,就是假裝問題根本不存在。)

▶ *Exercises*

請勿改變例句的句型,用a)、b)詞組代換下列例句。　(解答見268頁)

1. Domestic cigarette consumption is declining.

   a) domestically
   b) falling

2. The bottom line is all that counts in M&A situations.

   a) the name of the game
   b) making a quick profit

3. There will be a package for employees who are made redundant.

   a) lose their jobs
   b) we will provide

◆◆◆◆◆◆◆◆◆◆◆◆◆◆ 簡短對話 ◆◆◆◆◆◆◆◆◆◆◆◆◆◆◆

Owens: You know, Maria, Ray isn't the only one who's put a lot of good years into this company.

Cortez: Oh, I didn't mean to imply that. I realize there are a lot of people who've made a major commitment of time and effort, you included.

Owens: When you get to be my age, let me tell you, the thought of starting out fresh in a whole new organization is pretty daunting.

Cortez: So you'll stay on?

Owens: No, I didn't say that. After all, as Eric says, the decision may not be mine to make.

---

imply 意指; 暗示　　**daunting** 可怕的; 令人失去勇氣的

Lesson 27

Takeover (4) (企業購併)

●預習 — *Sentences*

- It's going to be done through the company-wide E-mail system.
- When do you think the transition will start?
- I'm sure they'll want to get us integrated as soon as possible.
- That's all I have for you now.
- I'd rather stay and face the challenge.

●*Vignette*

Turner: He's arranging it so that employees at every level will have access to accurate information on the situation as it unfolds and how it's likely to affect them personally.

Winchell: How's that going to work?

Turner: It's going to be done through the company-wide E-mail system. You'll be able to access the latest information through your own terminal. The computer will be programmed to tell you precisely what your own package consists of in case your job is eliminated.

Cortez: Eric, when do you think the transition will start?

Turner: Probably sooner than you might expect. The acquisition is subject to the approval of shareholders and the relevant regulatory authorities, but ACR is real go-go company and I'm sure they'll want to get us integrated as soon as possible. Anyway, that's all I have for you now but I promise to keep you informed. Oh, Shoichi, can I talk to you for a second? Just the two of us.

Sawasaki: Sure.

Turner: In view of what's happening you have the option to either return to the Tokyo office immediately or remain here through the transition. What's your preference?

Sawasaki: No question about it. I'd rather stay and face the challenge— if I'm wanted, that is.

Turner: Good. I'm glad you feel that way. Your talents both as a liaison person with Japan and as an excellent food marketer are bound to be in great demand in the new organization.

　　這次的購併定案後，澤崎被迫要做個抉擇：即刻調回東京公司，或是繼續留待美國總部。澤崎毫不猶豫地選擇了後者。他似乎企盼能有機會看到即將發生的變局。

透納：　他這樣安排，是為了使各階層的員工，在事情進展的同時，都可以掌握最正確的資訊，並且知道他們個人會受到甚麼樣的影響。

溫謝爾：　這要怎麼進行呢？

透納：　經由全公司的電子郵件系統。你可以透過自己的電腦終端機，獲得最新的消息。他們也會設計電腦程式，以便正確地告訴你，萬一你的工作被裁了，公司給你的遣散方案裡頭會有些甚麼東西。

古岱茲：　艾瑞克，你認為甚麼時候會開始換手？

透納：　可能比你預期的要快。這個購併需得經過股東和相關管理當局的認可才會有效。不過 ACR 的活動力相當強，我確信他們會儘快地把我們兼併過去。不過，我能告訴你們的也就這些了。但是，一有任何消息，我保證一定讓你們知道。哦，昭一，我可以跟你講一下話嗎？就我們兩個。

澤崎：　當然可以。

透納：　考量目前的狀況，你可以有兩個選擇 —— 立刻調回東京，或是留在這裏度過這次的轉變，你希望怎樣？

澤崎：　毫無疑問地，我寧願待在這裏，面對這個挑戰 —— 當然，前提是如果他們要我的話。

透納：　太好了。我很高興你這麼想，不管是身為與日本之間的聯絡人，或是優秀的食品市場開發者，你的才幹在我們新的組織中一定會十分搶手的。

Words and Phrases

accurate	正確的	regulatory authorities	管理當局
company-wide	全公司的	go-go *adj.*	活躍的
E-mail (electronic mail)	電子郵件	integrate	整合; 統合
terminal	終端機	preference	喜好
eliminate	除去; 消除	No question about it.	毫無疑問。
acquisition	取得	liaison [liˋezən] person	聯絡人
shareholder	股東	marketer	市場開發部負責人
relevant	相關的	be in demand	有需要

Vocabulary Building

● **have access to**　　可以取得⋯

The subsidiary has access to virtually unlimited financing from the parent company.

(子公司幾乎可以無限量地從母公司獲得財務支援。)

● **as it unfolds**　　隨著事情逐漸明朗; 隨著事態繼續發展

Thomas has promised to keep us posted on the latest developments as they unfold.

(湯瑪斯向我們保證, 隨著事態發展, 若有任何變動, 他會立刻讓我們知道。)

● **sooner than one might expect**　　比某人預期的要來得快

I'm sure you'll find a new job sooner than you might expect.

(我確定你會比你所預期的更快找到工作。)

● **be subject to**　　必須獲得⋯的批准; 會受⋯影響的

cf. John's mood is subject to violent ups and downs.

(約翰的情緒常是大起大落的。)

請勿改變例句的句型，用a)、
b)詞組代換下列例句。

▶**Exercises** (解答見269頁)

1. Employees at every level will have access to accurate information on the situation.

   a) be given
   b) every member of the workforce

2. The computer will be programmed to tell you precisely what your own package consists of.

   a) your immediate supervisor will be happy
   b) let you know

3. You talents are bound to be in great demand in the new organization.

   a) people like you
   b) will be valued

◆◆◆◆◆◆◆◆◆◆◆◆◆ 簡短對話 ◆◆◆◆◆◆◆◆◆◆◆◆◆

Sawasaki: I must say, though, this is a bit of a shock for me. In Japan it's quite rare for a company to be taken over against its will.
Turner: Let me tell you, Shoichi, it comes as a shock for all of us.
Sawasaki: But aren't people in this country used to the M&A game?
Turner: Sure, intellectually we know it happens. But deep down inside I think we all expect it will never touch us personally.

---

against one's will 違背某人意願地 **be used to** 習慣於… **intellectually** 外在知識上 **deep down inside** 在內心深處

Lesson 27

Takeover ——總結

■　　■　　■

　　M&A (mergers and acquisitions) 是所謂「吸收兼併」的簡稱。但這在美國商人眼中，還是個相當駭人的字眼。

　　話雖如此，回顧過去二十年間 M&A 的歷史，幾乎在任何情況下，它都可以達到裁減人員的目的。 M&A 的世界是相當現實的，就像漢克‧歐文斯所言， "The bottom line is all that counts in M&A situations."

　　ABC 食品公司在業績低落時被其他公司乘虛而入，而造成 hostile takeover (非善意的購併)。因此，一個企業若要防止購併的事情發生，就必須多加注意它的股價和股東。要能保障公司的經營權，它的股市價格不能太低，而且該公司的持股人必須對公司有信心，能夠長期保有他手中的股票。

　　所以，經營者必須一一去認識所謂的 investor relations，這廣義說來就是一般的宣傳、銷售活動。而與 investor 更具體相關的，則有年度報告、股東通信，發行投資者取向的刊物，以 road show (巡迴演出)的方式舉辦針對投資者訴求的公司說明會，還有證券分析師的評估會議 security analyst meeting 等等。

　　隨著 M&A 的增加，如何讓投資者了解企業的現況、未來的展望、以及公司的經營戰略，都將益發顯出其重要性，而成為關鍵課題。

Corporate Shakeup

（公司內部的人事變革）

◆ Lesson 28 的內容 ◆

新公司將定名為「尼爾森 ABC 食品公司」。儘管公司的合併還要一段時間才能完成，但是公司內部已接連產生了很大的變化。首先，艾瑞克・透納要調任寵物食品部門，對於這個營運狀況向來不佳的部門，是要重新起步或關門大吉，就看透納的決斷了。漢克・歐文斯決定辭職，他打算要籌辦個青少年的野外訓練營。瑪莉亞・古岱茲則準備要結婚，她原先就有意要開創自己的事業，現在正是大好時機，她得加快步伐了。

Well, I've decided to accept the special package and leave.

Corporate Shakeup (1) (公司內部的人事變革)

●預習 —Sentences

- I'm not sure if it's an upward move, though.
- That pet food company has been bleeding for years.
- Then I'll have to either close or sell.
- That's the real-life world of M&A.
- Alex DeMarco will run the new combined company.

●Vignette

Sawasaki: Hi, Eric. I just saw the announcement that you've been appointed president of the pet food operation. Congratulations.

Turner: Thanks, Shoichi. I'm not sure if it's an upward move, though. As you know, that pet food company has been bleeding for years. My mandate is to go over there and see if it can be pulled into shape before the merger takes effect.

Sawasaki: And if not?

Turner: Then I'll have to either close or sell. I may be working to put myself out of a job.

Sawasaki: That would mean giving a lot of other people the ax too, I suppose.

Turner: Yep. And as operations continue under the new parent company, more job duplications and positions with overlapping responsibilities will be uncovered. That's the real-life world of M&A.

Sawasaki: Who's going to replace you as head of Corporate Marketing?

Turner: Probably nobody. There's a hiring freeze now. Besides, there will be some restructuring of the marketing function at head office. Alex DeMarco, president of Nelson, will run the new combined company, which will be known as Nelson ABC Foods.

Sawasaki: I've heard him likened to boot camp training sergeant.

Turner: He's more than just that.

■狀況

　　所謂總裁只是虛有其表，透納實際上是調到一個連年虧損的部門。如果不能經營重建的話，只好關閉或賣掉。不管怎樣，這都不會是件好差事。

澤崎：　嗨，艾瑞克。我剛剛看到公告說，你被任命為寵物食品部門的總裁了。恭禧。

透納：　謝了，昭一，雖然我並不十分確定這是一種晉升。就如你所知道的，那個寵物食品部門年來一直在虧損。上面的命令是要我到那裡去，看看能不能在公司合併生效前把它搞好，弄得像樣一點，不要老是赤字。

澤崎：　如果弄不好呢？

透納：　那我只好把它關了或賣了。我可能是在努力走向失業之路。

澤崎：　我想這也表示很多人會因此而丟掉飯碗。

透納：　沒錯。而且，業務在新的母公司控制下持續運作的結果會是，那種兩個人掛名做同樣工作的情形和工作性質重疊的職務將一個個地被挑出來。這就是企業購併的現實面。

澤崎：　那誰會取代你成為行銷部門的總經理呢？

透納：　可能不會有人。現在人事已經凍結了，不再聘用新人。此外，總公司的行銷部門可能會重組。尼爾森的總裁，亞力士‧迪馬哥將會經營這個合併後的公司，這家公司將命名為尼爾森 ABC 食品公司。

澤崎：　我聽說人家把他跟新兵訓練營的士官相比耶！

透納：　他還不只是那樣呢！

Lesson 28 Corporate Shakeup (1)

Words and Phrases

mandate [`mændet] 指示; 命令	overlapping *adj.* 部分重疊的
pull into shape 使成形; 使站得起來	be uncovered 被暴露出來
take effect 生效	real-life world 現實世界; 世態
close or sell 關門或出售	M&A 企業購併
put oneself out of a job 使自己	restructuring 重組
失業	liken 將…比喻做 (某物)
give the ax 解雇	boot camp training sergeant
job duplication 工作重複	新兵訓練營的士官

Vocabulary Building

- **shakeup** (人事上的)大變動; 激烈的變革; 改組
  Many employees were dismissed or demoted as part of the shakeup following the acquisition.
  (在公司換手後的人事變動中, 很多員工不是遭到裁撤就是被降職了。)

- **upward move** 晉升; 升遷
  Chris decided not to take the job in L.A., even though it would have been
  an upward move for her.
  (儘管洛杉磯那份工作對克莉絲而言是個晉升, 但她還是決定不去了。)

- **bleed** 出現赤字; 敲詐
  Product liability claims have bled the company dry.
  (產品責任訴訟的事件已經把公司榨乾了。)

- **hiring freeze** 人事凍結〈不再聘人〉
  The hiring freeze has resulted in understaffing even of some essential
  functions.
  (人事凍結的結果是, 甚至連一些重要的職務都有人員不足的現象。)

▶ Exercises

請勿改變例句的句型, 用a)、
b)詞組代換下列例句。　　　　　　(解答見269頁)

1. You've been appointed president of the pet food operation.

    a) Eric was just
    b) to head

2. Who's going to replace you as head of Corporate Marketing?
    a) when will I
    b) succeed Eric

3. There will be some restructuring of the marketing function.
    a) a total revamping
    b) you can expect to see

◆◆◆◆◆◆◆◆◆◆◆◆ 簡短對話 ◆◆◆◆◆◆◆◆◆◆◆◆

Sawasaki: Have you ever worked in the pet food business before?

Turner: No, the closest I've come is opening cans of the stuff for my cat at home. Still, I'm looking forward to the chance to test my abilities in a new field.

Sawasaki: Having a pet of your own is a start, I suppose.

Turner: Cats are such individuals, though. Are you a cat person yourself, Shoichi?

Sawasaki: A cat person?

Turner: Sorry, I mean do you like cats?

Sawasaki: Not really. I guess you could call me a dog person.

---

closest one has come 某人所做過最接近的 (一件事)　　**stuff** (像…種類的) 東
西　　**cat person** 愛貓的人

Lesson 28

Corporate Shakeup (2) （公司內部的人事變革）

● 預習 —*Sentences*

- I have a lot of personal respect for him.
- I'm sure you'll enjoy working with him.
- I'm going to do whatever I feel is good for the company.
- That sounds like a really good mindset.
- The company has asked me to do some part-time consulting work.

● *Vignette*

Turner: Alex is extremely intelligent, pragmatic, ruthless and energetic. I have a lot of personal respect for him. I'm sure he'll be able to turn around the company very quickly but there'll be some casualties too. He's a tough boss but I'm sure you'll enjoy working with him.

Sawasaki: I'm looking forward to meeting him. You know, Eric, I've decided to take a positive outlook on the whole thing and try to overcome the anxiety I've been feeling since I heard of the takeover. I'm just going to do whatever I feel is good for the company and trust that management will recognize my value.

Turner: That sounds like a really good mindset. The new managers will need a lot of assistance to get things off the ground. My advice is to stay calm, supportive, and objective. Oops, I'm running behind schedule. Listen, I just dropped in to say good-bye. I'm off to Des Moines, Iowa, where I'll be based. Stop by if you're in that area. Anyway, so long, Shoichi. It's been a pleasure working with you.

Sawasaki: Good-bye, Eric. And good luck.

Turner: Thanks. I'll need it.

* * *

Owens: Well, I've decided to accept the special package and leave. The company has asked me to do some part-time consulting work. I'll probably do that for a while, then open a camp where young people can come and find out about nature and themselves. It'll be a version of Outward Bound training for younger kids, something my wife and I have talked about doing since our children were still small.

尼爾森的總裁亞力士‧迪馬哥似乎是個真正專業的經營者。
透納說：「我個人相當尊敬他。」

透納： 亞力士非常地聰明，講求實際，不講情面，而且精力充沛。我個人相
當尊敬他。我確信他很快就能扭轉公司目前的局勢，但也會有人成為其下
的犧牲者。他是一個強悍的上司，但我相信你會很喜歡與他共事的。

澤崎： 我期待見到他。艾瑞克，事實上我已經決定要抱持正面的態度來看待
這整件事了。我在開始聽到公司要被購併時，就開始憂心，但現在我要試
著克服那種不安的感覺。今後，任何會對公司有益的事，我都打算去做，
相信管理階層會明白我的價值。

透納： 聽來像是個相當不錯的思考態度。新任的經理們會需要很多協助來使
公司業務上軌道。我的建議是，保持冷靜，提供援助，而且要站在客觀的
立場。糟了，我快趕不上時間了。聽著，我只是順道進來跟你說再見的。
我要前往愛荷華州的迪摩因。那裡將成為我的據點。如果你到那附近去，
要來看看我。就這樣了，再見，昭一，跟你共事是件愉快的事。

澤崎： 再見，艾瑞克。祝你好運。

透納： 謝了。我會需要的。

＊　　＊　　＊

歐文斯： 事實上，我已經決定接受公司的資遣方案離開。公司要我做一些兼
職性的顧問工作。我可能會做個一陣子，然後辦個營隊，讓青少年藉以發
現自然，也能找到自我。這是野外訓練營的青少年版。在我們孩子還小的
時候，我太太和我就在討論這件事了。

Lesson 28 Corporate Shakeup (2)

Words and Phrases

pragmatic　實用主義的	荷華州的一個城市)
ruthless　無情的	stop by　路過順便停留一下
energetic　精力充沛的	so long　再見
casualties　犧牲者; 死傷者	Outward Bound training　一種在
oops　糟糕; 哦	野外舉行的訓練, 藉以使參加的各公
Des Moines [dɪ'mɔɪn]　迪摩因(愛	司主管能有更新更開闊的視野

Vocabulary Building

- **turn around**　恢復; 重整
  Morris managed to turn the losing operation around in less than a year.
  (莫里斯成功地在不到一年的時間內逆轉公司營運不斷在吐血的虧損狀態。)

- **mindset**　思考態度; 想法模式
  Gail tried to overcome the conservative mindset of her colleagues.
  (蓋兒試圖打破同事們的保守思想。)

- **get things off the ground**　使事情開始進行
  The personnel reshuffle was part of the new president's drive to get things off the ground.
  (人事異動是新任總裁的策略之一, 期使公司業務能順利上軌道。)

- **run behind schedule**　比預定計畫落後
  cf. We can make up the 45-minute delay in departing from London and will arrive in New York right on schedule.
  (雖然從倫敦啟程時晚了四十五分鐘, 但我們可以在行程中補回來, 並在預定時間抵達紐約。)

▶ *Exercises*

請勿改變例句的句型, 用a)、
b)詞組代換下列例句。

(解答見270頁)

1. I'm sure he'll be able to turn around the company very quickly.

   a) there's no doubt
   b) achieve dramatic results

2. He's a tough boss but I'm sure you'll enjoy working with him.

   a) get along well
   b) demanding

3. The company has asked me to do some part-time consulting work.

   a) I've been asked
   b) be a part-time consultant

◆◆◆◆◆◆◆◆◆◆◆◆◆◆ 簡短對話 ◆◆◆◆◆◆◆◆◆◆◆◆◆◆◆

Sawasaki: How does Evelyn feel about the move to Des Moines?

Turner: Oh, she's not coming with me.

Sawasaki: She's not?

Turner: She just got promoted at the company where she works, and she doubts she could find anything comparable in Iowa. So we'll have a long-distance marriage, at least for a while.

Sawasaki: Really? That's not unusual in Japan, but I didn't know Americans did that sort of thing.

Turner: It's becoming increasingly common with the rise in two-career families.

---

get promoted 被擢升　　**comparable** 可以比擬的　　**long-distance marriage** 夫妻分隔兩地的婚姻　　**for a while** 暫時　　**rise** 上升; 增加　　**two-career family** 雙薪家庭; 夫婦都在工作的家庭

Lesson 28

Corporate Shakeup (3) （公司內部的人事變革）

●預習 —*Sentences*

- I can picture you doing something like that.
- And yet it was too early to go into retirement.
- You're not leaving, are you?
- He's getting restless in his current bank job.
- We'll speed up our plans and get started.

●*Vignette*

Owens: Get the kids to think strategically and work as a team, you know. We've got a couple hundred acres in the country that would be perfect for it.

Sawasaki: That sounds great, Hank. I can picture you doing something like that.

Owens: Yeah, I got a few offers after the news of the takeover came out, but the food business just didn't sound fun to me anymore. And yet it was too early to go into retirement. At any rate, thanks to the "sweetener" deal given to employees aged 55 or older, I didn't have to dig too deeply into my planned retirement funds.

Sawasaki: How about you, Maria? You're not leaving, are you?

Cortez: To be honest, there's something about working for a tobacco company that doesn't sit well with me. You know my fiancé Geoff and I've been planning on starting our own business. He's getting a little restless in his current bank job and since ABC Foods is being restructured, it seemed like a good time for us to take advantage of the special offer. We'll speed up our plans and get started . . . and get married at the same time.

Sawasaki: Oh, that's fabulous news! Congratulations, Maria.

Owens: I'm so happy for you, Maria!

Cortez: Thank you, both of you.

歐文斯：　你知道的，就是使孩子們能作戰略性的思考，而且，學會團隊工作，不要一人單打獨鬥。我在鄉間購置了幾百英畝的地，用來做這個再適合也沒有了。

澤崎：　漢克，聽起來很不錯。我幾乎可以看到你做這些事的樣子。

歐文斯：　是蠻不錯的。其實，在購併的消息傳開後，有一些公司向我招手，只是，食品業對我而言已經不好玩了。而現在退休又稍嫌早了一點。不管怎樣，還多虧了公司付給五十五歲以上員工的那筆額外給付，使我可以不要動用太多我計畫中的退休基金。

澤崎：　妳呢，瑪莉亞？妳還會留下吧，對不對？

古岱茲：　老實說，為一家菸草公司工作有點不太對我的味。你知道我未婚夫傑夫和我一直打算要開始我們自己的事業。他對他目前在銀行的工作有點不滿意，再加上 ABC 食品公司要改組了，又有這筆特殊的資遣金，似乎該好好利用一下。我們會加速計畫的進行，開始我們的事業…同時，結婚。

澤崎：　哇，這消息太棒了！恭禧，瑪莉亞。

歐文斯：　我很為妳高興，瑪莉亞。

古岱茲：　謝謝你們。

Words and Phrases

acre	英畝 (一英畝約等於 4,047 平方公尺)	dig into	動用
		to be honest	老實說
picture	在眼前浮現圖畫	restless	不滿的
come out	(消息)傳出	speed up	加速進行
go into retirement	進入退休狀態	fabulous	好極了

Vocabulary Building

- **offer**　　提議; 提供; 出價
  cf. I'm asking $100 for the sofa, but I'll take the best offer I get.
  (這張沙發我要價一百美元, 不過我會賣給出價最高的人。)

- **sweetener**　　(為達特殊目的而在原來金額外再予添加的)優渥津貼
  cf. They eased Tom out by offering him a sweetened deal for his severance package.
  (公司在原本的退職金之外, 又多付了湯姆一筆錢, 以使他自動離職。)

- **sit well with**　　與…合得來
  Pam's casual attitude on the job did not sit well with her superiors.
  (潘在工作上那種漫不經心的態度使她與上司合不來。)

- **take advantage of**　　利用…
  Don't take unfair advantage of other people's weaknesses.
  (不要不當地利用他人的弱點。)

1. We've got a couple hundred acres in the country.

   a) weekend cottage
   b) Hank owns

2. Geoff and I've been planning on starting our own business.

   a) given a lot of thought to
   b) the two of us have

3. It seemed like a good time for us to take advantage of the special offer.

   a) I decided I should
   b) capitalize on

◆◆◆◆◆◆◆◆◆◆◆◆◆◆ 簡短對話 ◆◆◆◆◆◆◆◆◆◆◆◆◆◆◆◆

Turner: But now you've surprised me, Shoichi. Didn't I just hear you say long-distance marriages are common in Japan?
Sawasaki: Yes, not unusual, anyway.
Turner: But my image of the Japanese woman is somebody who docilely follows her man wherever he goes.
Sawasaki: Well, in a lot of cases, the wife stays behind for the sake of the children's education. People don't like to move their kids if they're already in a good school, especially when they're studying for their college entrance exams.

---

docilely　溫順地　　**for the sake of**　為了⋯的緣故

Corporate Shakeup (4) (公司內部的人事變革)

● 預習 —*Sentences*

· What kind of work are you and Geoff going to do?
· I'm not familiar with that term.
· You can consider it synonymous with niche marketing.
· Consumers make most buying decisions while they're shopping.
· Many consumers are single; many are old.

● *Vignette*

Owens: What kind of work are you and Geoff going to do?

Cortez: We're setting up a small agency specializing in micro marketing.

Sawasaki: I'm not familiar with that term. Micro marketing?

Cortez: Not many people know it, but you can consider it more or less synonymous with niche marketing. We'll work with retailers and find out who their customers are, where they live, what they want. Then we'll go into their stores and rearrange product displays on shelves and direct specific messages to specific customers.

Owens: And how do you do that?

Cortez: Because consumers make most buying decisions while they're shopping, we put ads on supermarket loudspeakers, shopping carts, and point-of-purchase displays. The days of mass marketing are gone. It doesn't do any good anymore to saturate the airwaves with commercials hammering product names into people's skulls. It's a different world out there. For one thing, women aren't sitting at home watching the soaps the way they used to. Many consumers are single; many are old; many don't speak English; and some can't even read.

Owens: I get your point. You're saying that the retailers have to do more stratified marketing to reach specific groups through targeted media.

Cortez: Or non-media. We also plan to help organize sports events, festivals, and other activities to reach local or ethnic markets.

Sawasaki: Sounds like you have a big challenge ahead of you too, Maria.

　　古岱茲想要成立一家專門做小眾市場行銷的公司。她說，大眾市場行銷的時代已經過去了。

歐文斯： 你和傑夫打算走哪一行？

古岱茲： 我們要成立一家小代理商，專門做小眾市場行銷。

澤崎： 小眾市場行銷？我不太熟悉這個詞。

古岱茲： 知道它的人是不太多，不過你可以把它想成是有點類似於利基行銷。我們要與零售商併肩工作，找出他們的顧客是誰，住在哪裏，需要甚麼。然後我們到他們店裡去，重新調整他們架上貨品的位置，並使特定的顧客看到特定的廣告訊息。

歐文斯： 那你們要怎麼做呢？

古岱茲： 由於客戶多半是在購物的同時才決定要買甚麼，所以我們要在店裡頭做廣告，可以利用的，有超級市場裡頭的擴音機，購物推車，以及店頭的 POP 廣告。大眾市場行銷的時代已成過去。那種充斥在媒體中作強迫推銷的商業廣告也不是那麼有用。時代不一樣了。像是說，婦女不再像從前一樣坐在家裡看連續劇。而且，有很多消費者是單身新貴；很多是銀髮族；很多不會說英語；有些甚至不識字。

歐文斯： 我瞭解妳的意思了。妳是說零售業者必須經由目標媒體來進行分層更細的行銷工作，期能觸及那些特定的族群。

古岱茲： 或者是用一些非媒體。我們也打算協助策畫體育活動，民俗節慶，和一些其他的活動，以使我們的行銷觸角能達到那些少數民族的市場。

澤崎： 這樣聽起來，瑪莉亞，擺在你們前頭的也會是個極大的挑戰囉！

Words and Phrases

agency　　代理商

synonymous [sɪˈnɑnəməs]　　同義的

point-of-purchase display　　店頭
　展示〈POP廣告〉

(the) days of something are gone
　　　…的時代已經過去了

saturate　　使飽和; 使充滿

airwaves　　電波

hammer　*v.*　　強迫灌輸 (觀念)

skull　　頭蓋骨; 腦袋

for one thing　　一則

I get your point.　　我瞭解你的意思
　了。

stratified　　分層化的

non-media　　非媒體的

ethnic market　　少數民族的市場

Vocabulary Building

● **niche** [nɪtʃ]　　利基; 特定的客戶群〈針對特定的產品或服務〉
Multimedia language instruction is an interesting niche worth considering investing in.
(多媒體語言教學是個吸引人的利基, 值得考慮是否要把錢投資進去。)

● **it doesn't do any good**　　一點好處都沒有
It doesn't do any good to get angry about what you can't change.
(對於無法改變的事, 生氣是於事無補的。)

● **It's a different world out there.**　　時局變了; 情況不一樣了。
cf. It's a whole new world out there.
(現在情形完全改觀了。)

● **soap** (soap opera)　　連續劇
cf. I started watching the new soap opera, but the interpersonal situations are so tangled and complicated that I can't follow the plot.
(我開始看那齣新的連續劇, 可是它裡頭的人物關係錯綜複雜, 我看得一頭霧水, 搞不清劇情發展。)

1. We're setting up a small agency specializing in micro marketing.

   a) Maria works at
   b) that offers media training

2. Women aren't sitting at home watching the soaps.

   a) there are a lot fewer people
   b) just cooking meals or

3. We also plan to help organize sports events.

   a) find sponsors for
   b) with Hispanic marketing

◆◆◆◆◆◆◆◆◆◆◆◆◆ 簡短對話 ◆◆◆◆◆◆◆◆◆◆◆◆◆

Sawasaki: I must say, you sound really excited about your new work. And if anybody can make a go of it, you can, I'm sure.

Cortez: Thanks, Shoichi, I hope you're right. I've got a confession to make, though.

Sawasaki: Oh?

Cortez: To tell the truth, I was starting to get cold feet about our plans.

Sawasaki: You? Cold feet? That's hard to believe. It sounds so unlike you.

Cortez: Really, though, I was. But this merger gave me just the shove I needed to go ahead and take the plunge.

---

make a go of 在…上面獲得成功　　**confession** 告白　　**get cold feet** 感到膽怯　　**shove** 推　　**take the plunge** 突然採取決定性步驟;（在躊躇思索之後）決定要冒險一試

Lesson 28

Corporate Shakeup — 總結

■　■　■

我們來綜觀一下 ABC 食品公司最近接連發生的各種變動。

首先是艾瑞克‧透納要調到連年赤字的寵物食品部門。而他目前的職位則後繼無人。透納要從紐約調到愛荷華州的鄉下，說得好聽點，是去那邊作總裁，但以實際情形來看，這跟降職其實沒有太大差別。這時，透納唯一能確定的存活方式，就是把這個部門好好地整頓一番。當然他也可以省點力氣，把公司關閉或賣掉。但如此一來，他也會和公司面臨同樣的命運，走上失業一途 (I may be working to put myself out of a job.)。

漢克‧歐文斯是年齡超過五十五歲的員工，他拿了一筆額外給付，辭職了。這是所謂的 golden handshake，也就是為了鼓勵員工提前退休而給付的獎金。(相反地，也有稱為 golden handcuffs 的慰留金，藉以留住員工，不令其離職。)

歐文斯暫時要在公司做 part-time consulting work (然後自己要辦個野外訓練營)，這種工作大概會持續個一、兩年，而領到的薪水則是原先的一半左右。

另外，美國人在年老之後，通常會去做義工，或投入一些有意義的社會活動，有人甚至選擇到外地去傳教。

瑪莉亞‧古岱茲想要結婚，和先生兩人共同成立小公司。

在美國，受到 M&A (企業合併) 風氣的影響，大約有五百家公司受到波及，雇員總計少了三百五十萬人。而在美國勞動人口當中，有百分之六十都是受雇於一百人以下的小公司 (small business)，這樣算來，到 2000 年為止，就業機會將只有今天的一半。

雖說在 1980 年代，每年都有二十萬左右的小企業誕生，但其中有百分之二十四在兩年內就不見了。總而言之，這個世界是殘酷的。

New Corporate Culture
（新企業文化）

◆ **Lesson 29 的內容** ◆

　　據聞，自從四十三歲的亞力士·迪馬哥接任了尼爾森食品飲料公司的總裁之後，尼爾森的企業文化有了明顯的轉變。原先是日式的溫情主義，現在則是一味地向錢看齊，競爭成了尼爾森每日的生活。而這也多少透露出迪馬哥本人的性格: 精明、幹練、冷血。

Say, Shoichi, did you read Ken Bulow's column in this morning's paper?

Lesson 29

New Corporate Culture (1)（新企業文化）

●預習 — *Sentences*

- He makes reference to DeMarco's business philosophy.
- What have we gotten ourselves into?
- It's out with values like that and in with "lean and mean."
- That doesn't jibe with the view of Nelson I got in Japan.
- Obviously their corporate culture has changed drastically.

●*Vignette*

Winchell: Say, Shoichi, did you read Ken Bulow's column in this morning's paper? He describes Nelson Food & Beverages' corporate culture as— brace yourself for this— the sort of greed that was the hallmark of the money-money-money decade of the 1980s. Later on in the article, he makes reference to Alex DeMarco's, quote, make money or perish, unquote, business philosophy. Interesting, isn't it?

Sawasaki: To say the least. If what he says is true . . .

Winchell: What have we gotten ourselves into, right?

Sawasaki: It sounds like quite a contrast to the care and nurture of employees that Ray Weston used to uphold.

Winchell: It's out with values like that and in with "lean and mean," I guess.

Sawasaki: You may be right, Brad, but that doesn't jibe with the view of Nelson I got in Japan. They seemed to be as paternalistic as the typical Japanese company, complete with company picnics and all that. And they had an excellent reputation for corporate philanthropy.

Winchell: Yeah, that was my perception of Nelson too, but obviously their corporate culture has changed drastically.

Sawasaki: But how's that possible? Culture is usually long term and difficult to change. It's rooted in deeply held beliefs and values.

208

專欄作家肯‧布洛直稱尼爾森的企業文化為「物慾」，他也將亞力士‧迪馬哥的經營理念描述為「不賺錢就請走路」。

溫謝爾： 昭一，你看了今早報紙上肯‧布洛的專欄嗎？他把尼爾森食品飲料公司的企業文化描述成 —— 要有心理準備哦 —— 金錢物慾，這曾經是80年代錢錢錢的代表精神。接下來的文章中，他提到亞力士‧迪馬哥的經營理念，他是這樣說的，「不賺錢就請走路」。有趣吧，對不對？

澤崎： 是還蠻有趣的。如果事情真像他說的那樣…

溫謝爾： 看我們把自己搞進甚麼裡頭去了！你是不是想這麼說？

澤崎： 我想到雷‧威斯敦對待員工一向是愛護培植有加，現在這樣聽起來簡直差了十萬八千里。

溫謝爾： 我想啊，那樣的價值觀是過去式了，現在呢，人事會開始減肥，甚至會減到該有的肉都沒了。

澤崎： 布雷，你可能是對的，可是這跟我在日本聽到有關尼爾森的看法並不一致。他們就像典型的日本公司一樣，滿是溫情主義，還有公司野餐甚麼的。而且，他們公司的慈善事業還是出了名的呢！

溫謝爾： 是啊，我所瞭解的尼爾森也是像你所說的一樣，不過，顯然地，他們的企業文化已經徹底改變了。

澤崎： 可是，那怎麼可能呢？文化是長期形成而且不容易改變的，它乃是深深紮根於信念與價值觀。

Lesson 29 New Corporate Culture (1)

Words and Phrases

corporate culture 企業文化	uphold 支持
hallmark 特徵	out with/in with 走了…, 來了…
money-money-money decade 錢、錢、錢的十年	value 價值觀; 價值標準
make reference to 提到…; 提及…	paternalistic [pə,tɜnəˈlɪstɪk] 溫情主義的
quote . . . unquote 引用別人話語時的用字	complete with 附帶有…的
"make money or perish" business philosophy 「不賺錢就請走路」的經營理念	and all that …等的
	corporate philanthropy [fəˈlænθrəpɪ] 企業的慈善行為
nurture 養育; 滋養	perception 理解
	root in 紮根於…

Vocabulary Building

- **brace yourself** 使自己預備好 (接受…)
  You'd better brace yourself for a major shock.
  (你最好準備好接受一個重大的打擊。)

- **to say the least** 最起碼; 以最低限度而言
  Alex is ambitious, to say the least.
  (最起碼來說, 亞力士是個有野心的人。)

- **lean and mean** (在公司人事上) 不只沒有贅肉, 連該有的肉都不見了; 精簡且刻薄
  The new "lean and mean" approach means more work and fewer people to do it.
  (公司新的人事政策是「精簡加刻薄」, 這表示工作量會增加, 但員工卻相對地減少。)

- **jibe with** 〔美俚〕與…一致
  Tom's report on office productivity doesn't seem to jibe with reality.
  (湯姆的辦公室生產力報告看來與事實並不相符。)

▶ **Exercises**　請勿改變例句的句型, 用a)、
b)詞組代換下列例句。　(解答見 270頁)

1. Did you read Ken Bulow's column in this morning's paper?

   a) the interview with DeMarco
   b) what did you think of

2. They seemed to be as paternalistic as the typical Japanese company.

   a) ABC Foods isn't nearly
   b) concerned with market share

3. It's rooted in deeply held beliefs and values.

   a) a function of
   b) people's behavior is

◆◆◆◆◆◆◆◆◆◆◆◆◆ 簡短對話 ◆◆◆◆◆◆◆◆◆◆◆◆◆◆

Sawasaki: You know, when I left International Foods, one of the major attractions of this company was the way managers really seemed to care about the people working for them. I suppose we'll be seeing a lot less of that from now on.

Winchell: I'm afraid you're right. That kind of approach will probably go out the window after DeMarco takes over.

Sawasaki: It's going to be hard adjusting to the new style, especially for a foreigner like me.

Winchell: No offense, Shoichi, but I wish you'd cut out that "foreigner" business. I mean, I realize you're not an American, but you don't have to harp on it.

Sawasaki: Sorry about that.

---

attraction 吸引力　　**see less of** 看到的…愈來愈少　　**go out the window** 消失不見　　**take over** 接管　　**No offense.** 沒有惡意。　　**cut out** 停止　　**harp on** 反覆地說…

Lesson 29

New Corporate Culture (2) (新企業文化)

●預習 — *Sentences*

- Alex DeMarco was probably responsible for the rapid change.
- What do you know about him, Brad?
- She may be able to shed some light on this subject.
- Just packing up my stuff in this cardboard box.
- I was in charge of their account for five years at Drachman.

●*Vignette*

Sawasaki: And any member of a group who deviates from that group's cultural <u>norms</u> is pressured to conform.

Winchell: I'm not sure, Shoichi, but my guess is that Alex DeMarco was probably responsible for the rapid change.

Sawasaki: Eric Turner described DeMarco as extremely bright but ruthless. What do you know about him, Brad?

Winchell: Not much except that he's done so well <u>at the helm of</u> Nelson in only one year that he's already reputed to be one of the strongest candidates to succeed the chairman of A.C. Raleigh. De-Marco is still young—in his early 40s, I believe. <u>I'll tell you what,</u> Shoichi. Let's go find Chris Compton. She may be able to shed some light on this subject.

*   *   *

Sawasaki: Hello, Chris. What are you doing?

Compton: Just packing up my stuff in this cardboard box.

Winchell: What? You're not leaving us, are you?

Compton: Afraid so. It's been nice working with you, but I decided to join a friend of mine from the Drachman Institute who's just starting her own agency. I just didn't think I'd be able to <u>survive</u> in Nelson's cold-blooded cultrue.

Sawasaki: So you're familiar with Nelson?

Compton: Yeah, I was in charge of their account for five years at Drachman.

令澤崎不解的是，為何一個企業文化能在如此短的時間內，就有如此巨大的轉變？克莉絲‧坎普敦提出了她的看法。

澤崎：　而且，一個團體中，若有成員偏離了該團的文化基準，那他會受到壓力而規正過來。

溫謝爾：　昭一，我不太確定耶，不過，我猜想那些急劇的變革可能是出自亞力士‧迪馬哥之手。

澤崎：　艾瑞克‧透納形容迪馬哥是個十分精明幹練，卻冷酷無情的人。布雷，你知道他些甚麼？

溫謝爾：　不多。我只知道他接任尼爾森的總裁還不到一年，卻幹得有聲有色，所以大家都認為他是最有可能接手 A.C. 勞雷的人選。迪馬哥還很年輕 —— 四十出頭吧，我想。昭一，我告訴你怎麼著，我們去找克莉絲‧坎普敦，她在這個問題上也許可以告訴我們一些甚麼。

*　　*　　*

澤崎：　哈囉，克莉絲。妳在幹甚麼？

坎普敦：　我正在把我的東西裝到這個厚紙箱裏。

溫謝爾：　甚麼？妳不會是要離開我們了吧？

坎普敦：　恐怕就是這樣了。跟你們共事是很好，不過我決定要投奔我一個原本在達奇蒙協會工作的朋友，她剛剛成立了自己的代理行。我只是覺得自己在尼爾森的冷血文化下不會有存活的機會。

澤崎：　那就是說妳還蠻熟悉尼爾森的囉？

坎普敦：　是啊，以前在達奇蒙時，我負責他們這個客戶有五年之久。

Lesson 29 New Corporate Culture (2)

Words and Phrases

deviate	違背; 脫離	shed light on	對 (某問題) 給與一些線索
conform	配合; 順從	cardboard box	厚紙箱
ruthless	冷酷無情的	cold-blooded	冷血的
repute	認為; 評為	account	客戶; 主顧
candidate	候選人		
succeed	接續; 繼任		

Vocabulary Building

- **norm** 基準; 標準
  Thirteen-hour workdays are the norm for Stan.
  (史坦的標準是一天工作十三個小時。)

- **at the helm of** 掌權; 領導
  cf. Things have changed drastically since Alex took the helm.
  (自從亞力士開始接管公司之後, 事情有了徹底的改變。)

- **I'll tell you what.** 我告訴你怎麼做。
  You look pale. I'll tell you what. Just go home and forget about work.
  (你看起來臉色不好。我告訴你怎麼做, 你現在回家去, 別去想工作了。)

- **survive** 生還; 還活著
  He survived three heart attacks in two years.
  (他在兩年內三次心臟病發作, 但還是活下來了。)

▶**Exercises** 請勿改變例句的句型, 用a)、
b)詞組代換下列例句。

(解答見270頁)

1. Eric Turner described DeMarco as extremely bright but ruthless.

   a) painted
   b) the columnist

2. She may be able to shed some light on this subject.

   a) fill me in
   b) I thought you could

3. I just didn't think I'd be able to survive in Nelson's cold-blooded culture.

   a) wondered how
   b) African jungles

◆◆◆◆◆◆◆◆◆◆◆◆◆◆ 簡短對話 ◆◆◆◆◆◆◆◆◆◆◆◆◆◆

Sawasaki: Chris, I hate to see you leaving like this. It feels like I just met you, and already it's good-bye.
Compton: I know. It's hard on me too. I was just getting settled here, and then this darn merger came along. But I just couldn't bring myself to stay.
Sawasaki: Still, you're lucky to have an opening like that to take.
Compton: Yeah, the woman I'll be working for was my boss for a while at Drachman, and we really got along well. So I'm sorry to go, but at the same time I'm looking forward to my new job.
Sawasaki: Lots of luck to you, Chris.

---

be hard on 對…而言很不好受　　**get settled** 安定下來　　**darn** 該死的
(damn的委婉說法)　　**bring oneself to** 使自己決意…　　**opening** (職位
的)空缺　　**get along well** 處得很好　　**Lots of luck to you.** 祝你好運。

Lesson 29

New Corporate Culture (3) （新企業文化）

●預習 — *Sentences*

· He made his name there by proving his marketing skills.
· Did they expect DeMarco to turn the whole place upside down?
· There was a lot of opposition to his appointment.
· John Nelson identified him as the agent of change.
· Nelson is aiming to be the world's most competitive corporation.

●*Vignette*

Sawasaki: What do you know about DeMarco's background?

Compton: Well, he got his undergraduate degree in advertising at UCLA and then he joined a well-known ad agency in Los Angeles. He did a brilliant job there on a number of consumer accounts. Ten years later he was hired away by a client, Golden Farm Produce Co., as corporate vice president of marketing. He made his name there by proving his marketing skills and turning around their ailing family restaurant business. Then last year he joined Nelson as president at the age of 43.

Winchell: Did they expect DeMarco to turn the whole place upside down?

Compton: Absolutely. In fact, there was a lot of opposition to his appointment among the other officers, as he had the reputation of being abrasive and cold. But John Nelson, the chairman and founder, identified him as the agent of change needed to keep the company successful in the face of a rapidly shifting business environment. And the two of them agreed that the company had to completely revamp its culture and mode of operation. Nelson is now aiming to be the world's most competitive corporation by being number one in every line of business they're in. Every day it's compete, compete, compete.

216

聽了坎普敦的敘述，澤崎覺得迪馬哥是一個強悍的經營者。而在這每日「競爭、競爭、競爭」的企業文化中，澤崎能否順利過關，就看他自己了。

澤崎： 對於迪馬哥的來歷，妳知道多少？

坎普敦： 這個嘛，他畢業於洛杉磯加大廣告學系，離開學校之後，他進到洛城一家知名的廣告代理商工作。在那兒，他為幾家生產消費性商品的公司做過廣告，出色極了。十年後，那家廣告代理商的一個客戶，黃金農產品公司，把他挖走去擔任他們公司行銷部門的副總裁。他在那家公司展現了他的行銷手法，把他們奄奄一息的餐館關係事業整個救活起來，給自己博得相當高的評價。之後，就在去年，他四十三歲的時候，加入了尼爾森，成了尼爾森的總裁。

溫謝爾： 他們以為迪馬哥能夠翻轉整個情勢嗎？

坎普敦： 就是這樣。事實上，當初他被任命擔任這個職務時，上面有不少人反對，因為他的風評就是霸道而且冷血。可是公司的創辦人兼董事長強森‧尼爾森認為，迪馬哥是個能夠帶來轉變的作用劑，面對這個急劇變遷的商業環境，公司若要成功，沒有這作用劑是成不了的。他們兩人同意，公司的文化和運作形態必須作番徹底的改造，尼爾森要在每項事業上都拔得頭籌，它正企圖成為世界上最具競爭力的企業。競爭、競爭、競爭，這就是在尼爾森每日的生活寫照。

Lesson 29 New Corporate Culture (3)

Words and Phrases

background 經歷；背景	ailing 有病的
undergraduate degree 學士學位	Absolutely. 當然；正是。
UCLA (University of California at Los Angeles) 加州州立大學洛杉磯分校	appointment 任命
	abrasive 易起摩擦的；霸道的
	in the face of 面臨著…
brilliant 優秀的；才氣縱橫的	business environment 商業環境
trun around 把…從劣勢扭轉過來	mode of operation 運作型態

Vocabulary Building

● **make one's name** 得到名聲
Mike made his name as a brilliant marketer.
(麥可是個優秀的市場開發負責人，他以此而著稱。)

● **turn the place upside down** 把整個地方都翻轉過來；大肆改革
I want to get out of here before the new management turns the place upside down.
(在新的老闆把這裡搞得天翻地覆之前，我要先走一步了。)

● **agent of change** 造成改變的作用劑；轉變的原動力
You can be sure that Noel will be an agent of major change throughout the organization.
(諾爾一定會成為為整個公司組織帶來重大改變的作用劑。)

● **revamp** 改造
I intend to revamp the entire headquarters operation within the next three months.
(我打算在未來三個月內將整個公司總部的運作重新改造。)

（解答見 271 頁）

▶ Exercises

請勿改變例句的句型, 用a)、b)詞組代換下列例句。

1. He did a brilliant job on a number of consumer accounts.

   a) projects
   b) very well

2. Ten years later he was hired away by a client.

   a) given a job offer
   b) just after he got promoted

3. Nelson is now aiming to be the world's most competitive corporation.

   a) now intends
   b) efficient

◆◆◆◆◆◆◆◆◆◆◆◆◆ 簡短對話 ◆◆◆◆◆◆◆◆◆◆◆◆◆

Sawasaki: Haven't a lot of heads rolled at Nelson since DeMarco took over?

Compton: Have they ever! I hear the head office staff is one-third of what it was before.

Sawasaki: You'd think that their morale would have really suffered.

Compton: Well, it has, but that hasn't prevented them from improving their profits immensely. One reason may be that everybody who's left is really running scared.

Sawasaki: Sounds kind of grim.

---

heads rolled 被殺頭; 被裁撤   **morale** 士氣   **run scared** 恐懼地跑來跑去   **grim** 殘酷的; 殘忍的

Lesson 29

New Corporate Culture (4) （新企業文化）

● 預習 — *Sentences*

· Did you ever meet DeMarco in person?
· All of a sudden, he just stood up and walked out on us.
· "Workaholic" may be a better word.
· Divorced his wife after 22 years of marriage.
· He's divested a number of operations.

● *Vignette*

Sawasaki: Did you ever meet DeMarco in person?

Compton: Yeah, a couple of times. The first time I met him, I was part of Drachman's presentation team. One of the presenters, not me, didn't have ready answers to some of Alex's questions. Then all of a sudden, he just stood up and walked out on us. He's really big on quick responses. We were told later that one of his tenets is "Procrastination is the mother of ineptitude."

Winchell: Does he have any hobbies?

Compton: No. He's something of a business junkie— "workaholic" may be a better word. Shows up at the office by 6 in the morning and works late into the evening. Never goes on vacation. Divorced his wife after 22 years of marriage to start playing the field again. But aside from all that, from what I've seen, he's always about five steps ahead of the game. He's a real strategist and a very astute businessman.

Winchell: What are some of the things he's done to change Nelson's culture and get the whole organization to be more competitive?

Compton: Well, he's divested a number of operations and fired over 12,000 people. He also reduced the layers of management to facilitate quicker decision-making. There are now five to six echelons of management between Alex and production workers. He wants to eliminate at least one more. Divesting weak businesses was, in itself, cultural change. Previously, the operations with low profitability had been subsidized by the more profitable ones. But in the new environment, each business has to stand on its own.

　　迪馬哥是一個標準的工作狂。早上六點就到辦公室，一直工作到深夜，連假也不休。據說，他甚至還跟他結婚二十二年的太太離婚…

澤崎：　妳見過迪馬哥本人嗎？

坎普敦：　見過幾次。我第一次看到他時，是在一個說明會中，那時我是達奇蒙解說小組的一員。有一個解說員，不是我，他對於亞力士提出的問題，沒能馬上回答。然後，迪馬哥突然就站起來，當著我們的面離開。他是相當重視反應迅速的。之後，別人告訴我們，他的信條之一就是：拖延是無能之母。

溫謝爾：　他有沒有甚麼嗜好？

坎普敦：　沒有。他是個事業狂的絕佳例證 —— 或者說他是「工作狂」會更合適。他每天早上六點就到辦公室，一直工作到很晚才回去。從來不休假。他跟他結婚二十二年的妻子離了婚，好再追求更多其他的女人。不過，撇開這一切不說，就我所看見的，他在商業競賽中永遠領先別人五步。他是個真正的戰略家，一個十分有洞察力的實業家。

溫謝爾：　為要改變尼爾森的企業文化，以使整個組織更具競爭力，他都做了哪些事？

坎普敦：　我看看，他砍掉了一些個單位，裁了超過一萬二千人，他也使管理階層的層數減少，以加快決策的步伐。現在，亞力士和生產線員工之間只有五到六個階層，但他至少還要再裁掉一層。其實，就裁撤獲利不佳的事業單位這件事來看，它本身就是一種文化變革了。先前，賺不到錢的部門會由獲利較豐的的部門來提供財務支援。但在新環境裏，每一項事業部門都必須自力更生了。

Words and Phrases

meet in person	見到本人	layers of management	管理的階層
tenet	信條		
ineptitude	愚蠢; 無能	facilitate	使便利; 促進
something of	…的絕佳例證	echelon [ˈɛʃəˌlan]	階層
business junkie	事業狂	eliminate	減去; 消除
workaholic	工作中毒者; 工作狂	profitability	獲利率
strategist	戰略家	subsidize	資助
astute [əˈstjut]	有洞察力的	stand on one's own	自立更生
divest	放棄; 脫手		

Vocabulary Building

- **be big on**　　熱中; 偏愛; 重視

  He's really big on the concept of empowerment.

  (他相當看重權限委讓的概念。)

- **procrastination**　　拖延; 延遲

  cf. Don't put off till tomorrow what you can do today.

  (今日事, 今日畢。)

- **play the field**　　同時與很多異性交往

  Nat started playing the field again the same day his wife died.

  (奈特在他太太死了的當天, 馬上就跟別的女人交往起來了。)

- **ahead of the game**　　走在前面

  They managed to keep ahead of the game by constantly searching for new market niches.

  (藉著不斷地探索搜尋新的市場利基, 他們總是能夠在商場中保持領先。)

(解答見 271 頁)

▶ *Exercises*

請勿改變例句的句型, 用a)、
b)詞組代換下列例句。

1. Did you ever meet DeMarco in person?

   a) face-to-face
   b) have you ever met

2. One of the presenters didn't have ready answers to some of Alex's questions.

   a) wasn't able to answer
   b) quick

3. He's divested a number of operations and fired over 12,000 people.

   a) sold off
   b) let go of

◆◆◆◆◆◆◆◆◆◆◆◆◆ 簡短對話 ◆◆◆◆◆◆◆◆◆◆◆◆◆◆

Winchell: So what do you say, Shoichi? After everything Chris had to say about DeMarco, are you still gung-ho about working for the new organization?

Sawasaki: Gung-ho, no, but I'm still looking on the bright side. I mean it's a chance to test myself. The way I see it, if I can make it in DeMarco's organization, I can probably make it anywhere.

Winchell: You've got a point there.

---

gung-ho 狂熱的; 滿腔熱血的　　**make it** 成功　　**You've got a point.** 那倒是一個理由。

Lesson 29

New Corporate Culture —— 總結

■ ■ ■

　　最近，大家有將 corporate culture 譯作「企業文化」的趨勢，但它真正的涵意還是頗令人費解。所謂 culture，基本上是指一個公司內的活動，或其意見基礎所賴以成形的價值觀 (corporate values)。就像每個人都有每個人的 personal style 一樣，每個企業也各有其不同的風格。

　　比方說，辦公室不能聊天、員工一律著制服上班、利益至上、重視傳統、標榜革新等等，這些都是展現企業文化、特質和風格的地方。企業文化會表現在其經營理念、 mission statement、或是不成文規定 (unwritten rules) 上面。對於某些無法清楚定義其企業文化的公司，我們也可從經營者的 personal behavior (是否常加班到很晚，是否懂得照顧員工、是否慳吝等等)、其企業經營的優先順序 (priorities)、對待員工或顧客的基本態度等，而窺知一二。

　　一般而言，廣告公司的 culture 和銀行的 culture 會有很大的差別。而大企業和中小企業、重型工業和一般廠商之間也會有落差。這些差異點有時會以 formal vs. informal, busy vs. relaxed, elegant vs. practical 等詞彙來表現。

　　「企業文化」的功用，從 1970 年代末期開始受到矚目。而 1980 年 10 月 27 日當週的商業週刊更以 corporate culture 為其 cover story，其封面的副標是 "the hard-to-change values that spell success or failure" (一成形就難改動的價值觀，事業成敗的關鍵點)，這給企業文化下了相當的註解。亦誠如澤崎所言， culture is usually long term and difficult to change，但尼爾森卻能在極短的時間內確立其「競爭、競爭、競爭」的企業文化，這也許是迪馬哥本人強悍的個人風格使然吧！

Lesson 30

Moving On
（勇往直前）

◆ Lesson 30 的內容 ◆

　　接受電視訪談的亞力士‧迪馬哥看來就是個相當精悍的天才戰略家。他精簡且冷靜的對答裡流露出其傲慢冷酷的性格。但澤崎卻因這場訪談對他產生好感，覺得迪馬哥似乎是位深具領袖氣質的企業家，也對透納所言：「我個人相當尊敬他」的涵意有了更多的體會。總之，事已至此，回顧以往也無濟於事，只能勇往直前囉！

Lesson 30

Moving On (1) (勇往直前)

●預習 ── *Sentences*

- I see nothing morally wrong with the cigarette business.
- Cigarettes may present a health risk.
- Smoking is a matter of personal choice.
- I just happen to choose not to.
- Smoking is an adult custom, like social drinking.

●*Vignette*

[*In a TV studio*]

Reporter: We have in our studio this morning Alex M. DeMarco, president of A.C. Raleigh's food business unit, which has just been renamed Nelson ABC Foods, Inc. Following the hostile takeover of ABC Foods recently, this company is now the world's fourth largest manufacturer of food products. Good morning, Alex.

DeMarco: Good morning, Georgia.

Reporter: What do you think of the morality of a cigarette manufacturer owning a food company?

DeMarco: I see nothing morally wrong with the cigarette business. Cigarettes may present a health risk, but so does cholesterol. It's up to the consumer to decide whether to eat eggs or to smoke.

Reporter: Do you smoke?

DeMarco: No.

Reporter: Why not?

DeMarco: Smoking is a matter of personal choice. I just happen to choose not to.

Reporter: Do you want your teenage children to be smokers?

DeMarco: Most cigarette company employees will tell you they'd prefer their children did not smoke. Smoking is an adult custom, like social drinking or making love. Young people should be urged *not* to smoke until they have enough years, knowledge, and experience in life to make mature and informed decisions.

226

[在一個電視攝影棚]

記者： 今天早上我們請到了亞力士·迪馬哥，他現在是改名後的尼爾森 ABC 食品公司的總裁，這個公司是 A.C. 勞雷的食品事業單位之一。在 ABC 食品公司新近被惡意地買收兼併進來之後，這家公司現在已成為世界上第四大食品製造廠。早安，亞力士。

迪馬哥： 早安，喬治亞。

記者： 你覺得，以一個菸草製造商擁有一家食品公司，這件事在道德上來說如何？

迪馬哥： 我看不出來菸草事業有甚麼不道德的。香菸的確有礙健康，不過膽固醇也會。不論是吃蛋或是抽菸，要不要這麼做的權利在消費者手中。

記者： 你抽菸嗎？

迪馬哥： 不抽。

記者： 為甚麼？

迪馬哥： 抽不抽菸是個人的選擇。我只是正好選擇了不抽。

記者： 你會希望你的青少年子女抽菸嗎？

迪馬哥： 很多在菸草公司上班的人會告訴你，他們希望自己的小孩不要抽菸。抽菸是成年人的習慣，就像應酬喝酒或與人發生性關係一樣。該要有人告誡青少人不可吸菸，除非他們年齡夠大，知識和生活歷練也夠老道，能自行做出成熟且正確的決定了，那麼，他們可以選擇抽菸。

Lesson 30　Moving On (1)

Words and Phrases

studio [ˈstjudɪˌo]　攝影棚；錄音室；
　工作室
hostile takeover　帶有敵意的收買
morality　道德

cholesterol [kəˈlɛstəˌrol]　膽固醇
make love　發生性關係；做愛
urge　力勸；催促
mature　成熟的

Vocabulary Building

● **move on**　遷移到另一處 (工作或住所)
After five years with the company, Paula decided to move on to a higher-paying job.
(寶拉在這家公司工作已經五年了，她決定要換一份薪水較高的工作。)

● **health risk**　健康危機
Are you aware of the health risk posed by being overweight?
(你瞭解肥胖會給身體健康帶來甚麼樣的危機嗎？)

● **social drinking**　應酬喝酒
My doctor told me that even social drinking was out.
(我的醫生告訴我，甚至連應酬喝酒都不可以。)

● **informed decision**　正確的決定
I want my kids to grow up into people capable of making mature and informed decisions.
(我要我的孩子們在長成之後，都能自行做出成熟且正確的決定來。)

▶ *Exercises*

請勿改變例句的句型, 用a)、
b)詞組代換下列例句。

(解答見 271 頁)

1. This company is now the world's fourth largest manufacturer of food products.

   a) one of my clients is
   b) Chicago's biggest

2. I see nothing morally wrong with the cigarette business.

   a) there's
   b) about smoking

3. Young people should be urged not to smoke.

   a) minors
   b) to remain non-smokers

◆◆◆◆◆◆◆◆◆◆◆◆◆◆ 簡短對話 ◆◆◆◆◆◆◆◆◆◆◆◆◆◆◆◆

Reporter: But ACR's advertising makes heavy use of sports celebrities and other figures popular with young people. Isn't that part of a strategy to get them hooked on the cigarette habit?

DeMarco: Smoking is not an addiction, like heroin or the other hard drugs that are now ravaging our society. To my mind, we should be focusing on the drug problem and not worrying so much about a habit that has been accepted for centuries.

Reporter: So you don't have any qualms about cigarette advertising.

DeMarco: Not in the least.

---

sports celebrity 體育界的名人　　**get someone hooked** 〔口語〕使某人上癮
addiction 上癮　　**ravage** 毀壞; 荼毒　　**focus on** 把焦點擺在…　　**don't have any qualms about** 對於…不覺得良心不安

Moving On (2)（勇往直前）

●預習 ─ *Sentences*

- ABC Foods is unlikely to add much to your profits.
- We're already trimming some of the deadwood off the tree.
- That's all I can say at this early stage.
- Good luck to both of you.
- Don't know what I'll do without her.

●*Vignette*

Reporter: Alex, you have an excellent track record of turning around two companies in very short periods of time. But some industry sources say that ABC Foods is unlikely to add much to your profits. Do you think you can live up to your reputation as the profitability guru?

DeMarco: We see this merger as an opportunity to make a lot of structural changes that ABC Foods has been needing for some time. We're already trimming some of the deadwood off the tree. And I don't think the positive effects of this remedy are going to take very long to show up in our bottom line. That's all I can say at this early stage.

Reporter: Thank you. That was Alex DeMarco, president of Nelson ABC Foods, Inc.

*　　*　　*

Cortez: Hi, Shoichi. I hear you and Brad are transferring to the new corporate headquarters in Chicago. Good luck to both of you.

Sawasaki: Thanks, Maria. I'm only sorry I can't take along Roz. Don't know what I'll do without her. Anyway, though, I was looking for you. Here's a little present.

Cortez: Oh, Shoichi, thanks but you know you shouldn't have.

Sawasaki: It's just a little trinket. Go ahead and open it.

Cortez: How nice! It's very unusual. Did it come from Japan?

Sawasaki: Yes, it's called a Daruma doll.

Cortez: Thank you.

記者：　亞力士，你曾經在極短的時間內使兩家公司的營運狀況由虧轉盈，業績可說是十分優秀。不過業界方面有人說， ABC 食品公司可能無法為你輝煌的戰績再添一筆。你向來都以善於創造利潤著稱，這次，你有把握再創佳績嗎？

迪馬哥：　我們把這次的合併視作一個轉機，一個能大大改變公司結構的機會，這是 ABC 食品公司一直以來的需要。我們現在已經在裁撤一些不必要的人員了。我想，要不了多久，就可以從公司帳面上看見此一策略的正面療效了。目前，初步上我所能說的就這些了。

記者：　謝謝。以上看到的是亞力士・迪馬哥，尼爾森 ABC 食品公司的總裁。

＊　＊　＊

古岱茲：　嗨，昭一。我聽說你和布雷要調到公司在芝加哥新成立的總部去了。祝你們好運。

澤崎：　謝了，瑪莉亞，我只是覺得遺憾不能帶羅絲一起過去。沒有她，我簡直不知道該怎麼辦。不管怎樣，我正好在找妳。這是一點小禮物。

古岱茲：　哦，昭一，謝謝，你曉得你不該這樣的。

澤崎：　沒甚麼，只是一點不值錢的東西。打開來看看。

古岱茲：　哇，真好，這東西很少見，日本來的嗎？

澤崎：　是啊，這叫做達摩娃娃。

古岱茲：　謝謝。

Lesson 30　Moving On (2)

Words and Phrases

track record　業績	bottom line　　帳本底行〈顯示公司
be unlikely to　不可能…	的盈虧狀況〉
live up to　使自己達到…	transfer　調職
structural change　結構性的改變	corporate headquarters　　總公司
trim　削減	trinket　不值錢的東西

Vocabulary Building

- **industry source**　業界方面

Many industry sources identify DeMarco as the brightest executive in the food business.

(業界方面多半將迪馬哥視作食品界最耀眼的一個主管。)

- **guru**　權威; 專家

The computer hardware company hired a quality-control guru to help overcome its reputation for shoddy products.

(那家電腦硬體設備公司聘了一位品管專家來協助克服品質不良的產譽。)

- **deadwood**　冗員; 枯木

It's high time we cleared out some of the deadwood from this overstaffed department.

(現在正是給這個人員過剩的部門減減肥的大好時機。)

- **remedy**　藥物; 治療

The remedy is worse than the disease.

(這個治療比疾病本身更糟糕。)

▶ Exercises

請勿改變例句的句型, 用a)、
b)詞組代換下列例句。

(解答見 271 頁)

1. Do you think you can live up to your reputation as the profitability guru?

   a) you'll be able to maintain
   b) are you confident that

2. We see this merger as an opportunity to make a lot of structural changes.

   a) regard
   b) bring in

3. I hear you and Brad are transferring to the new corporate headquarters.

   a) somebody told me
   b) relocating to Chicago

◆◆◆◆◆◆◆◆◆◆◆◆◆ 簡短對話 ◆◆◆◆◆◆◆◆◆◆◆◆◆

Reporter: Does this acquisition represent a move by your parent organization to lessen its dependence on the cigarette business, which—whatever you might say—has a questionable future?

DeMarco: No. ACR has no intention of abandoning its major line of business. We at Nelson saw this as a good opportunity to broaden our operations.

Reporter: What are your plans for the old ABC Foods organization? Can we expect to see some major layoffs in the near future?

DeMarco: No more than necessary. But I will expect every single employee to pull his or her own weight in making a profit for our shareholders.

---

parent organization 母公司 **lessen** 減低 **dependence** 依賴 **questionable** 令人存疑的; 不確定的 **abandon** 放棄; 捨棄 **line of business** 營業項目 **pull one's own weight** 盡自己的本分

Moving On (3) （勇往直前）

●預習 —*Sentences*

· I admire you for taking such a big step.
· Sure, we know it'll be tough at the outset.
· Sixty percent of them are gone before their sixth birthday.
· Geoff and I are trying to be realistic about the whole thing.
· Don't think you're going to get rid of me so easily.

●*Vignette*

Sawasaki: You know, Maria, I admire you for taking such a big step.

Cortez: Well, I'm not taking it alone, after all. I'm going to be the marketer and Geoff will be the finance man. Sure, we know it'll be tough at the outset. After all, one out of every four new businesses fails in the first two years. And 60 percent of them are gone before their sixth birthday. But Geoff and I are trying to be realistic about the whole thing. We've made provisions for just about every scenario, including the worst.

Sawasaki: I'm sure you'll do well but I'll certainly miss you. I've really appreciated your friendship and advice.

Cortez: Hey, don't think you're going to get rid of me so easily. We're moving to Chicago too to open up our agency. Let's stay in touch.

Sawasaki: Oh, that's great. You probably can teach me a thing or two about micro marketing.

Cortez: You bet.

Sawasaki: How about heading out to Joe's Bar for a quick one? We ought to drink to our respective futures, don't you think?

Cortez: You go ahead. I'll finish packing and be down in another ten minutes or so.

*　　*　　*

　　澤崎在臨別之時送了日本的達摩娃娃給瑪莉亞‧古岱茲。
待會兒，他們要去喬的酒吧為彼此的將來乾杯。

澤崎：　瑪莉亞，妳知道嗎？我欣賞妳能跨出這一大步。

古岱茲：　不過，我終究不是一個人來做這件事。我會負責行銷，傑夫則主管
　　　　財務。當然了，我們知道一開始會很艱苦。畢竟，在新興的事業中，有四分
　　　　之一在頭兩年就垮了。而百分之六十則撐不到他們的六周年紀念。不過，
　　　　傑夫和我會試著從現實的角度來看待這整件事。我們已經預先設想了各種
　　　　可能發生的狀況，並做好準備。就是最糟的狀況發生，我們也有底了。

澤崎：　我確信妳會做得很好的，但，我也一定會想念妳的。我真的很感激妳
　　　　所給我的友誼和忠告。

古岱茲：　嘿，別想說你這麼容易就甩掉我了。我們也要搬到芝加哥去，在那
　　　　兒成立我們的代理行。保持聯絡吧！

澤崎：　哇，那真是太好了。也許妳還能教我一點有關小眾市場行銷的東西。

古岱茲：　一定。

澤崎：　我們現在到喬的酒吧，快快喝他一杯如何？我們該為彼此的未來乾一
　　　　杯，不是嗎？

古岱茲：　你先去。我把東西打包好，十分鐘左右就到。

＊　　　＊　　　＊

Words and Phrases

marketer	行銷負責人	miss	想念
one out of every four	四分之一	get rid of	擺脫…
be gone	消失; 走了	drink to	乾杯祝…
scenario [sɪˈnɛrɪˌo]	設想狀況		

Vocabulary Building

- **take a step** 跨出一步
  cf. Steps must be taken immediately to reduce industrial waste.
  (為減少工業浪費, 必須儘速採行一些步驟。)

- **at the outset** 最初; 一開始
  Harold made it clear at the outset that the job would be tough.
  (哈洛德一開始就講明了, 這工作會很艱難。)

- **make provisions for** 為…作準備
  What sort of provisions have you made for a temporary power outage?
  (為因應暫時的停止供電, 你們都做了甚麼防備動作?)

- **stay in touch** 保持聯絡
  cf. "Good-bye." — "Keep in touch."
  (「再見。」「保持聯絡」)

(解答見 272 頁)

▶ **Exercises**   請勿改變例句的句型, 用a)、b)詞組代換下列例句。

1. I admire you for taking such a big step.

   a) congratulate you on
   b) bold

2. Geoff and I are trying to be realistic about the whole thing.

   a) more careful
   b) how we spend our money

3. I'll be down in another ten minutes or so.

   a) at the outside
   b) within an hour

◆◆◆◆◆◆◆◆◆◆◆◆◆◆ 簡短對話 ◆◆◆◆◆◆◆◆◆◆◆◆◆◆◆

Sawasaki: Any particular reason you're setting up in Chicago?
Cortez: Isn't it obvious? I wanted to be close to you.
Sawasaki: What?
Cortez: Oh, Shoichi, you're so serious! I was just kidding you.
Sawasaki: Wow, you really had me worried there for a second. Anyway, what's the real reason, if you don't mind telling me?
Cortez: Not at all. What it is is that Geoff comes from the Chicago area and he went to school there too, so he has some good contacts for our new business.

---

set up 立足; 開業   **kid** v. 對…開玩笑   **contact** 聯絡人

237

Moving On (4) (勇往直前)

●預習 —*Sentences*

- Did you see the Alex DeMarco interview on television?
- I sort of liked his no-nonsense style.
- I get the impression that he's a real sharp strategist.
- I still remember the day you told me about the takeover.
- I don't know, and naturally I have some worries.

●*Vignette*

Winchell: Hey, Shoichi, did you see the Alex DeMarco interview on television this morning?

Sawasaki: Yeah, I did. I sort of liked his no-nonsense style.

Winchell: I agree. I get the impression that he's a real sharp strategist.

Sawasaki: With a taste for competition.

Winchell: Like a shark's taste for blood.

Sawasaki: Sure is a switch from the measured pace of the Ray Weston days. I still remember the day you told me about the takeover. At that time I didn't quite realize how drastically it would affect us.

Winchell: Do you think we're headed in the right direction?

Sawasaki: Honestly, I don't know, and naturally I have some worries. You know, so much has changed since I arrived in New York a year ago.

Winchell: But it's been interesting, hasn't it?

Sawasaki: Never a dull moment. Anyway, it's no use looking back. Let's see what the future has in store for us.

　　對澤崎而言，紐約這一年真是風波頻繁的一年，但也是他所經歷過最最充實的一年了。今後，在澤崎前面的道路還會更加「多采多姿」呢！

溫謝爾：　嘿，昭一，你有沒有看到今早電視上亞力士・迪馬哥的訪問？

澤崎：　有啊，我看了。我有點喜歡他那種實事求是的調調。

溫謝爾：　我同意。他給我的印象是：一個相當狡點的戰略家。

澤崎：　而且喜好競爭。

溫謝爾：　就像鯊魚嗜血一樣。

澤崎：　雷・威斯敦時代的整齊步調鐵定要有所轉變了。我還記得你告訴我公司要被購併的那一天，那個時候，我還不是十分瞭解這會給我們帶來多麼劇烈的影響。

溫謝爾：　你覺得，我們現在前進的方向正確嗎？

澤崎：　老實說，我不知道，而且，我當然是有些憂慮。你知道的，從我來到紐約這一年來，很多事情都變了。

溫謝爾：　不過很有趣，不是嗎？

澤崎：　是啊，這裡的日子可從來沒有無聊過。不管怎樣，回首從前是沒有用的，且看未來在我們身上會發生甚麼事吧！

Lesson 30　Moving On (4)

Words and Phrases

sharp strategist　　有才幹的戰略家　　be headed in the right direction

taste for　　喜好…　　　　　　　　　　朝正確的方向前進

switch from　　從…轉換過來　　　dull　　乏味的；無聊的

days　　(…的)時代

Vocabulary Building

- **no-nonsense**　　實事求是的；正經的
  Jack has a hard-nosed, no-nonsense approach to hiring and firing decisions.
  (在決定要聘用或解雇人員之際，傑克總是穩紮穩打，實事求是。)

- **measured pace**　　整齊的步調
  The near-bankrupt securities company introduced the changes at a measured pace.
  (那家快破產的證券公司在一步步、有規律地引進改革策略。)

- **it's no use**　　無用的；無意義的
  It's no use letting other people's critical comments get you down.
  (讓別人的批評把自己搞得心情沮喪是沒有意義的。)

- **what the future has in store**　　未來會怎樣
  cf. What does the future hold in store for the street children we saw in Brazil?
  (我們在巴西街頭上看到的那些孩子將來會怎樣呢？)

（解答見272頁）

▶ **Exercises** 請勿改變例句的句型, 用a)、
b)詞組代換下列例句。

1. I get the impression that he's a real sharp strategist.

   a) have a feeling
   b) shrewd

2. I still remember the day you told me about the takeover.

   a) was terribly shocked when
   b) I heard the news of

3. So much has changed since I arrived in New York a year ago.

   a) my English has improved
   b) started working

◆◆◆◆◆◆◆◆◆◆◆◆◆ 簡短對話 ◆◆◆◆◆◆◆◆◆◆◆◆◆

Sawasaki: You know, Brad, I'm going to miss a lot of the people we've worked with here, especially Eric and Roz.
Winchell: My sentiments exactly.
Sawasaki: But there's one person I'm going to be happy never to see again.
Winchell: Who's that?
Sawasaki: That old so-and-so at the cash register in the cafeteria.
Winchell: Didn't you hear? She's transferring to Chicago too.
Sawasaki: I can't—wait, you're pulling my leg, aren't you?
Winchell: Finally you're beginning to catch on.

---

so-and-so 某某人　　**transfer** 調職　　**pull one's leg** 欺騙某人　　**catch on** 理解

Lesson 30

Moving On — 總結

■ ■ ■

尼爾森的企業文化就像 80 年代「錢、錢、錢」的「物慾」(greed)潮流一樣。而其總裁亞力士‧迪馬哥的經營理念 ——「不賺錢就請走路」,則更為駭人。

在尼爾森簡直就是金錢至上,公司裡的每一項決策,包括人事制度,都是以利益為其考量,絕對沒有「體貼員工」這種事。

至於迪馬哥本人,有人說他是 extremely intelligent, pragmatic, energetic, 也有人說他是 ruthless, abrasive, 不一而論。且從外界說他是工作狂、從不休假,拋棄結褵二十二年的妻子等這些評論來看,他似乎是個具有強烈性格的經營者。

但對澤崎而言,雖說是透過電視訪談初次見到迪馬哥,但卻莫名地對這位總裁產生了好感,覺得迪馬哥是個深具領袖特質的領導者。他也漸漸能夠體會,為何連透納這樣的人都會說出像「我個人相當尊敬他」的話來。或許,對於澤崎,這正是個學習另一種美國企業經營方式的良機呢!

透納也說了, " . . . We should remember that the ability to face and accommodate change is one of the pillars on which our country's prosperity has been built." (我們應該記得的是,我國得以繁榮的支柱之一,就是國人善於處變的能力。) 沒有轉變就沒有進步! 讓我們祝福決心迎向人生更大目標的澤崎吧!

Lesson 31

To Chicago

（到芝加哥）

◆ **Lesson 31** 的內容 ◆

　　因為合併的關係，所以尼爾森 ABC 食品公司的總部將遷至芝加哥。現在，澤崎身邊的老同事只剩下溫謝爾一個了。在異鄉的紐約，澤崎好不容易才走過這一年，也算融入 ABC 總部這個環境了，但現在發生這些事，著實令他覺得不安。不過，這也許是學習新時代美式經營的一個機會也說不定。但在這樣急劇的變化中，澤崎能否達成目的呢？在飛往芝加哥的班機上，澤崎一面和溫謝爾閒聊，一面，他的心仍舊惶惶不定。

Lesson 31

To Chicago (1) （到芝加哥）

●預習 — *Sentences*

- I asked a saleslady to lend me a pair of scissors.
- It was barely long enough to go around my waist.
- I havn't been so embarrassed in years.
- I also learned to like the taste of black coffee.
- Brad, weren't you about to say something?

●*Vignette*

Flight attendant: Cream or sugar?

Sawasaki: No thanks. I'll take it black.

Flight attendant: Here you are, sir.

Winchell: So, Shoichi, you've really gone on a diet.

Sawasaki: That's right. I told myself I simply had to get back in shape after a really awkward experience I had recently.

Winchell: What was that?

Sawasaki: It was when I went shopping for a new belt at a department store in Tokyo. I picked one I liked and asked a saleslady to lend me a pair of scissors. You know, to cut the belt to the proper length. She brought the scissors and asked me to put it on to see how much it had to be trimmed. Well, it didn't. I mean it was just barely long enough to go around my waist. I haven't been so embarrassed in years.

Winchell: I see. But you've actually lost some weight, haven't you?

Sawasaki: Uh-huh. I also learned to like the taste of black coffee, which I used to hate. They say it helps with your digestion and keeps your breath fresher that way. But Brad, weren't you about to say something just before they brought the coffee around?

Winchell: Yeah, it's about how DeMarco says we're going to have to work harder. You know, I can't imagine doing that. Even before the takeover, we were all burning both ends of the candle trying to pull out of our sales slump.

Sawasaki: It's true. We've all been under a lot of pressure.

　　不知是否受到購併壓力的影響，澤崎最近又胖了。不過，令他下定決心要開始減肥的，是發生在東京一家百貨公司的購物插曲。

空服員： 要加奶精或是糖嗎？

澤崎： 不用，謝謝。我喝黑咖啡。

空服員： 這是您的咖啡，先生請用。

溫謝爾： 所以，昭一啊，你真的在節食了。

澤崎： 沒錯。最近我有過一次很令人困窘的經驗。之後，我告訴自己，我一定得要回到原來的身材。

溫謝爾： 你碰到甚麼事了？

澤崎： 那次我在東京逛一家百貨公司，想要買條皮帶。我選中了一條，於是請售貨小姐借我一把剪刀。你知道的，就是把皮帶改成適合的長度。她拿來了一把剪刀，要我把皮帶繫上，看該剪多少。結果，不用剪。我是說，那條皮帶往我腰部一圈，還險些不夠長。我有好多年沒那麼丟臉過了。

溫謝爾： 原來如此。不過，你真的瘦了一點了，不是嗎？

澤崎： 是啊，以前我最恨黑咖啡的，現在我都學會喝了。聽說黑咖啡能幫助消化，使口氣清新。不過，布雷，剛剛他們還沒把咖啡端上來時，你不是正要說些甚麼嗎？

溫謝爾： 哦，對了，是有關迪馬哥說我們今後必須再加把勁工作的事。你知道，我簡直無法想像那種情形。即便是在購併這件事還沒有發生之前，為了試圖把下滑的銷售額往上拉，我們就都已經做得要死要活了。

澤崎： 沒錯。我們是都承受太多壓力了。

Lesson 31 To Chicago (1)

Words and Phrases

flight attendant	空服員	trim	修剪
take coffee black	喝不加奶精和	waist	腰部
糖的咖啡；喝黑咖啡		lose weight	減重
Here you are.	這是你的，請用。	black coffee	不加奶精和糖的咖
get back in shape	使身材回復	啡；黑咖啡	
awkward [ˈɔkwəd]	令人困窘的	takeover	購併；買收
scissors	剪刀	sales slump	銷售下滑

Vocabulary Building

- **go on a diet**　開始節食
  When I found that none of my suits fit me anymore, I decided it was time to go on a diet.
  (當我發現所有的西裝都穿不下時，我決定開始節食了。)

- **digestion**　消化
  Worrying is not only useless but it's also terrible for your digestion.
  (憂慮不僅於事無補，而且對你的消化作用也有十分不良的影響。)

- **burn both ends of the candle**　過度消耗體力
  cf. George was a gifted and hardworking accountant, but it's small wonder he died young. He simply was burning the candle at both ends.
  (喬治是個有天賦、工作又勤奮的會計師，不過，對於他的英年早逝，我們並不太訝異。因為他實在是太過消耗他的體力了。)

- **under pressure**　受壓；承受壓力
  Some people can work only under the pressure of a deadline.
  (有些人只有在期限快到了的壓力下才能工作。)

(解答見 272頁)

▶*Exercises*

請勿改變例句的句型, 用a)、
b)詞組代換下列例句。

1. I went shopping for a new belt at a department store in Tokyo.

   a) was looking
   b) to replace the one I lost

2. You've actually lost some weight.

   a) gained a lot of
   b) friends

3. They say it keeps your breath fresher.

   a) not smoking
   b) I've been told

◆◆◆◆◆◆◆◆◆◆◆◆◆ 簡短對話 ◆◆◆◆◆◆◆◆◆◆◆◆◆◆

Sawasaki: I've got to admit, though, there is one problem with taking my coffee black.
Winchell: What's that?
Sawasaki: Now that I know each cup has zero calories, I find myself drinking a lot more of the stuff than I used to.
Winchell: Too much caffeine can do a real job on your nerves.
Sawasaki: So I've discovered.
Winchell: Maybe you should switch to decaffeinated.
Sawasaki: I'll give it a try.

---

zero calories 零卡路里; 無熱量　　**stuff** 東西; 飲料　　**caffeine** 咖啡因
do a real job on someone's nerves 使神經過度興奮　　**switch to** 轉換成…
decaffeinated 除去咖啡因的　　**give it a try** 試試看

Lesson 31

To Chicago (2) （到芝加哥）

●預習 ── *Sentences*

· DeMarco isn't the only slave driver.
· I've never worked a 40-hour week.
· Nine-to-five is a thing of the past.
· These days, competition is global.
· It makes you think that something is wrong.

●*Vignette*

Winchell: But DeMarco isn't the only slave driver among America's CEOs these days. Nose to the grindstone is a pretty common battle cry with the market the way it is now. And you know what? We aren't the only ones complaining about our workload.

Sawasaki: Yeah, I read that most CEOs expect their high-level executives and middle managers to put in 50−60 hours a week and some are expecting 60−70 hours.

Winchell: You know, I've never worked a 40-hour week and neither have most of my friends. Nine-to-five is a thing of the past. These days, competition is global and so are our markets. And now document creation and communication is so easy that you feel you should stay in the office to whip up a proposal or to hang around waiting for a telephone window.

Sawasaki: I know what you mean. It's really easy to rack up 60 hours even on a week when things are relatively slow.

Winchell: It makes you think that something is wrong, if not with the system then with the people in it.

Sawasaki: The article I read also said that 77 percent of American CEOs think everyone is going to have to work harder. Only nine percent thought America was working too hard.

Winchell: When I started in business there was a lot of talk about working smarter. It didn't take too long to realize that was just a euphemism for working longer and harder. The only way to keep time for yourself these days seems to be by getting off the fast track.

一週工作四十個小時的生活似乎已成為過去的遺物了。大部分的 CEO 都期望中高級主管每天能工作十個小時，甚或十四個小時。

溫謝爾： 不過，近來在美國的執行長中，迪馬哥並不是唯一善於壓榨員工的老闆。隨著現今的市場走向，工作、工作、工作已經是一種相當普遍的口號了。而且，你知道嗎？我們並不是唯一在抱怨工作量過多的人。

澤崎： 是啊，我讀過報導說，多數的執行長希望他們底下的高級和中級主管一週工作五十到六十個小時，有些甚至要求六十到七十個小時。

溫謝爾： 你知道，我一週從來沒有工作到四十個小時過，而我大部分的朋友也沒有。但朝九晚五的工作型態已經是過去式了。近來講的都是全球性的競爭，而我們的市場走的也是國際路線。現在文件的製作和兩地的通訊又那麼容易，讓你覺得應該要待在辦公室裡趕一份企劃案，或者是在辦公室晃來晃去，等個較容易接通電話的時段。

澤崎： 我懂你的意思。就算是在一個業務比較清淡的星期，也很容易在工作上花掉六十個小時。

溫謝爾： 這令人感覺好像有甚麼地方不對勁，不是體制本身，就是裡頭的人有問題。

澤崎： 我讀到的那篇文章也說，美國的執行長中，有百分之七十七認為大家還不夠努力。只有百分之九覺得美國人太過勤奮了。

溫謝爾： 我初出社會的時候，有很多關於怎樣在工作上做個聰明人的說法。不多久我就瞭解，那其實就是要人在辦公室待晚一點，勤奮一點，只是說得比較委婉罷了。看來，在現在這種時代，若想給自己保留一點時間，就只能選擇退出這競爭激烈的商場了。

Lesson 31 To Chicago (2)

Vocabulary Building

- **slave driver**　壓榨員工的老闆
  If Chuck had been a bit less of a slave driver, morale in the company might not be so bad.
  (假如查克不要那麼樣壓榨他底下的員工，也許公司的士氣還不至那麼糟。)

- **nose to the grindstone**　不停地工作
  Jonathan walks around the office a lot just to make sure everybody's keeping their nose to the grindstone.
  (強納森之所以在公司上下走來走去，就是為了要確定大家都好好地在工作崗位上工作，沒有偷懶。)

- **nine-to-five**　朝九晚五的工作型態
  My brother became a taxi driver because he said he couldn't stand the thought of a nine-to-five office job.
  (我弟弟說，一想到那種朝九晚五的辦公室生活，他就受不了，所以，他開計程車去了。)

- **window**　某個特定的時段
  Try to catch the chairman during the half-hour window between 11:15 and 11:45. That's the only time you'll find him in his office today.
  (想辦法在十一點十五分到四十五分這半小時之間逮到總裁。今天他只有在那時候會在辦公室。)

250

▶ *Exercises*

請勿改變例句的句型, 用a)、
b)詞組代換下列例句。

(解答見 272 頁)

1. Some are expecting 60−70 hours.

   a) demanding that we put in
   b) a lot of overtime

2. You feel you should hang around waiting for a telephone window.

   a) I don't want to
   b) your boss to return to the office

3. It makes you think that something is wrong.

   a) strikes you
   b) has gone

◆◆◆◆◆◆◆◆◆◆◆◆◆◆ 簡短對話 ◆◆◆◆◆◆◆◆◆◆◆◆◆◆

Sawasaki: It's not just the long hours at the office either.

Winchell: You're talking about taking work home, right? A lot of people do that, especially on the weekends.

Sawasaki: Sure, there's that, but actually I was thinking about the tyranny of the telephone.

Winchell: Tyranny?

Sawasaki: Nowadays people think nothing of placing an international call. The result is I get calls from Tokyo at home, even about trivial matters. And even if people allow for the time difference, they often forget to allow for daylight saving time. So there's no telling when the phone may ring.

---

take work home 把工作帶回家做　　**There's that.** 是有這麼一回事。
tyranny 暴虐; 壓制; 虐待　　**think nothing of** 不以為…有甚麼大不了
trivial 微不足道的　　**time difference** 時差　　**daylight saving time** 日光
節約時間　　**there's no telling** 誰也不知道

Lesson 31

To Chicago (3)（到芝加哥）

● 預習 — *Sentences*

· There'll be less red tape involved.
· It's scary in a way.
· Sometimes I feel like chucking it all.
· You wouldn't be the first one.
· People are starting to get fed up.

● *Vignette*

Sawasaki: Well, at least now that a huge layer of upper- and middle-level management was wiped out in the restructuring process I suppose there'll be less red tape involved in getting something new implemented.

Winchell: You're right. Sad to say but trimming the management head count is apparently one of the biggest benefits in companies that are merged or acquired.

Sawasaki: It's scary in a way, but the next century is probably going to bring even more change than the '90s. For example, who can say what's going to happen in Eastern Europe and China in the next few years?

Winchell: As if the changes in our own industry weren't enough to make our heads spin. Sometimes I feel like chucking it all.

Sawasaki: You wouldn't be the first one. I've met a number of people who got burned out in high-level positions and gave them up for something with a little more relaxed pace.

Winchell: Yep, people are starting to get fed up but it's not an easy topic to broach. People will use phrases like "high-commitment manager" out in the open but words like *karoshi* only get whispered behind closed doors.

Sawasaki: Karoshi? You mean the Japanese word for death due to overwork?

Winchell: Yeah. I've read about it in some business magazines.

溫謝爾說，為自己爭取時間的唯一方法，就是放棄這條出人頭地之路。而澤崎也遇見過不少因為精疲力竭，而決定急流湧退的經營者。

澤崎： 不過，至少在企業重組的過程中，上級和中級管理階層都被大幅砍殺，我想日後若要施行甚麼新政策，可因此省掉不少繁文縟節。

溫謝爾： 沒錯。這講起來是有點令人難過，不過，在公司被兼併或買收後，看起來最大的好處之一就是能夠砍掉管理階層的人員編制。

澤崎： 從某方面來看，這還怪恐怖的。不過，下個世紀可能會帶來比 90 年代更多的變革。舉例來說，沒人能清楚預知，在往後幾年中，東歐和中國大陸將有甚麼樣的變局。

溫謝爾： 聽來像是我們自己產業內部的轉變還不夠把我們攪得暈頭轉向似的。有些時候，我真不想幹了。

澤崎： 你可不是第一個這麼想的人。我碰到過一些人，他們在高高在上的崗位中搞得精疲力竭，之後捨棄了原來的職位，寧可要輕鬆一點的步調。

溫謝爾： 就是啊，人們已經開始受不了了。不過，這種事不好拿出來當話題講。在公開場合，大家還是會用些像是「完全獻身事業的經營者」這一類的詞兒，可是門一關起來，就開始有耳語聲在談論過勞死之類的事了。

澤崎： 過勞死？你是說那個意指工作過度勞累而死的日本字嗎？

溫謝爾： 是啊，我在一些商業雜誌上看到的。

Words and Phrases

layer	層	high-level position	高層地位
upper- and middle-level manage-ment	上級、中級管理階層	get fed up	受夠了
		broach	提出 (話題)
be wiped out	一掃而盡	high-commitment	有高度責任感
restructuring	企業重組		的; 獻身的
implement	實施; 施行	out in the open	公然地
trim	修剪	whisper	低聲說話
scary	恐怖的	death due to overwork	過勞死
get burned out	精疲力竭; 失去幹勁		

Vocabulary Building

- **red tape**   官僚的形式主義
  At any large organization you're bound to run into a certain amount of red tape.
  (在任何大型組織中, 你少不了一定要碰上某些官樣的繁文縟節。)

- **head count**   人員定額
  I'll never get permission to increase the head count in sales. Can we hire some part-timers to carry the work load during the Christmas season?
  (我想在銷售部門再增加一些人, 但這絕不會得到批准的。可是為要應付聖誕季節增加的工作量, 我們可以找一些兼職人員嗎?)

- **make someone's head spin**   使某人頭暈眼花
  You're way ahead of me and your numbers make my head spin. Can you please speak in layman's language?
  (你的話實在很難懂, 而你那些數字又搞得我頭昏眼花。可不可以請你用平民化一點的語言?)

- **chuck it all**   全部放棄
  Denny decided to chuck it all and go on a hitchhiking trip across South America.
  (丹尼決定把一切都丟開, 一路搭便車遊遍整個南美。)

1. The next century is probably going to bring even more change.

    a) years to come are
    b) usher in

2. People are starting to get fed up.

    a) tell me they're
    b) a lot of my friends

3. I've read about it in some business magazines.

    a) several major newspapers
    b) there have been articles

◆◆◆◆◆◆◆◆◆◆◆◆◆ 簡短對話 ◆◆◆◆◆◆◆◆◆◆◆◆◆◆

Sawasaki: You know what really burns me up about this restructuring and streamlining business? It's the way they're so quick to cut out jobs without eliminating the work that those people were doing.

Winchell: So those of us who are lucky enough to avoid getting the ax end up with a heavier workload.

Sawasaki: Exactly. Personally I think I've just about reached my limit.

Winchell: I think I reached mine a couple of years ago.

---

burn up〔口語〕使人怒氣上升　　**restructuring** 企業重組　　**streamlining** 精簡化的　　**cut out** 去掉　　**eliminate** 消除　　**get the ax** 被解雇　　**workload** 工作量　　**reach one's limit** 達到自己的極限

Lesson 31

To Chicago (4)（到芝加哥）

●預習 — *Sentences*

- People in Japan put in an unbelievable number of hours.
- How do they keep it up?
- America will be heading in that direction.
- They seem to be using money as the carrot.
- It gives you something to think about.

●*Vignette*

Winchell: Even the concept would have been unimaginable for people not too far ahead of my generation. But Shoichi, I've heard that people in Japan put in an unbelievable number of hours. How do they keep it up?

Sawasaki: I don't really know. But I can tell you that it really takes a toll on people's health and on their family relationships.

Winchell: I suppose that America will be heading in that direction. Especially with the big guys telling us that what's to come will make our current schedules seem like a walk in the park.

Sawasaki: They seem to be using money as the carrot. Our compensation is more incentive-based than ever.

Winchell: It's true. A recent poll I saw said that 83 percent of today's managers have more incentive-based compensation in their pay packages than they did ten years ago. It gives you something to think about when you're wondering why you're still in the office at 8 on a Friday evening or canceling your golf game on Saturday to get caught up on work.

Announcement: Ladies and gentlemen, we'll be landing at Chicago's O'Hare Airport in just a few minutes. Please put your tray tables and seat backs in their upright positions and fasten your seat belts.

Winchell: Well, Shoichi, are you ready for this?

Sawasaki: As ready as I'll ever be.

　　日本的「過勞死」也曾在歐美的傳播媒體上掀起討論的熱潮。他們如何能在工作上花掉那麼長的時間？這是個令人費解的問題。

溫謝爾：　就算是那些比我早不了幾代的人，他們也沒有辦法想像居然會有這種觀念。不過，昭一，我聽說在日本，人們的工作時數長到令人難以置信。他們如何可以這樣一直持續下去？

澤崎：　我也不是很瞭解。不過，我可以告訴你，這種情形嚴重影響到他們的身體健康和跟家人的關係。

溫謝爾：　我猜想，美國正在朝著那個方向前進。尤其是那些上面的人還在告訴我們，日後要來的情形會令我們覺得現今每日的行程有如在公園散步那般輕鬆。

澤崎：　他們好像把錢當作蘿蔔一樣。我們的報酬從來沒有這樣地趨向獎金制過。

溫謝爾：　沒錯。我看到有一個最近的調查報告說，與十年前相比，今天的經營者有百分之八十三傾向在薪資制度中採取獎金報酬制。這真的是個耐人尋味的問題，尤其是當你在想，為何星期五晚上八點，你還在辦公室，或者是，為何你不得不取消一場週六的高爾夫球賽，就為了趕工作進度？

廣播：　各位女士先生，我們再過幾分鐘就要降落在芝加哥的歐哈爾機場了。請把您的餐桌和椅背放直，並繫上安全帶。

溫謝爾：　那麼，昭一，你準備好迎接這一切了嗎？

澤崎：　我已經蓄勢待發了。

Words and Phrases

concept　　概念

unimaginable　　無法想像的

head *v.*　　朝⋯的方向前進

big guy　　大人物

compensation　　報酬

incentive-based　　獎金制的

poll　　調查

Vocabulary Building

- **keep it up**　　保持

  cf. Sales are up this quarter compared with last year. Just keep up the good work.

  （跟去年相比，這四個月來的銷售額上升了。要保持下去。）

- **take a toll on**　　造成⋯的犧牲

  All these interruptions are taking a toll on my productivity.

  （這些一而再、再而三的中斷使我的生產力都降低了。）

- **carrot**　　紅蘿蔔

  cf. My boss used a carrot-and-stick approach—raises for top achievers and pay cuts for underperformers.

  （我老闆採用了一種「恩威並施」的方法 —— 業績表現優秀的人，加薪，低於水準以下者，扣薪水。）

- **get caught up on**　　趕上工作進度

  You can go home, Mari. I have to get caught up on the work that's piled up during my business trip.

  （瑪莉，妳可以回家了。我出差時桌上案子堆積如山，我得快快把他們消化掉。）

▶ **Exercises**　　　請勿改變例句的句型, 用a)、
　　　　　　　　　　b)詞組代換下列例句。　　　　（解答見 273 頁）

1. Even the concept would have been unimaginable.

   a) the very idea
   b) out of the question

2. People in Japan put in an unbelievable number of hours.

   a) work long
   b) amazing

3. You're wondering why you're still in the office at 8 on a Friday evening.

   a) I can't understand
   b) what Maria is doing

◆◆◆◆◆◆◆◆◆◆◆◆◆ 簡短對話 ◆◆◆◆◆◆◆◆◆◆◆◆◆◆

Sawasaki: What you said about Japanese working long hours reminds me of my father.

Winchell: Did he have to work late a lot when you were growing up?

Sawasaki: Yeah, although it wasn't just work that kept him out late. He also went out drinking with his coworkers pretty often, and sometimes he played mah-jongg with them till after midnight. He claimed that it was part of his job.

Winchell: I bet your mother didn't see it that way.

Sawasaki: She didn't complain much, but I felt sorry for her. I thought I could avoid that lifestyle by working for an American company.

---

coworker 同事　　　**mah-jongg** 麻將　　　**claim** v. 聲稱

Lesson 31

To Chicago — 總結

在美國，80年代可說是 Decade of Greed (金錢物慾的十年)。美元開始成為弱勢貨幣，而商場則因市場擴及全球而競爭加劇。常有企業在大量裁員，至於 M&A 以及企業重組 (restructuring) 更是家常便飯。在這種現象背後，我們可以看到一股以利益取向的貪婪潮流。

這時，許多工作狂的出現，協助了公司維持其理想的營運狀態。這些工作狂大部分都是在戰後嬰兒潮中出生的。他們為了要與日本人競爭，也像日本人一樣，在工作上投注大量的時間與精力。這種工作型式甚至還獲得廣泛的認同。

就這樣，到了80年代末了，工作者變得疲乏不堪，但他們期望從上司口中得到一些稱讚與鼓勵。不過，事與願違，經營者幾乎都異口同聲，「80年代還馬馬虎虎，90年代還要更加嚴格。」為甚麼呢? 也許，與80年代相比，90年代的變化要來得更大，步調也會更快吧!

在這樣的環境下，美國商人的工作量更大了。90年代之初，財星雜誌曾作過調查，多數 CEO 都希望高級主管每週平均能工作五十四個小時，中級主管人員則要求四十九個小時。

為此，不只要用鞭子 (stick)，連胡蘿蔔(carrot) 也不可少。優秀人員的薪資愈來愈高。而年終獎金配合業績發放，以及依業績配給股票等的誘因，也都成為報酬制度的一環。

同時，所謂權限委讓 (worker empowerment) 的概念在工作上也愈來愈普遍了。

Answers to Exercises

Lesson 18

(1)

1. a) Fine, if it weren't for my lost luggage at JFK.
   b) Not bad, except for my lost luggage at JFK.
2. a) I've learned many things about you.
   b) I've heard many rumors about you.
3. a) Shall I install the phone in your new office?
   b) Shall I take you to the conference room?

(2)

1. a) Japanese names can be difficult to pronounce.
   b) Oriental names can be hard to say.
2. a) Aren't those the Catskill Mountains that I see over there in the distance?
   b) Aren't those the World Trade Center buildings that I see over there in the mist?
3. a) This desk resembles an airplane cockpit.
   b) This desk is built like an airplane cockpit.

(3)

1. a) He wanted to have lunch with you today.
   b) He was hoping to take you out for lunch today.
2. a) I'll reserve a table for you at Tavern on the Green.
   b) I'll book a table for the two of you at Tavern on the Green.
3. a) She'll be coming over with the children during their school break.
   b) She'll be moving with the kids during their school break.

(4)

1. a) It may be a good idea to come to Greenwich for some golf.
   b) You'll have to come to Greenwich for dinner.
2. a) If you have any questions, you should speak up.
   b) Whenever you have any questions, my door's always open.
3. a) He doesn't like being by himself in that office.
   b) He may get lonely without anyone to talk to in that office.

Lesson 19

(1)

1. a) People hustle to survive in New York.
   b) People struggle to survive in the Big Apple.

2. a) Some liberal Americans have been insisting drugs should be legalized.

   b) Some radicals are saying drugs should be legalized.

3. a) It's not apparent to me what good that would do.

   b) I don't see why it should be done.

(2)

1. a) That's required only for pre-employment applicants.

   b) The physical examination is mandatory only for pre-employment applicants.

2. a) Maria Cortez and I were just discussing drugs at lunch.

   b) Maria Cortez and I were just talking about drugs over breakfast.

3. a) No one gets hired without being certified as drug-free.

   b) Nobody gets hired without drug-testing.

(3)

1. a) Drugs are so rare in Japan I wouldn't even know what they look like.

   b) Drugs are so uncommon in Japan I wouldn't even know what to look for.

2. a) We can show you a video if you're interested.

   b) We have a video if you'd like to see it.

3. a) I'll return afterwards to answer any questions.

   b) I'll come back afterwards to chat with you.

(4)

1. a) Don't some people think all this testing an invasion of their privacy?

   b) Don't some people consider all this testing a waste of time?

2. a) Most people just want to get away from it all.

   b) Most people only wish they could be let alone.

3. a) Someone has to pay for it.

   b) The person responsible has to pay the bill.

Lesson 20

(1)

1. a) It's an administrative aphorism that whatever is least expected to will go wrong.

   b) It's a rule of thumb that whatever can go wrong will go wrong.

2. a) Say, did you just move from Japan, Shoichi?

   b) Incidentally, did you just move to the United States, Shoichi?

3. a) It's basically a checklist of ways to maximize security.

   b) It's basically a package of tools to improve security.

(2)

1. a) I appreciate exactly what's going on in your mind.
   b) I understand exactly how you feel.
2. a) Fear is not a useful weapon in overcoming the situation.
   b) Fear won't help you at all in self-defense.
3. a) Whatever you do, don't antagonize any intruder or attacker.
   b) By all means, avoid confronting any intruder or attacker.

(3)

1. a) You'll soon get to know the other staff.
   b) You'll gradually get used to them.
2. a) It's a community movement that began in the early '70s.
   b) It's a social movement that started in the early '70s.
3. a) It's considered to be quite effective.
   b) It's proven to be exceedingly effective.

(4)

1. a) I once joined a neighborhood patrol in Japan looking for a rapist.
   b) At one time I joined a neighborhood patrol in Japan looking for an arsonist.
2. a) The participants collaborate with the local police force.
   b) The volunteers work in close cooperation with the local police force.
3. a) The sign is intended to discourage the potential burglar.
   b) The sign is supposed to deter the potential crime.

Lesson 21

(1)

1. a) Do you want the collision insurance?
   b) Do you need the collision coverage?
2. a) I've moved here from Japan to be with ABC Foods.
   b) I've been transferred here from Japan to work for ABC Foods.
3. a) It's imperative for you to get a New York license soon.
   b) You'll need to apply for a New York license soon.

(2)

1. a) I'm afraid it's invalid here.
   b) I suspect it's not valid here.
2. a) How long have you been in this country?
   b) How long have you lived in the United States?
3. a) While my partner checks the information through our computer, please describe to me exactly what happened.

b) While my partner checks the information through our computer, please tell me how this has happened.

(3)

1. a) The stop sign is partially hidden by that tree branch.
   b) The stop sign isn't really visible because of that tree branch.
2. a) It may be necessary for you to appear in court sometime in the next seven days.
   b) You're going to have to testify at the trial sometime in the next seven days.
3. a) We also have to give you a ticket for not observing a stop sign.
   b) We also have to cite you for failing to observe a stop sign.

(4)

1. a) I heard you've inquired about your court hearing tomorrow.
   b) I understand you've made an inquiry about your court hearing tomorrow.
2. a) You have an excellent case and our legal representation should be unnecessary.
   b) You have an excellent case and so a lawyer won't be necessary.
3. a) The officer noted that the stop sign at the intersection was partially hidden.
   b) The officer noted that the stop sign at the crossing was out of sight .

Lesson 22 ————————————————————

(1)

1. a) You told me you were engaged to an international banker.
   b) You said you were about to be married to an international banker.
2. a) We plan to get married next spring as soon as we manage to arrange a date.
   b) We plan to get married next spring provided we're still interested in each other.
3. a) We don't intend to have a baby until we've started up our own business.
   b) We don't intend to start a family until we've made it.

(2)

1. a) What type of business will you go into?
   b) What kind of business will you start?
2. a) Could you explain why being an entrepreneur is so appealing?
   b) Why do you think being an entrepreneur is so attractive?
3. a) Now the annual sales come to well over $10 billion.
   b) Now it's worth something like $10 billion.

(3)

1. a) They account for nearly half of the U.S. adult population.

b) They make up close to half of the U.S. adult population.

2. a) How would you describe their characteristics?

    b) What would you say are their special qualities?

3. a) Harriet stays home to look after the perfect house and adorable kids.

    b) Harriet is the typical housewife to take care of the perfect house and adorable kids.

(4)

1. a) He encouraged the participants to express their honest feelings.

    b) He gave people plenty of room to feel free to state their honest feelings.

2. a) They wanted to be counted as excellent performers among their peers.

    b) They wanted to stand out as top players among their peers.

3. a) They can't afford to neglect their personal relationships.

    b) Their jobs force them to neglect their hobbies.

Lesson 23 ────────────────────────────

(1)

1. a) Did you find any strong candidates for staff additions?

    b) Do you have any strong candidates to fill the vacancies?

2. a) I questioned him what he was good at.

    b) I asked him what his strengths are.

3. a) Americans may delay a business conference to tell the latest jokes.

    b) Americans may hold up a business conference to exchange the latest jokes.

(2)

1. a) Some types of language are often rejected as inappropriate in a business context.

    b) Laughter is often rejected as inappropriate on formal occasions.

2. a) Everybody thought that laughing made them look undignified.

    b) The idea was that laughing made them look silly.

3. a) You can develop abilities you were missing before.

    b) You may see things you were missing when you were younger.

(3)

1. a) If you don't get enough sleep, your sense of humor deteriorates.

    b) When you're depressed or nervous, your sense of humor is likely to be lost.

2. a) I was ticketed twice in Manhattan in a single week.

    b) I got two parking tickets in Manhattan as soon as I bought a car.

3. a) Life in New York is a real pain at times.

    b) Life in New York can be tough for all of us.

(4)

1. a) We also have a great deal of experience with computers.
   b) We also joke a lot about ourselves.
2. a) Do you know the one about the ultimate computer hacker?
   b) Have you heard about the ultimate entrepreneur?
3. a) One of my favorites is a joke that goes back to the Edo era.
   b) I like the story from the Edo era.

Lesson 24

(1)

1. a) I purchased a carton of your ice cream and it had a nut in it.
   b) I bought a carton of your ice cream and it had a metal piece in it.
2. a) Let me ask you what you're going to do about it.
   b) I want to know how you will handle it.
3. a) On the front of the package you'll find the date of manufacture.
   b) On the front of the package it shows the weight of the product.

(2)

1. a) Eric suggested I take you along on a complaint response visit.
   b) Eric suggested you should come along on a complaint response visit.
2. a) I've made an appointment to visit him on my way to the office.
   b) Dennis promised to visit him at 3 this afternoon.
3. a) It keeps me in better touch with competitors' moves.
   b) One should stay in better touch with customers' feelings.

(3)

1. a) Dennis managed to come to a preliminary agreement with the customer on a fair settlement.
   b) The aim is to sign an agreement with the customer on a fair settlement.
2. a) Is there anything I should not say?
   b) Can you think of anything I should be careful of saying?
3. a) ABC Foods receives many complaints about prices.
   b) We also get letters from customers complaining about prices.

(4)

1. a) We sometimes actively solicit negative feedback about the nutritive value of our products.
   b) We sometimes get comments from our customers about the nutritive value of our products.

2. a) Value for money is still a key issue among American consumers.
   b) Nutrition is still the biggest concern of American consumers.
3. a) Do you ever get people who won't forgive no matter what you do?
   b) What do you say to people who can't be satisfied no matter what you do?

Lesson 25 ─────────────────────────

(1)
1. a) Everybody at the office in Tokyo is easy to get along with.
   b) Everybody I know was really thrilled.
2. a) Ray is grateful of the contribution you've made in the frozen foods area.
   b) I appreciate the contribution you've sent to the magazine.
3. a) Business seems to be the most important consideration over there.
   b) Customer service seems to be a lot better over there.

(2)
1. a) I don't think he cares much about being interviewed by reporters.
   b) I am not sure if he cares much about being in the limelight.
2. a) It never occurred to me that he'd remember my name.
   b) I didn't expect that he'd remember who I was.
3. a) Ray never forgets what he ate for lunch at a restaurant a year ago.
   b) Ray remembers who he met for lunch at a restaurant a year ago.

(3)
1. a) He would rather have the company plow the money back into R&D.
   b) He prefers to have the company invest in R&D.
2. a) Ray isn't the same as the standard Japanese company president.
   b) Ray's superior to the standard Japanese company president.
3. a) He started at the bottom and climbed the ladder.
   b) He started in the mailroom and worked his way up.

(4)
1. a) It's one of the things that makes him stand out.
   b) His true sense of devotion is one of the things that separates him from the pack.
2. a) His knowledge of marketing is one of the main reasons for his success.
   b) His skill in handling employees is one of the main reasons for his rise in the company.
3. a) He's a hands-on manager who's willing to get his hands dirty.
   b) He's an operations guy who's willing to roll up his shirt sleeves.

Lesson 26

(1)

1. a) All I'm telling you is that it's going around on the grapevine.
    b) All I'm saying is that it's going around in the office.
2. a) I have to see him at 2 about a new advertising campaign.
    b) I've got a meeting with him at 2 to discuss next year's budget.
3. a) They heard some rumors about a massive staff cutback here at headquarters.
    b) They say that there's going to be a severe downsizing program here at head-quarters.

(2)

1. a) We're under tremendous pressure to economize everywhere.
    b) We're under tremendous pressure to increase profits everywhere.
2. a) We're already very agile, in my opinion.
    b) We're already very lean, if you care for my opinion.
3. a) Will you do anything about this one?
    b) Are you going to do anything to keep it from spreading?

(3)

1. a) I recommend against secrecy unless it's really necessary—and possible.
    b) I don't do that except in cases where it's really necessary—and possible.
2. a) A hush-hush attitude breeds unneeded mistrust among employees.
    b) Withholding information breeds unneeded speculation and suspicion.
3. a) It's a relief to hear it's just a lot of hot air.
    b) I'm glad to find out it's just a lot of hot air.

(4)

1. a) I thought we were ready to get official authorization.
    b) I was positive we were ready to sign the papers.
2. a) It's been on the grapevine that a takeover may be likely this month.
    b) Rumor has it that a takover may be in the offing.
3. a) Nobody can be sure what steps Ray Weston is going to take.
    b) I wonder how much money the project is going to take.

Lesson 27

(1)

1. a) I have several announcements to share with you this morning.
    b) I have a very important message to convey to you this morning.
2. a) The Executive Council and the board carefully considered a number of op-tions.

b) The Executive Council and the board looked into a number of ways to survive.
3. a) So it seemed that the company had to be taken over one way or another.
   b) So we had to be taken over in spite of all the efforts.

(2)
1. a) Our investment bankers said we should avoid tactics of that sort.
   b) Our investment bankers advised against doing anything hasty.
2. a) Ray is slated to announce his retirement today.
   b) Ray is expected to step down today.
3. a) They know that the business upswing won't last forever.
   b) They're reminded that their cigarette profits won't last forever.

(3)
1. a) Domestically cigarette consumption is declining.
   b) Domestic cigarette consumption is falling.
2. a) The bottom line is the name of the game in M&A situations.
   b) Making a quick profit is all that counts in M&A situations.
3. a) There will be a package for employees who lose their jobs.
   b) We will provide a package for employees who are made redundant.

(4)
1. a) Employees at every level will be given accurate information on the situation.
   b) Every member of the workforce will have access to accurate information on the situation.
2. a) Your immediate supervisor will be happy to tell you precisely what your own package consists of.
   b) The computer will be programmed to let you know precisely what your own package consists of.
3. a) People like you are bound to be in great demand in the new organization.
   b) Your talents will be valued in the new organization.

Lesson 28

(1)
1. a) Eric was just appointed president of the pet food operation.
   b) You've been appointed to head the pet food operation.
2. a) When will I replace you as head of Corporate Marketing?
   b) Who's going to succeed Eric as head of Corporate Marketing?
3. a) There will be a total revamping of the marketing function.

b) You can expect to see some restructuring of the marketing function.

(2)

1. a) There's no doubt he'll be able to turn around the company very quickly.
   b) I'm sure he'll be able to achieve dramatic results very quickly.
2. a) He's a tough boss but I'm sure you'll get along well with him.
   b) He's a demanding boss but I'm sure you'll enjoy working with him.
3. a) I've been asked to do some part-time consulting work.
   b) The company has asked me to be a part-time consultant.

(3)

1. a) We've got a weekend cottage in the country.
   b) Hank owns a couple hundred acres in the country.
2. a) Geoff and I've given a lot of thought to starting our own business.
   b) The two of us have been planning on starting our own business.
3. a) I decided I should take advantage of the special offer.
   b) It seemed like a good time for us to capitalize on the special offer.

(4)

1. a) Maria works at a small agency specializing in micro marketing.
   b) We're setting up a small agency that offers media training.
2. a) There are a lot fewer people sitting at home watching the soaps.
   b) Women aren't just cooking meals or watching the soaps.
3. a) We also plan to find sponsors for sports events.
   b) We also plan to help with Hispanic marketing.

Lesson 29

(1)

1. a) Did you read the interview with DeMarco in this morning's paper?
   b) What did you think of Ken Bulow's column in this morning's paper?
2. a) ABC Foods isn't nearly as paternalistic as the typical Japanese company.
   b) They seemed to be as concerned with market share as the typical Japanese company.
3. a) It's a function of deeply held beliefs and values.
   b) People's behavior is rooted in deeply held beliefs and values.

(2)

1. a) Eric Turner painted DeMarco as extremely bright but ruthless.
   b) The columnist described DeMarco as extremely bright but ruthless.
2. a) She may be able to fill me in on this subject.
   b) I thought you could shed some light on this subject.

3. a) I wondered how I'd be able to survive in Nelson's cold-blooded culture.

   b) I just didn't think I'd be able to survive in African jungles.

(3)

1. a) He did a brilliant job on a number of projects.

   b) He did very well on a number of consumer accounts.

2. a) Ten years later he was given a job offer by a client.

   b) Just after he got promoted he was hired away by a client.

3. a) Nelson now intends to be the world's most competitive corporation.

   b) Nelson is now aiming to be the world's most efficient corporation.

(4)

1. a) Did you ever meet DeMarco face-to-face?

   b) Have you ever met DeMarco in person?

2. a) One of the presenters wasn't able to answer to some of Alex's questions.

   b) One of the presenters didn't have quick answers to some of Alex's questions.

3. a) He's sold off a number of operations and fired over 12,000 people.

   b) He's divested a number of operations and let go of over 12,000 people.

Lesson 30

(1)

1. a) One of my clients is now the world's fourth largest manufacturer of food products.

   b) This company is now Chicago's biggest manufacturer of food products.

2. a) There's nothing morally wrong with the cigarette business.

   b) I see nothing morally wrong about smoking.

3. a) Minors should be urged not to smoke.

   b) Young people should be urged to remain non-smokers.

(2)

1. a) Do you think you'll be able to maintain your reputation as the profitability guru?

   b) Are you confident that you can live up to your reputation as the profitability guru?

2. a) We regard this merger as an opportunity to make a lot of structural changes.

   b) We see this merger as an opportunity to bring in a lot of structural changes.

3. a) Somebody told me you and Brad are transferring to the new corporate head-quarters.

   b) I hear you and Brad are relocating to Chicago.

(3)

1. a) I congratulate you on taking such a big step.
   b) I admire you for taking such a bold step.
2. a) Geoff and I are trying to be more careful about the whole thing.
   b) Geoff and I are trying to be realistic about how we spend our money.
3. a) I'll be down in another ten minutes at the outside.
   b) I'll be down within an hour or so.

(4)

1. a) I have a feeling that he's a real sharp strategist.
   b) I get the impression that he's a real shrewd strategist.
2. a) I was terribly shocked when you told me about the takeover.
   b) I still remember the day I heard the news of the takeover.
3. a) My English has improved since I arrived in New York a year ago.
   b) So much has changed since I started working in New York a year ago.

Lesson 31 ────────────────────

(1)

1. a) I was looking for a new belt at a department store in Tokyo.
   b) I went shopping for a new belt to replace the one I lost.
2. a) You've actually gained a lot of weight.
   b) You've actually lost some friends.
3. a) They say not smoking keeps your breath fresher.
   b) I've been told it keeps your breath fresher.

(2)

1. a) Some are demanding that we put in 60–70 hours.
   b) Some are expecting a lot of overtime.
2. a) I don't want to hang around waiting for a telephone window.
   b) You feel you should hang around waiting for your boss to return to the office.
3. a) It strikes you that something is wrong.
   b) It makes you think that something has gone wrong.

(3)

1. a) The years to come are probably going to bring even more change.
   b) The next century is probably going to usher in even more change.
2. a) People tell me they're starting to get fed up.
   b) A lot of my friends are starting to get fet up.

3. a) I've read about it in several major newspapers.
   b) There have been articles in some business magazines.

(4)

1. a) The very idea would have been unimaginable.
   b) Even the concept would have been out of the question.
2. a) People in Japan work long hours.
   b) People in Japan put in an amazing number of hours.
3. a) I can't understand why you're still in the office at 8 on a Friday evening.
   b) You're wondering what Maria is doing in the office at 8 on a Friday evening.

Key Words and Idioms

high-commitment 有高度責任感的；獻身的 (252)

high-level executive 高階層的主管 (248)

high-level position 高層地位 (252)

hinder 妨礙 (158)

hire 錄用 (100)

hiring freeze 人事凍結〈不再聘人〉 (190)

Hispanic marketing 對美國境內講西班牙語或葡萄牙語的美籍拉丁人所進行的市場拓展。 (22)

hit the rumor mill 謠傳開來 (158)

hock 典當 (112)

hold hostage 挾持人質 (112)

hold off 延期 (166)

hold up 打斷 (100)

Honestly. 真的。 (104)

horror story 令人戰慄的言語 (50)

hostile takeover 懷有敵意的購併 (172)、(226)

hot air 大言大話；吹牛 (162)

house hunting 找房子 (22)

hulk 大個子 (82)

hunch 直覺；預感 (176)

hush-hush 祕密的；機密的 (162)

I

I almost forgot. 我差點忘了。 (18)

I get your point. 我瞭解你的意思了。 (202)

I see your point. 我瞭解你的意思了。 (54)

I suppose that's all right. 我想應該沒問題。 (18)

identification 身分證明 (64)

identify 確認 (58)

if you'd like 如果你要的話 (36)

I'll be darned. 太突然了；怎麼會這樣。〈有 I'm very surprised. 之意〉 (72)

I'll tell you what. 我告訴你怎麼做。 (212)

impairment 損害；減低價值 (176)

impending 迫近的；逼近的 (172)

implement 實施；施行 (252)

in a [business] context 在 [商業] 場合 (情況) 中 (104)

in any case 不管是甚麼情況 (58)

in cooperation with 與…配合 (協力) (58)

in someone's honor 向某人表示敬意；為紀念某人 (140)

in the distance 在遠處 (14)

in the face of 面臨著… (216)

in the meantime 於其時；另一方面 (22)

in the offing 即將發生 (166)

inappropriate 不適當的 (104)

incentive-based 獎金制的 (256)

incentive prize 獎勵品 (108)

individual 個人 (40)

industry source 業界方面 (230)

ineptitude 愚蠢；無能 (220)

inevitable 無可避免的 (180)

inferior 劣質的 (130)

informative 提供知識的 (36)

informed decision 正確的決定 (226)

initiate 發起；開始；著手做… (58)、(130)

inquire 詢問 (76)

insecure 不安全的；擔心的 (112)

insurance certificate 保險憑證 (68)

integrate 整合；統合 (184)

integrated 綜合的；統合的 (14)

interacting 互動；相互影響 (94)

International Human Resources 國際人資部門 (32)

interrupt 打斷 (22)

intersection 交叉口；十字路口 (76)

interview 面試 (100)

intruder 入侵者；闖入者 (50)

invasion （權利的）侵犯；入侵 (40)

investment banker 投資銀行（家） (176)

issue 問題所在 (94)

it doesn't do any good 一點好處都沒有 (202)

It's a different world out there. 時局變了；情況不一樣了。 (202)

it's no use 無用的；無意義的 (238)

I've heard many things about you. 我聽過很多關於你的傳聞。 (10)

K

keep a lid on 保守祕密；控制情勢 (162)

keep in touch with 與…保持聯絡；取得…的近況 (122)

keep it up 保持 (256)

keep time 保有時間 (248)

Keep up the good work. 幹得好，繼續保持下去。 (136)

L

label 標籤 ；在…上貼標籤；予以分類 (118)

labor force 勞動人口 (90)

lag 落後；減退 (158)

last thing 萬萬想不到的事 (100)

law-enforcement 執法的〈警官、檢察官等〉 (28)

layer 層 (252)

layers of management 管理的階層 (220)

lean （人事）精簡 (158)

lean and mean （在公司人事上）不只沒有贅肉，連該有的肉都不見了；精簡且刻薄 (208)

left-hand side 左側 (68)

legalization 合法化 (28)

legalize 使合法化 (28)

legend has it that 傳聞說… (140)

letter of the law 法律條文 (76)

liability 責任 (126)

liaison person 聯絡人 (184)

lifestyle 生活方式 (90)

liken 將…比喻做（某物） (190)

live up to 使自己達到… (230)

live up to one's reputation 夠得上某
人所得到的名聲　　(130)

look into 調查　　(172)

lose someone to 某親屬死於…
(140)

lose weight 減重　　(244)

lost luggage 遺失的行李　　(10)

loud and clear 清清楚楚的　　(130)

low-key 低調的; 不顯眼的　　(148)

lucrative 有利的; 有利可圖的
(28)

M

M&A 企業購併　　(180)、(190)

make a point of 照例; 必定　　(130)

make it a point to 照例要; 一定會
(144)

make love 發生性關係; 做愛　　(226)

**"make money or perish" business
philosophy** 「不賺錢就請走路」的
經營理念　　(208)

make one's name 得到名聲　　(216)

make provisions for 為…作準備
(234)

make reference to 提到…; 提及…
(208)

make someone's head spin 使某人頭
暈眼花　　(252)

make the list of 入選為…　　(136)

make the rounds 巡視; 巡迴　　(162)

mandate 指示; 命令　　(190)

mandatory 必須的; 強制的　　(32)

marijuana 大麻　　(36)

marketer 市場開發部負責人　　(184)、
(234)

massive 大量的　　(154)

master plan for life 生涯規畫　　(82)

masterless 沒有主子的; 沒有主人的
(112)

mature 成熟的　　(226)

mean 故意要…; 想要…　　(22)

Meaning what? 甚麼意思呢?　　(90)

meant 視作…; 意指…　　(100)

measured pace 整齊的步調　　(238)

medical treatment 治療; 醫療
(126)

meet in person 見到本人　　(220)

merger 合併　　(172)

mindset 思考態度; 想法模式　　(194)

mishandled complaint 處理不當的申
訴　　(130)

miss 想念　　(234)

**MIT (Massachusetts Institute of
Technology)** 麻省理工學院
(112)

mode of operation 運作型態　　(216)

model (車子的)年型　　(144)

modular 組合式的　　(14)

mold 黴菌　　(126)

money-money-money decade 錢、
錢、錢的十年　　(208)

morality 道德　　(226)

motivate 使有做事的動機　　(82)、
(144)

motorcyclist 摩托車騎士　　(72)

move on 遷移到另一處(工作或住所)
(226)

mug 〔美俗〕從背後襲擊勒住被害者的
脖子　　(28)

My pleasure. 我的榮幸；很樂意。
　(22)

needlessly 不必要地　　(50)

negative feedback 負面回饋　　(130)

neglect 忽視；忽略　　(94)

negotiate 交涉　　(166)

neighbor 鄰居；鄰近的人　　(22)

nervous 緊張的；焦急的　　(108)

niche 利基；特定的客戶群〈針對特定的
　產品或服務〉　　(202)

nine-to-five 朝九晚五的工作型態
　(248)

no doubt 無疑地　　(172)

no ifs, ands, buts, or maybes 沒
　有「如果」、「而且」、「但是」、「也
　許」；不講條件；不容情　　(130)

no problem 沒問題　　(36)

No question about it. 毫無疑問。
　(184)

non-media 非媒體的　　(202)

no-nonsense 實事求是的；正經的
　(238)

nope ＝no　　(36)

norm 基準；標準　　(212)

nose to the grindstone 不停地工作
　(248)

not long ago 不久前　　(108)

Not that I can remember. 我不記得
　有過(這麼一回事)。　　(108)

not to my knowledge 不在我所知的範
　圍以內　　(158)

nurture 養育；滋養　　(208)

nutritive value 營養價值　　(130)

nuts and bolts 螺帽和螺絲釘；實際作
　用的部分；實務　　(118)

occur to someone 使某人想到
　(140)

offer 提議；提供；出價　　(198)

office politics 辦公室內的權力鬥爭(政
　治活動)　　(86)

on-line 線上的；網路上的　　(14)

on target 不偏離正題；正對目標進行
　(94)

on the same wavelength 有相同的波
　長〈喻興趣、思想相同〉　　(122)

one out of every four 四分之一
　(234)

one way or another 無論如何；不管怎
　樣　　(172)

Only kidding. 只是開玩笑的。　　(82)

oops 糟糕；哦　　(194)

operation 事業　　(136)

operations guy 做事的人〈不是只有嘴
　巴講講而已〉　　(148)

operative 生效的；運轉的　　(72)

opium 鴉片　　(104)

option 選擇　　(172)

organized crime 組織犯罪　　(36)

orientation meeting 新進人員講習
　(22)

out in the open 公然地　　(252)

out of sight 不在視線範圍內；看不到
　(76)

out with/in with 走了…，來了…
　(208)

outplacement service 為解聘員工安排

·伍史利的大日記 I、II
—————————— 哈洛森林的妙生活

Linda Hayward 著

三民書局編輯部 譯

來！ 和哈洛森林中的動物一起狂歡，
慶祝季節的交替吧！

·100%頑童手記

Wilhelm Busch 著

陸 谷 孫 譯

搗蛋鬼麥克斯與毛里斯
又想出什麼把戲來惡作劇？

中、英文寫成的雙行押韻詩，將滑稽有趣的
內容，巧妙地融入詩句的律動中，配上生動
的插圖，讓每一個故事都鮮活起來。

·非尋常童話

Wilhelm Busch 著

陸 谷 孫 譯

九篇獨立精彩的故事詩，
幽默詼諧的內容，
流暢的詩韻和活潑的插圖，
篇篇都讓你開懷大笑！

一天一篇，故事看完，
英文也學好了！